MOTHER SAVANT

A. L. HAWKE

PHANTOM HEART, LLC

Copyright © 2020 by A.L. Hawke

All rights reserved. No portion of this book may be reproduced, distributed or transmitted in any form or by any electronic or mechanical means, including information storage and retrieval systems, without permission in writing, except by reviewers who may quote brief passages for a review.

ISBN: 978-1-7329563-4-6 (ebook)

ISBN: 978-1-7329563-5-3 (paperback)

ISBN: 978-1-953919-15-1 (hardcover)

Library of Congress Control Number: 2019919884

This is a work of fiction. It all comes directly from the imagination of the author's mind. This includes names, characters, places, and incidents. Any public names are used solely for creative purposes. Any resemblance to actual people, living or dead, or to companies, institutions or locales is entirely coincidental or accidental.

Line edited by Paul Witcover

Proofread by Eliza Dee of Clio Editing Services

Cover Design © 2019 by Damon Za

Images by Shutterstock

Published by Phantom Heart, LLC

27702 Crown Valley Pkwy D-4, #201

Ladera Ranch, CA 92694, USA

Printed and bound in the United States of America

First printing January, 2020

Learn more about A.L. Hawke at www.alhawke.com

Correspondence: contact@alhawke.com

❀ Created with Vellum

CHAPTER 1
FOR ANOTHER XY

Savant Sara Holmes leaned forward in her metal chair, nearly spitting at the woman seated across from her. They were in matching silver chairs, Sara dressed in her tight lime-green leather Savant jumpsuit and the prisoner with long pepper-gray hair wearing a white lab coat, her hands tied behind her back.

"Tell me where *now!*"

The room was quite lovely. It was a small observation deck built at the top of Team Mother's newly made crystal Sky City with a transparent glass ceiling opening up into the darkening azure sky. The walls were paneled by glass windows on three sides and a beige wall with a steel door on the fourth. A large surgical light with folded spiderlike mechanical arms hung above the door. The room had been designed for tissue experimentation, but tonight, the laboratory workstation was replaced for quite different purposes. The sun had just set, and only a yellow-red shine from the horizon bounced off the checkered steel walls of Arkite City and reflected over the steel floor. The windows afforded a gorgeous view of the pyramidal city of Arkite, with the massive spire of Sector One's HQ Civic Building looming on one side, flanked by a dozen or so other pyramidal structures with their brightening, twinkling lights, and the vast green of Central Park on the other. Sara could even make out the faint remnants of an orange-red sunset over the distant desert sands—like she cared at the moment.

"Goddamnit! Tell me where the drive is!" Sara leaned forward again. "Now!" she shouted. "Where is it!" Never had Sara wanted to hurt someone so badly. She pulled her silver pistol from her belt and pressed the barrel against Dr. Teller's forehead.

Dr. Florence Teller had once been among the most prized scientists in Arkite. She had worked under Reyburn in Allele Corporation for twenty years. She had led the company in producing more efficient embryo machines by lining them in rows in the factory, proving that even human reproduction could be enhanced by industrial mass-production techniques. Combining the ancient lessons of Henry Ford with the achievements of the crop field machines of Sanborn and Tritch, Dr. Teller had brilliantly sped the velocity of human reproduction. The machines oddly resembled lines of twentieth-century washing machines, save for the growing female fetuses visible through their round central windows. Dr. Teller and Reyburn had successfully ruled Allele Corporation until Team Mother Elise Jackson had personally gunned down every lead scientist, dissolving the corporation.

Dr. Teller's eyes were wide open and leaking tears. She shook under the barrel of Sara's gun. In a trembling voice, she said, "I will only speak with your leader." She had repeated that phrase over ten times in the past hour.

After Elise's massacre, Dr. Teller had escaped. Tracked down, she had spent a couple of years in Station One Court, Arkite's maximum-security prison. But after two years of exemplary behavior, she had been released. Sara wondered in amazement why Elise hadn't executed her. Then none of this mess would have happened.

The prisoner turned her forehead, her stringy gray hair drifting over the pistol. With one hand, Sara yanked Dr. Teller's hair, pulling her head back, while with the other she pressed the barrel harder against the old woman's skull. Sara had never wanted to shoot anyone so badly in her life.

To stop herself from pulling the trigger, she whacked Teller over the head with the barrel of her silver gun.

"*Bitch!* Tell me! Where? Where is the XY! Where is Dr. Lilith Carloff? Where is my neural net!"

Then she hit Teller's head a few times with the butt of the gun, which yielded a more satisfying crack. But even as blood mingled with tears, her prisoner just winced and closed her eyes, saying nothing. That's when the gun slipped out of Sara's hands, tumbled over her tight lime-green rubber thigh, bounced, and clanged metal to metal against the steel floor. Sara caught a flash of the steel from her silver pistol reflecting off the outdoor light from the glass ceiling.

"*You bitch!*" Sara screamed.

Sara reached down, grabbed her gun, and pressed the barrel against Dr. Teller's forehead one last time. She had every intention of killing her. "Tell me now where you've taken it, where they are, or so help me I swear I will shoot!"

"I will only speak with your leader," the doctor muttered again.

But Dr. Teller was worn out. She had been given no food or water for the past day and a half and had already pissed herself —Sara could smell it. Now the gray-haired former Savant sat trembling with her eyes closed, waiting for the bullet.

"Enough!" said Sara. "I won't shoot you. That would be too merciful." Sara raised her free hand. "Give it to me now, Rex!"

Sara held up her hand, waiting for the mainframe to lower a laser scalpel from the ceiling. But nothing happened. She felt stupid with her hand raised and nothing happening.

Dr. Teller opened her eyes and squirmed in the chair.

"Now, Rex!" Sarah commanded.

"I apologize, Savant Holmes," came the unemotional robotic voice of the mainframe. The mechanical arms dangling above jerked, unfolded, but then froze. "I seem to be having some difficulty lowering the arm. It appears to be locked. Just a moment. Just a moment."

"Now, Rex!"

"Sorry, Savant Holmes," said Rex. "I am having difficulty with the mechanical arms. Just a moment. Just a moment."

Sara felt perspiration drip down the back of her tight lime-green rubber Savant suit. Her stomach roiled with nausea. Despite her threats, the idea of actually cutting this criminal's withered flesh made her sick. She wasn't used to doing this kind of thing. She had never done anything like this before. She hadn't even interrogated anyone. But she was furious.

Finally, a thin metal mechanical arm slowly lowered from the ceiling, holding a laser scalpel. Dr. Teller stared at the tip of the laser scalpel with wide-open eyes.

"Judging by your lab coat, Doctor," Sara said sarcastically, "you know what this is."

Without waiting for a reply, Sara lit the flame at the end of the silver scalpel and brought it close to the prisoner's cheek. Dr. Teller's eyes bulged as Sara ran it close to one eye, which squeezed shut at the heat.

"Cut me if you wish," said the doctor, her voice trembling more than ever. She took a deep, shuddering breath. "I can't tell you anything, Savant. I don't know where Lilly is. She made sure not to tell me. She knew I'd be taken."

"Why'd you help her?"

"For the people. For our future. I only know that Lilly has

asked for an audience with your dog of a leader at Primdon Street. She will exchange your precious cargo at Primdon. I promise you'll have the drive back for an exchange of exit from the city. I won't tell you anything else. I . . . I can't, for Lilly made sure I wouldn't know."

"But who's to say I won't shoot her?" asked another voice in the room.

Sara stepped back and looked around. Dr. Teller searched the room too. But it was as empty as ever.

"Elise?" she asked. Of course it was Elise. Elise didn't need to be physically present to see and hear what went on in her city. Sara knew that more than most, yet her rage had made her forget.

"Who's to say I won't shoot her, Flo?" repeated Elise's voice.

"Lilly will be armed," answered Dr. Teller with a nod. "And she carries your neural net."

"So she wants to trade the net for her freedom." Elise's voice sounded amused as it echoed through the room. "Where will she go?" Sara could hear the working of Elise's jaw, the steady chomping as she chewed the stimulant gum to which she was as addicted as she was to cruelty. "Do tell, Flo. One of the reasons I stopped chasing the rats was because I believed they were content to hide in their hovel. Now you're provoking me. Tell me where they are. I know a thing or two about Sara, and she very well might cut you. She's sweet, you see, but if you cross her and play with her Candy, God help you. She will have no qualms about systematically shredding your flesh off your shriveled-up dollface. So, come, come, spare us the trouble of making a mess, won't you, and tell us where the drive is. There's no reason for you not to. You'll be sent back to Station Court, and I will provide clemency in thanks for your cooperation. You may live. That's a hell of a lot more merciful than me leaving you to Sara right now."

"Let me cut her, Elise!" yelled Sara. "Goddamnit, let me melt her fucking dollface!"

"Tsk, tsk, Sara. I think you need to take a deep breath," came Elise's voice. "Breathe in and out, in and out, nice long deep breaths and calm down. Relax and quiet yourself."

"I can't tell you anything," Dr. Teller said, her head drooping. "I don't know."

"Well, Flo, then how about telling me why you did it," Elise said. "Surely you know your fate. I already let you go free once. That was a mistake. I won't do it again."

They waited. Dr. Teller kept her head down. When Sara brought the blade up again, ready to scalp her, and a small waft of gray smoke appeared over her skin, the former Savant spoke. "The boy, Adam. Adam will save us. The boy's more important than me or you. Freedom from Rex . . . freedom from the mainframe."

"The XY?" Elise asked with a laugh. "You're a criminal for him? An XY?"

"He will save Arkite, Mother."

"Why do you think Arkite needs saving?"

"For another XY!" cried Sara. "Please, Elise. Please. Say the word. I'm gonna kill her!"

Sara dropped the blade from her hands. It landed on the doctor's thigh, cutting deep into her leg. Dr. Teller screamed. Then the scalpel fell to the floor. Had it been an accident? Sara wasn't sure. She didn't care.

"Did you cut her, Sara?" asked Elise with a sigh.

"Just dropped the blade by accident, Mother."

"If my sister wants to meet with me, Sara," Elise said, "I think we should give her a royal welcome. I think the whole city should welcome her. We're family, after all."

There was silence. Just the sizzling sound of the scalpel lying on the steel floor and Dr. Teller whimpering in pain as blood oozed from the wound in her leg.

"Enough of this unpleasantness," ordered Elise sternly. "Transfer Dr. Teller to Station Three Court. I need her unharmed—for now. There may be more in her traitorous head. But be warned, Flo, execution or not, I don't think my orders will stop Sara from slicing you in half if you damaged the drive."

CHAPTER 2
EVERYBODY CALM DOWN
AND TAKE A DEEP BREATH

Team Mother Elise Jackson wanted to look good for her guest. She wore a lovely formal black lace dress with a draping dark cape, long dark leather boots, and a sharp silver choker around her neck that resembled the rings of Saturn—sharp enough to guillotine her head off. She had applied black mascara and black lipstick, and her black hair was slicked back and tied in a ponytail.

Leaning an elbow on Sara's green rocket cycle, she stood beside Sara in front of her black bike. Sara, wearing her tight shiny lime-green Savant jumpsuit, had her hands on her hips. She was blowing large red bubbles from the Mint she was chewing—the same sweet, stimulant-laden, highly addicting gum Elise favored. A small army of over fifty Officers from the Guard stood at attention behind them. It was quiet enough for Elise to hear the Officers' lips smacking. They were chewing Mint too.

They stood near the exit of Primdon Street, the only opening out of the checkered megatruss pyramidal wall of Arkite City. It was one thirty in the afternoon on a clear bright sunny day, the day following Dr. Teller's interrogation.

It wasn't often that an army of police stood before the exit of the city. Citizens watched along the sidewalks, nearly a hundred of them in drab gray suits, waiting for whatever their supreme leader was about to do. Above circled a swarm of small copter drones. Automated cars were backed up in traffic on the one-lane street—not because they were traveling out of the city, for nobody ever did that, but because so many people were watching and refusing to turn off the road.

Elise ran a hand down Sara's lovely long blond mane and then glided her fingers down the side of her assistant's slick lime-green Savant jumpsuit. Sara was so hot. She reminded her of Candice.

That's why they were here—for Candice. Elise lived for her Candy.

A rocket cycle, white and shiny, finally appeared through the clouds from the direction of Sector Two. Escorting it was a formation of a hundred copter drones piloted by Rex. In unison, the Officers lifted their rifles from inside their coats behind Elise and aimed at the approaching bike. One of the Officers, whose name was Gena, turned to Elise. "Say the word now, Mother, and we'll bring her down."

Gena was a hefty bald woman towering over six and a half feet in height. The Officer had been engineered in the embryo farms to be stronger than most women, selected all the way back in childhood to be an Officer of Arkite. Gena was Elise's favorite. Usually stoic and cold, vicious and loyal—but today Gena looked anxious. She was never nervous, but Elise knew why. The criminal was related to her. Gena and Dr. Lilith Carloff were assigned from birth to be raised together in the same household as "sisters."

"Steady, Gena," said Elise. "Your sister has the disk. No action until my order."

"Yes, Mother."

The cycle came close. It was particularly lustrous, reflecting the light of the midday sun as though built for no other purpose. There were two occupants on board. Dr. Lilith Carloff and a smaller passenger holding on to her waist from behind. Their ragged clothes contrasted sharply with the bike's pristine polish. The operator wore what once had likely been a pearl-white Savant jumpsuit as lustrous as the white bike. Now it was gray, dirty and torn. Elise liked Lilly's hair: it trailed a deep red over her white uniform and bike. Elise stared at the "cargo" Lilly was bearing. It was the XY boy.

"She deserves to die," snapped Sara. Sara had her pistol pointed at the rocket cycle too.

"Stay in line," repeated Elise.

The child got off the bike first. He was young but tall for his age.

He must be eight, Elise thought. *It was eight years ago when Lilith fled from Allele Corporation.*

The boy had a hardened expression, likely from scurrying under the earth and running from police all his life. It made him seem older. It was this boy that had once made Elise line up the scientists of Allele Corp, many of whom had been Elise's friends, in the main lecture hall and gun them down—the dastardliest act she had ever done. But she had never found the boy. Nor had she found Lilith.

Elise impatiently tapped her fingers over Sara's bike as Lilly and the boy approached, carrying their folded visor helmets under their arms. Elise's eyes widened as she noticed what was tucked under Lilly's other arm: a small silver metal case.

"Stop there," Gena said. "That's close enough."

"Sister," Lilly said to Gena. Gena nodded stoically. Then Lilly faced Elise with a scowl. She repeated "sister," this time referring to their political relationship.

"Search her," demanded Elise, staring into Lilly's eyes.

Lilly stepped back, dropped her helmet on the ground, and pulled out a pistol with her free hand from a holster concealed behind her back. She pointed it at Elise's head.

The Officers turned the muzzles of their rifles right back at Lilly.

"Back off!" yelled Lilly. "We have a deal."

"Calm yourself," said Elise with a smile, raising a hand. "Certainly you know you're surrounded. There's no escape."

"Drop the gun, Lilly," said Gena.

"I ask for freedom," Lilly said, addressing everyone. "Freedom from the city for Adam and me."

Then she dropped the metal case on the ground. Elise's eyes bulged. Her fingers closed into a gloved fist at the sound of the metal clanging against the asphalt. It nearly made her lose all reason.

Deep breaths. Remember, Elise, mindful meditation.

"There's your precious lover!" snapped Lilith. "Now let Adam and me go."

"The little man too?" Elise said.

The twerp looked right up at Elise, fearlessly meeting the leader of Arkite's gaze with challenging eyes.

"Yes," replied Lilith. "Safe passage from Arkite—both my son and me."

"Calm yourself," Elise repeated. "Everybody just take a deep breath and calm down. It's"—Elise gestured with her arms extended—"why, it's such a lovely day, isn't it? Lower your weapons. I get jumpy when people point guns. I was shot once, you know."

"You should have died," Lilly said.

"After all our work, Elise," cried Sara, "how dare she! Let me kill her."

"Sara, we don't kill. You know that. You're a Savant." Elise cocked her head back at her Chief Guard. "We have our Officers do that." She smirked, then continued. "Lilly, although I'm so very happy to see you, it's rather difficult to talk with a gun pointed at my head."

Lilly lowered her gun toward Elise's chest. Elise chuckled.

"Let us go," Lilly snapped.

"Don't you want to chat?"

"I'm here to leave with my son. Turn around and walk slowly to your bike without looking back. When you and your guards are far enough away, Adam and I leave."

"We'll just shoot you down the moment you're airborne," Elise said with a shrug.

"I have a kill switch." Lilith showed Elise a small black handheld device worn like a ring over her third finger in her free hand. "Do anything stupid, and I'll erase the drive completely."

"Clever," Elise said with a sly grin. "You've always been clever. If I remember, I even once considered recruiting you as Lead Savant. You're an attractive one too."

"And you're an animal."

"Well I must say, I admire a good bit of blackmail," said Elise. "But why? Why go through all this trouble just to kill yourself and the XY outside the city walls? You can't survive outside the Pyramid. Nobody can. You know that."

"Just turn around and walk slowly back to your bike. I don't have to tell you anything."

"Oh, yes, you do," Elise said. "You will tell me, or I won't give you a goddamn thing. You might have a gun pointed at me, but I have hundreds of drones above and over fifty rifles below aimed at your pretty little red head."

"I seek safe passage. You get the neural net back, and we're allowed to leave freely. That's all you need to know."

Elise shook her head. "Why?"

Lilith looked back, deadpan. Her son had the same impassive expression.

"What a lovely day for a family reunion," Elise said. She turned to Sara, who looked ready to tear the criminal apart with her bare hands. "Lilly was Reyburn's wife, Sara. Reyburn chose her after Reyburn turned over the city to me and Magnacourt. You probably recall Connie-con Reyburn, Sara. Remember Team Grandmother, the one who tried to kill me? But we should be nice to Lilly. See, once Lilly had to bend over for Connie-con too. I actually feel kind of sorry for her." Elise made a mockingly sad face.

"You disgust me," replied Lilly.

"Of course, Reyburn chose me 'cause I was a dollface," continued Elise with a shrug. Elise walked right up to Lilly's face, feeling the barrel of the gun press against her sternum. "I was once the cream of the crop when it came to dollfaces, not like the old shriveled-up prune you see before you now, Lil. Once I was quite attractive. But Lilly, you're still lovely, aren't you? No stringy hair yet. Still a flashy red. Sara, all Savants choose their Chief Savants to fuck—or fuck over. It's custom. The sexiest, fuckiest, hottest young girls—"

"Shut up!" cried Lilly. "I'll shoot! I can't stand your filthy mouth."

"Take advantage of ladies at the top of the class," Elise continued, ignoring her. "The cream of the crop. Indeed, I was your wife's little dolly, Lil. Before you were even hatched. That made me, like you, her bitch, you know."

"I'll shoot!"

"Do you know what your wife used to do to me?" Elise asked Lilith, narrowing her eyes and speaking in almost a whisper. "When she *recruited* me? She used to stand over me," Elise said more quietly still, leaning close to Lilith's ear, "order me to undress and kneel before her, and then have me lap up her legs like a thirsty stray dog, force me to lick and pleasure her, while tying a rope over my choker—the same choker I'm wearing now, dear—and tug at it until the bitch came, whimpering all over me."

"Enough!" cried Lilith, pushing Elise back with the gun pressed deep into her stomach. The Officers moved closer.

"Whenever it served her," Elise added as if the gun wasn't

there, "Connie-con would bind me with wires and tape, doing all sorts of kinky shit."

"The case!" Lilith shouted impatiently. "Shut the hell up and take it. Let us go."

"She'd make me run naked in frigid snow," continued Elise, looking up as if in fond remembrance. "Choke me before sticking things up my ass and cunt—without my consent, I might add. But she wasn't only a sick motherfucker. She was also a sadist. She would inspect my work and inflict pain. Once—"

"You sick bitch!" Lilith shouted. "Let us go. Don't say another word."

"Desperation changes a girl, I suppose," Elise drawled, shrugging her shoulders. Lilly dug the gun deeper. "And perhaps time can change one into an animal, Lilly. Yes. Yes, an animal. That's what you called me, right? An animal?"

"You are."

"*And who do you think made me this animal, you fuck!*" yelled Elise, finally enraged. Lilly stepped back at the sudden outburst. "How dare you take the only thing I care about in this world! What do you think I'm going to do? Set you free? I'd rather string you up by your goddamn toes than watch you roam free with that mutant freak by your side!" Elise closed her eyes, straightened her skirt, and took a deep breath. "Well, now you've upset me." She took another breath, tempering her rage. She forced a smile. "I've been trying very hard lately to learn to calm myself. Meditation is important to center oneself. Now you're fucking that up too. I . . ." Elise looked at Sara. "I didn't know Connie-con well during her last years of life, Sara. Not when she married Lilly. Who knows, maybe she changed and stopped being a sadistic abusive whore." Elise chuckled. "Well, Lilly, you may as well shoot. Without Candy-can, I'm as good as dead anyway. So shoot me. Ask the guards." Elise turned to

Gena. "Gena, do I fucking care to live since she took my Candy Doll?"

"You've been very unhappy, Master," Gena said.

"Yeah." Elise chuckled and pushed her body deeper into Lilly's gun, squinting her eyes and squirming a bit. "Notice what she says. She says *Master*. See, she calls me *Master*. Just like your bitch wife made me call her time and time again when she bent me down and—"

"Turn around and walk to your bike, Elise! No more words! Do it now, Mother, or I will pull the trigger! I won't warn you again."

"No," Elise said, staring into her eyes. "Kill me. Free me. If you damaged her, I don't really care to live anymore."

Lilly looked at her oddly, and Elise nodded as if urging her on.

"Mommy," said the boy, who stood beside his mother. It broke the tension. "Are we leaving the city now?"

Elise looked down at him and smiled. "Why don't you move your gun for a moment from my stomach, Lilly, so I can inspect the drive? If it's undamaged, who knows, I might do exactly what you ask."

Lilly hesitated but then lifted the gun and pointed it at Elise's head.

Elise carefully knelt down and picked up the small rectangular steel case from under their feet. It was the size of her palm. She removed a black leather glove and held it in her bare hand, looked it over, concerned that it could be damaged from the fall. There were small scratches along the sides, but it seemed intact. It was cold. Metallic. So cold. But running her finger along it warmed her heart.

"Is she here?" Elise asked. "Is my lover here? Or have you already killed her?"

The change of subject seemed to disarm Lilith. She relaxed a little and nodded. "Candice is safe."

Elise marveled over how this small tiny metal box meant more to her than anything. She turned to Lilith and smiled again. "Why'd you do this?" she asked. "You're asking to be banished to a radioactive desert. Why would I want to do that to you and your poor child? It would be better to have my guards kill you now and put you out of your misery."

"That's a lie," Lilith replied. "The radiation levels are safe outside the Pyramid walls."

"Rex," Elise asked, looking down at the screen permanently embedded in her left wrist, "what are the current radiation levels outside the city walls of Arkite?"

"Estimations, Mother, are background radiation levels around seven point six sieverts per year," said the robotic male voice of the mainframe.

"There's no radiation," Lilly said.

"Seven point six," replied Elise. "I know you've been away from the lab for a while, but surely you know, Lilly, that isn't livable."

"He's lying, Elise," Lilly said.

"I do not lie, Dr. Carloff," responded the robotic voice from Elise's wrist monitor. "I never lie. I am the mainframe."

"He might not be lying, Elise, but he doesn't know," replied Lilly. "He has nothing outside the walls to measure it."

"A big risk," Elise said. She stared at Lilith and the boy for a moment. The woman's plan was clever. It was, in fact, the only way she and the XY could leave Arkite. But why would she want to go outside the protective walls? It was suicide.

"Fucking bitch!" shouted Sara.

Elise spun around. She had completely forgotten about her Lead Savant.

"We were so close to bringing Candy back!" Sara shouted.

Elise addressed her wrist monitor again. "Rex, can you check the contents of the drive?"

"Candy is safe," interjected Lilly.

"I need to check," Elise said, flashing Lilly a fake smile.

"Yes, Mother," said Rex. "I can attempt an acoustic scan. Please bring the cartridge up to your wrist and I will scan it."

"She's unharmed," objected Lilly. "But Rex can't perform an adequate scan remotely."

Elise furrowed her brow and looked at Lilly suspiciously. She moved the silver box close to the screen along her arm.

"Just a moment," said Rex's voice. "Just a moment."

The "moment" was painful. Ever since the neural net had been stolen last week, Elise hadn't slept. This was the only complete network of Candice's neural synapses. It had taken Elise two years to replicate each pathway and connect the damaged parts and record it all digitally on a disk. It was, in essence, more Candice than Candice's actual brain left in the cryochamber. If the disk was damaged or lost, so would be Candice.

"Of course, Mother," said Rex after a long silence, "as Dr. Carloff states, I cannot completely analyze the disk from a quick acoustic scan. It would be better to study it in the lab."

"Cut the shit, Rex," Elise said. "What's Candice's condition?"

"The configuration appears to be the original copied one week after Savant Candice Harlow's death, Mother," Rex said. "This mapping is the initial digital transfer. However, it is incomplete. The mapping includes what was created based on the organic tissue not yet decomposed. This is, of course, very incomplete. It has not been repaired with your new mapping and bridge connections."

"What?" Elise snapped, glaring at Lilly. "What do you mean?"

Lilly anxiously shook her head.

"All additional connections you have made over the past year and a half have been erased," Rex explained.

Elise's eyes widened. "What did you do!" she shouted.

Lilith's face had gone pale. The boy, Adam, started crying.

"What did you do!" Elise screeched, her mouth inches from Lilith's face.

"She erased your work, Mother," answered Rex simply.

"The disk is sound, Mother," Lilly objected. "Rex can't be sure remotely that—"

"Like mother, like fucking daughter!" Elise shouted. "I can't believe it! How dare you! You redhead twitchy tweet fuck!"

"I didn't hurt her," Lilly insisted, shaking her head. "You can still revive her."

The heat rose to Elise's face. "The longer it takes me to revive her, the more Candy dies! Every day, her frozen body decays. I don't have time to re-synapse all the connections to make her whole now!"

Elise rushed away from everyone, taking deep breaths, trying to control herself. She had to think. If she couldn't control her rage, she was going to get everyone shot, including Sara and herself.

Deep breaths, Elise.

Then Lilith made it worse. "Let me go," Lilith said. "We had a deal. You have the disk. My freedom for your dead lover's."

That was when a crack echoed along Primdon Street. And then a scream—a child's scream. Lilly's body fell to the ground, Adam wailing beside her. Along the white Savant jumpsuited chest of Dr. Carloff was a large black smoking hole that leaked crimson. Lilly's eyes were shut. Elise turned; Sara held a smoking pistol from an outstretched arm.

Elise rushed over and grabbed Lilith's palm, yanking the plastic kill switch from her finger. Then she touched Lilith's neck to check for a pulse. It was weak and irregular. She wasn't breathing.

Sara had dropped the gun. She was crying into her hands. Officers had grabbed her.

"Shit!" Elise jumped up. "Shit! Shit! Mother . . . fucking *shit*!" She whirled on Sara. "You fucking idiot!"

Sara wept.

"What the hell is the matter with you!" Elise shouted at Sara.

Sara just kept crying.

"All right," Elise said, gesturing to the guards, who circled Lilly and the hysterical boy. Elise walked back to Sara's green rocket bike and leaned against it, rubbing her eyes. She took another deep breath. Sara and the boy were wailing so loudly she felt like shooting them both herself. "Calm down," she said. "Everybody just calm the fuck down."

"Sorry, Elise," Sara said between sobs.

"Shut up."

"She destroyed everything," Sara continued.

"Shut up."

"How could she?" cried Sara. "How could she kill—"

"Shut up! Do you have any idea how dumb you are? I could have questioned her, you fucking moron! She knew Reyburn's secrets!" Elise walked back over to Adam, who knelt beside his mother, cushioning her head in his lap. Lilly's eyes were shut, her face almost serene. Blood continued to run along her dirty white suit.

"What should we do with the boy?" asked Gena stoically, standing over them. Elise looked up at the bald-headed Chief Officer.

"He's an XY," Elise replied coldly. "Take him away."

"Not kill him, Mother?" Gena asked.

Elise didn't respond, but Gena had heard the order. Gena looked relieved. She crouched down to pick up Adam, but he kicked and punched her. With the help of another Officer, Gena scooped the boy up in her arms. Even then, the boy was reaching for Lilly, wailing.

"Elise, I would advise that you permit me to take Dr. Carloff to Angel of Hope Hospital immediately," Rex said.

"What are you going to do for her?" Elise asked. "She's got a hole in her chest."

"The wound appears to be fatal to the heart and lung," Rex said. "It is a critical wound, Mother. But if I work fast, I might still be able to revive her with a temporary pump in the hospital."

"Fine. Take her, Rex."

"Yes, Mother."

A large bright red metallic copter drone dropped down and with robotic arms carefully scooped up Dr. Carloff's body. The body was swiftly hauled up and placed inside the drone.

Elise looked at Sara, who was now handcuffed with her head down, being held by three Officers, still whimpering.

"How dare you disobey me, Sara," Elise said.

Sara couldn't reply. She whimpered some more.

Elise removed her right black leather glove. Then she walked up to Sara and struck her as hard as she could in the face with her bare hand. Sara fell to the ground, crying more than ever.

"Let her go," Elise said to the surrounding Officers. "She didn't do anything I didn't want to do."

The Officers uncuffed Sara. Sara tried to reply but was too choked up. She quickly mounted her green rocket cycle, launched into the air, and sped off.

Elise walked to her own black rocket bike.

"We're free to leave, Master?" asked another Officer.

Elise donned her black visor, a modified open helmet looking like a hard half eggshell with a transparent face shield. She turned on her black rocket bike and rose in the air.

"Bring me the disk, Elise, and I will see what I can recover of Candice," came Rex's voice through the speakers of her helmet. "There may still be enough records in our laboratory to rework it. There should be traces that are left unharmed and whole. And, anyway, Candice's cerebellum and brainstem remain complete and viable."

CHAPTER 3
SARA

SARA RUSHED BACK HOME, parked at the roof landing bay, leapt off her bike, and left the green rocket cycle to be taken into a garage by an attendant. She ignored the young bald girl in her formal double-breasted white suit. She had never ignored assistants before, because once upon a time that had been her job, and even though she was a Savant now, she didn't want to forget where she had come from. But today she brushed by without a word.

She ran into her blue dome-shaped kitchen, rushed to a countertop, and leaned her head in her hands, sobbing again.

She had never killed anyone. She had always thought that the act of murder would change her into something dirty or evil. She was surprised to feel nothing. In fact, she wasn't crying for Lilith at all; she was crying for Candy. Candice Harlow had been her lover more than Elise's. Sure, Elise had hired Candice. Elise had picked Savant Candice Harlow out of attraction and had even once planned to marry her. But in the months before Candice's death, Candice had lived with Sara. In those blissful months, Sara had been closer to Candice than Elise ever was.

Two years.

Sara had endured two long, horrible years under the leadership of a sadistic bitch—Team Mother Elise—all in order to revive Candice. She had accepted the prestigious position as Lead Assistant Savant under Elise upon Candice's death, but at the time, she had thought her work would involve completing the Lazarus Project. It hadn't. Elise had changed all their efforts and started this secret project alone. Elise had done it in defiance of the Savant Council and at the risk of losing everything —even her rule in Arkite. But when Sara had found out that the rogue project involved the possibility of resurrecting Candice, she'd enthusiastically helped Elise, risking her own future as well. Now their personal, perhaps more ambitious project of raising the dead was all but lost with the damage to the mapping of Candice's neural net. They had planned to take the electronic imprint, when completed, and use the neural net to regrow and carefully revive Candice's brain.

Sara wept into her hands for the longest time. Rex even said something, but she didn't listen. Then she felt the great irony in her predicament. Through the openings in her fingers, she could see the walls of her domed blue kitchen. This was where Candice had been murdered. Right there in Candice's kitchen, Lazarus had thrust a dagger into her chest. He had killed her after Sara had fought the beast.

Two years.

After Candice had died, Elise had commissioned a fifty-foot diamond monument in Central Park, at the precise center of the city, to remind her of her pain. But Sara didn't need a fifty-foot diamond to remember Candice. Every day, Sara labored over Candice's frozen body in HQ Laboratory.

The coffin buried under the diamond in Central Park had been empty. Shortly after the stabbing, when Rex had given up attempting to revive Candice in the hospital, Elise had ordered Gena to return Candice's body to HQ Lab and freeze it in cryopreservation. The body had arrived six hours later by air. From the time of the stabbing to the time of final freezing, a day and a half had passed. That amount of time, though seemingly insignificant, was a very long time in death—ample time for the lack of blood and oxygen to lead to severe decomposition of body tissue. Recovery would mean replacement of dead tissue that by then amounted to over a fourth of the muscular, vascular, and nervous system of the body. But far worse was what was left of the brain, the most important part of all: a sludge of white and gray matter riddled with holes, worse than the worst stroke patient ever tended to. Such damage could have no normal possible chance of recovery—hence two years of repair.

Two years.

Rex had told Elise and Sara it could not be done. Rex advised that they return Candice's body to the mausoleum in Central Park at once and forget it. Rex then offered to simply clone Candice. But Elise violently refused, referring to the last genetically engineered man Elise had created: Lazarus. Lazarus had murdered Candice in the first place, and Elise partly blamed her death on the creation by Rex of Lazarus's artificial brain.

Elise had utilized a theory, originally posited in Candice's dissertation at Arkite University, ironically, that damaged brain tissue could be repaired by following the paths of damaged neural connections. This could even prove restorative to memories themselves, if applied to the hippocampus. The theory went like this: every connection could be thought of as a puzzle. If the puzzle is worked out, then holes from ischemia could, theoretically, be filled based on mapping of all other viable connections. Axons and dendrites could be reconnected with nano tools and electron microscopy at the cellular level, based on the connections still intact. Such a map could be re-created even if the brain was over eighty percent damaged—as was the case with Candice. But plugging the holes meant a tremendous amount of puzzle-solving. Not only that, tissue still decomposed when frozen, though at a much slower rate. Every second that passed created more gaps in Candice's neural network and more tissue to be replaced.

Two years.

Now for nothing.

"Sara, excuse me, but there is a call coming in," said Rex's stale voice. "I told you before, but you did not answer me. Can you take it?"

"What?"

"A call, Savant Holmes. You are receiving a call on the 3-D Viewer."

"From who?"

"Viceroy Savant Leeto Gansey."

"Okay," Sara said with a sigh.

She forced herself into her adjacent living room. It was dimly lit, with only teal lighting coming from the molding on the floor. There was a small platform, like a small plastic stage, in the center of the room: the 3-D Viewer. Sara sat down on a black leather couch across from it. She hadn't bothered to change, still wearing her green Savant clothes. She straightened herself on the couch and tried to look as presentable as she could.

"Accept the call, Rex."

A Savant in a gunmetal-gray jumpsuit appeared, slightly translucent, in a half-egg-shaped chair at the center of Sara's dimly lit room above the Viewer. The Savant swiveled her chair to face Sara directly and flashed a phony grin.

Savant Leeto Gansey was pretty enough, but her small features made her the very definition of a dollface. It was like she literally had a small doll's face. The size of her head was bizarre. It just seemed too small for her body. It wasn't a mutation—that would have been rejected by the embryo farms. But it was just small enough to give her pretty face an odd ugliness. Leeto had long blond hair like Candice, but where Candice's face was beautifully and gorgeously proportioned, there was something perverse and immature about Leeto's head, as though it had stopped growing too soon. And it was made worse by her attitude. Sara knew Leeto to be the most conceited woman in all of the Savant Program—and in the midst of Savants, that was quite an achievement.

"Sara. It's been so long. I'm so happy to see you. How are you doing, sister?"

"Fine," Sara lied.

"I'm so glad to hear it. The weather has been very agreeable, I hope? I have tried to fan the city during the hot summer."

"Yes, Viceroy. Your weather has been very nice."

"But I haven't seen you in the park. I do hope Elise isn't working you too hard."

"I'm fine."

The lie made Leeto smile more. "Yes, well, since I know how busy you are, I'll get to the point. I heard news about Dr. Carloff. We all did. The whole city watched the showdown. It was great—really amusing fun. But . . ." Leeto furrowed her brow. "I'm having difficulty understanding why Elise let it go on for so long. I mean, here is an XY with the infamous outlaw Dr. Lilith Carloff, wife of the villainous Team Grandmother Connie Reyburn, finally showing themselves to all of Arkite. Why oh why the hell didn't Elise just shoot them the minute they showed themselves? Was Mother just providing us entertainment?"

"Perhaps you should ask her."

"I did," Leeto said with a broader grin. "But Mother has a habit of not answering her calls—especially when drinking."

"She's been very busy."

"Of course." Leeto paused and reached down outside of the hologram. Her arm vanished into the darkness of Sara's living room. Then she brought a glass of white wine to her lips. "Well . . ." Leeto sipped some wine. "I found the whole thing remarkable. You and Mother had such restraint. That is, until *you* finally shot her in the chest."

"She deserved to die."

"Exactly." Leeto furrowed her brow again. "That's what I'm saying. But why the show? Was Mother entertaining us?"

Sara looked away. She wondered if her eyes were red. Of course they were. She had been crying for the last hour. Would Leeto figure it was due to the trauma of her kill? Or could it be that Leeto was already aware of the stolen object Dr. Carloff had been carrying?

Leeto Gansey and the rest of the Savant Council knew by now that Elise had been working on resurrecting Candice. Elise had convinced the Council that bringing back Candice was really further research for the Lazarus Project. Elise had argued that if she could repair brain tissue, she could heal diseases such as Alzheimer's, seizures, multiple sclerosis, and Parkinson's disease. After all, these conditions would also have to be researched in order to ensure immortality. The Council had reluctantly capitulated, because it had felt powerless to do otherwise. But that would not continue for much longer. Even before this latest business, the Council had been growing restive. Elise had made it clear to Sara that they had little time left.

"I want you to know that I, Savants Granger and Myer, and many other Savants are very grateful for your brave action in executing Dr. Carloff," said Leeto. "It seemed, from our overhead view, that you acted alone. I think it was extremely courageous under such a . . . shall I say, strong leader. You risked being sent to prison. But . . . may I be frank?"

"Yes."

"Well," Leeto said, smiling another fake grin, "from the drone footage reviewed by me and many other Savants, it did not appear like Mother had any interest in killing them. On the contrary, even the boy still lives. The boy was placed into custody with Chief Officer Harding. But we all know that the XY is, by genetic blood, Gena's nephew. It seems Elise is acting out of kindness for her Officer, not considering the interests of the city at all."

"I can't speak for her on this, Leeto. I . . ." Sara looked away. She rubbed her eyes with her sleeve. She felt like crying again. "I didn't even know the XY was still alive."

"I want you to know, Sara, that we are very worried about Mother's mental well-being. She has not been acting herself. We are concerned that she is no longer fit to be our revered leader. I know that this sounds traitorous, and I'm quite sure Mother herself will review this message, and . . . that is well, because, you see, I have tried to contact her, and she repeatedly refuses my calls. So if she reviews the video, that is well. She needs to know how desperate the Council is becoming. I can only hold them back for so long. I believe that it is just a matter of time before they vote for dissolution of her Motherhood. But I think that, perhaps . . . you know, Sara, maybe it's time for her to step down."

"I don't see Elise ever stepping down," Sara said with a chuckle.

"No. She loves her revered job. And believe me, Sara, we love our Mother. But I am very concerned, you see, that she has become much too distracted over her personal problems. If she loses Motherhood, have you thought about where that leaves you, my dear?"

Yes. Sara had thought about that a lot. She was very worried about Elise—not because she cared what happened to her boss, but because she cared about her own fate. If Elise were overthrown, where would that leave her?

"I'm sure you have," Leeto added.

"I answer to Elise, Viceroy. I believe the Council will understand that any work I do is under her direct orders."

"Of course, Sara. You're safe. You're very loyal, and we'll

consider that. But whatever comes to be, know that many of the Savants are upset over the time wasted. We have seen some of our loved ones die. You and Elise may have loved Candice, but we have loved countless others too. And as you've squandered resources for Candice, you've taken them away from our friends and family.

"But don't misunderstand me. I messaged you today for two reasons. First, I and many of the rest of us commend you for shooting Dr. Carloff. Thank you for killing her. Hopefully, Rex will fail in reviving her."

"She's not dead?"

"No. But don't worry. Her condition is critical. Let us hope that you properly executed her. We all know she deserved it." Leeto smiled and raised her glass in a silent toast that made Sara consider just how evil this bitch really was. "But that is not the only reason I contacted you." She drank some more wine and then said, "You . . . you are Lead Savant, not Chief. Has it ever occurred to you that because of your purely business relationship with Mother, you have never been given respect from Mother as her rightful heir? If Team Mother is relieved of her duty, you will be cast aside because Elise never gave you Candice's title. That seems so unfair, Sara. And I feel for this injustice. Many of us do."

"I don't need to ever be Mother. I have accepted my title."

"Of course. I understand. Just know that, unlike Mother, we are very impressed with your research. We believe that, had Elise done the work that was advised by the mainframe, you would have finished Candice's work by now and be rightfully honored forever as the Savant who brought us our rightful eternal gift. Now we fear that you will be cast aside."

"I'm fine, Leeto. I'm content."

"Well, if you have a change of heart, contact me personally. Let me and the Council know. We can even transfer you before Mother endangers you even further. I would be happy to have you assist me in Sky City. We have a whole new Genetics department working on research from Pyramid Corporation over there in their modern laboratory now."

"Am I in danger, Savant Gansey?"

Such a direct question. How would this shifty bitch answer her?

Leeto responded with a sinister smile. Then she leaned forward. "You're running out of time, Sara. Consider my offer, if you understand my gist, Savant, and know that I'd love to work with you. I think I might just be a little fairer than Savant Elise Jackson."

"Thank you for your kind words and concern. But . . . I love Mother."

"And I love Mother too," Leeto said, leaning back in her chair. She swiveled a little playfully, drank down the rest of her wine, and said, "She's given us such great progress in the Lazarus Project, up until two years ago, that is. Consider what I'm offering you, Sara. I invite you to meet with me in person anytime. We should have lunch. And again, dear, thank you very much for shooting Dr. Carloff in the chest."

With that, her image faded from the room.

Sara leaned back in her couch, feeling even more hopeless. Leeto knew of the damage to the drive. She had to. Was she offering Sara a way out before the Council ruled on Elise's fate? And should Sara take it, turning her back on Elise? She feared her predicament. And yet she knew Elise and feared turning her back on Elise even more.

CHAPTER 4
CANDY 2.0

THERE COMES a time when rage no longer quenches the emptiness inside a broken heart. No matter how much glass is shattered, wood splintered, or flesh torn, the death of Candice remained. Elise used to just let herself rage, but rage did nothing. Her Candy Savant was gone. It was time to get over it.

She would never get over it.

Of course, Candice wasn't gone. Her naked body stood frozen upright in a metal cryochamber located in the shiny white-walled train car of HQ Lab with frost and ice crystals forming along the cold glass and distorting the image of her gorgeous face. Candice's naked body—once alluring—had lost its attraction within the silver metallic capsule. It was bad enough that Elise had to mourn for Candice; she also had to look at her dead, frozen body.

Even before her lover's death, Elise could not stand working in the lab. Any interest in science had been stifled long ago under the torture of Team Mother Reyburn. So in order to avoid the lab and the view of her dead lover, she did most of her work at the third floor of her penthouse office. She dealt most of the dirty work to her ditz assistant, Sara, who visited the icicle chamber often when it came time for tissue samples.

Elise shifted in her chair, bringing a shaky wine bottle up to her lips. She would get drunk tonight . . . or this afternoon . . . or morning. Whatever the fuck time it was. No, she was already very inebriated, drunk in the dark emptiness of her home. All the blinds were drawn closed outside along the slanted windows of her pyramid penthouse. But it was dark outside, she thought. She spun a little on her half-egg-shaped swivel chair, nearly dropping the bottle. She took another swig of wine—a very large one—down to the last drop, most of it dripping down her white robe.

She had been so close, so close to bringing Candice back. No one had ever been so close to bringing the living back from the dead. But Candice's neural decay had been too rapid. After a year and a half of failures, Elise had finally sought help from scientists in her newly constructed ultramodern research center in Sky City. She had sent her precious small silver disk there under armed guard. And it had been there, in Sky City, until that motherfucking Dr. Lilith Jerkoff had stolen her beloved and erased Candy from existence.

YOU FUCKING BITCH!

She hurled the empty wine bottle down her ramp, hearing it roll the three floors down and crash against a wall. Then she laughed.

Well, at least Rex hadn't been able to revive Dr. Jerkoff at Angel of Hope Hospital. Lilith Carloff was dead.

And now the Savant Council was about to overthrow her.

Elise had squandered everything for her lover. Her plan, perfect before Lilith had spoiled everything, had been to revive Candice, proudly present her to the Council as a sample of immortality, and be granted a delay in completing the Lazarus Project. Now Elise had nothing.

She closed her eyes.

∼

DISORIENTED, ELISE OPENED HER EYES. SHE WASN'T SURE HOW long she had slept. She found herself still reclining in her central half-eggshell gray swivel chair at the top of the three-story ramp of her penthouse. She looked at her slanted window. Her window angled down sharply, following the pyramidal shape of the outdoor high-rise. The blinds were closed, so there was nothing to see beyond the glass in front of her. She still wasn't sure what time it was, but she knew she was dizzy.

She swiveled in the darkness and hummed stupidly. Then she lifted her finger up to her long black hair to brush it back from her eyes, but her hand missed her bangs and her long black fingernail nicked her chin. She winced and then giggled.

"Rex," she said in the dark. "Rex."

"Yes, Mother."

"R-e-x," she drawled with a laugh.

"Yes, Mother."

"Show . . . show me . . . show me the file on 23-N."

"Where would you like her projected, Mother?"

"Right here, dope. Right in . . ." She pointed down the dark ramp and nearly fell out of her chair. She liked it dark. She wanted it completely dark and had even shut off the dim mood lights that ran down the ramp of her home. If not for the lines of light between the blinds on the outside glass, it would be pitch black.

"There!" she cried, after a long silence.

"Savant Jackson, please recall that I cannot see you. I cannot see *there*. I can only hear your words. And at the moment, with all the lights turned off, I could not see you anyway. Please be more specific."

"The *fucking* . . . *fucking* ramp, you idiot! Put her on the . . . the fucking ramp, you fucking useless plastic dick! And . . . dress . . . dress her . . . in something nice. Dress her in her . . . Savant clothes, the cherry-red ones. Mine. The fucking pre—"

She lifted her finger to her chin but missed it and hit her cheek again. "Or maybe that frilly colorful peacock one I made her wear that time at my parade, eh, Rex?" She burst into laughter. "Remember that? Do you remember that one, Rex, when I had Candy wear that?"

Candice Harlow appeared before her in the darkness wearing a fluffy rainbow-colored dress with her long blond hair tied in a ponytail. She stood on the ramp under Elise, and in the darkness, it appeared as if her ghost had materialized there. Elise stared at her glorious fat cheeks and pointy nose, then looked down where the top met her chest, displaying, ever discreetly, the cleavage of her plump full breasts. Her Candy Doll—the prettiest girl Elise had ever seen. But the dress was ridiculous. And it made Elise laugh harder.

"You bitch!" Elise said, pointing an unsteady finger amid gales of laughter. "Bitch!" Candice furrowed her brow. The laughter stopped. "You haunt me! You're always here. You never leave me alone, Candy. Go away!"

Instead, Candice walked closer to Elise. Then she ran her lovely fingers along her soft blond bangs. Candy straightened the multicolored dress. The dress was hideous, but even this monstrosity looked good on Candice. Only Candice could make such a ridiculous outfit look decent.

"I miss you, Can," Elise said. She was surprised at how choked up she sounded.

"I miss you too, Elise," said Candice. It was Candice's voice. Her same voice. And her exact expression. It made Elise's heart race.

"Go," Elise said, frowning. She leaned forward, and for a moment she lost her balance and nearly fell out of the chair again. "Come . . . come here. Say something. Let me hear more of your sweet voice."

"Elise."

Elise giggled. "Say it again."

"Elise."

"Say it again."

"Elise."

"What . . . what else can you do?"

Candice crouched down and ran her pale palm along Elise's cheek. Elise couldn't feel it, but she could see the image of those lovely dainty fingers. She wished she could feel the warmth of Candice's hand.

"Change her again, Rex," Elise said and giggled excitedly. "Change . . . change her into her Savant clothes. Not that stupid dress. I want to see her in my red one."

"Yes, Mother," said Rex.

Candice did not shift an inch, but instantly she was wearing her tight cherry-red Savant clothes. The rubber-leather polymer was tight over her bosom down to her hips and along her long legs. Her long blond hair flowed over the cherry-red latex.

"Twirl, " Elise commanded. She loosened the rope over her silk robe and reached inside, touching the curve of her breast. She ran a finger along her nipple, pretending that it was Candy's. "Twirl around a little, Can, so I can see you better, babe."

Candice obliged. With a hint of a smile, she stood up, turned, and cocked her head back, letting her hair dangle. Then she bent over, showing her hips. Elise stared at her plump ass. Candice looked back and smiled.

"Around. Go. Twirl round and round." Elise spun in her chair. "Round and around, round and round, my cherry cherry Candy Doll. Turn round and round for me."

Candice turned around like a model on a runway.

"You've always been one piece of ass, Can. Damn."

"You like . . . this?" asked Candice as she slowly unzipped

her suit, baring the contour of one pale breast. "I can take it all off, Elise. I can peel off your outfit." Elise jerked back, surprised by Candice's voice. She didn't like hearing her voice so clear. It creeped her out a little and almost broke the spell. But then she wanted to hear that voice again.

"Say . . ." Elise closed her eyes and ran her hand down between her legs. She reached into her panties and started touching herself. "Yes. Say . . . say something, say something again to me, babe."

"Do you like what you see, Mother?" Candice asked, perfectly pronouncing every wonderful word with her old familiar voice. Yes, it was clearly her voice.

"Of course I do, dope. You're hot. Why don't you strip that top of yours all the way down and bare your tits for your Mother?"

Candice slowly peeled down the top. The profile of her white breast showed along her side. It was irresistible. She stood directly above Elise. Elise ran her finger along the image of her soft skin with one hand while touching herself with the other. It seemed so real.

"Pull it down your legs and touch yourself for me. Make love to me, babe."

Candice ran her fingers over Elise's. The sight of those long, dainty fingers touching her own turned Elise on more than ever. Then Candy gestured for Elise to explore the curves of her breasts with her. Candice pinched the erect red nipple of one breast. Elise closed her eyes, rubbing herself. Up and down. Up and down.

"It certainly is getting hot in here, Elise." Elise wasn't sure if it was Rex's voice or Candy's. She didn't care anymore.

"Yeah . . . pull . . . pull off your underwear and come closer. I miss you so much, babe."

Elise opened an eye. Candy had a small red birthmark on her stomach under her right breast. Even that had been scanned and remembered by the mainframe. Elise looked at it and then down to her perfectly soft belly button.

"Now touch yourself," Elise said. "Show me your fingers between your legs."

Candice smiled. She slowly pulled down the rest of her suit, kicking free of it and then turning so that her ass faced Elise. She bent over and started fingering herself, sticking her dainty index finger in and out of her pussy and letting Elise watch her.

"Like this?" Candice asked.

Oh, how Elise missed her. And now, it took her over the edge. Elise rubbed herself harder. And as Elise rubbed her pussy harder, Candice did the same. Elise moaned, and Candice moaned with her. It felt so real. It felt wonderful.

"Oh, Candy. Shit!"

Elise reached out to touch Candy's ass, but her fingers passed right through the projection.

Candy froze. It was a computer error, freezing the image at the worst time. Elise fell off her chair.

"*Goddamnit!*" she shouted. "Fucking Rex! Shut it off! Shut it off now, you goddamn *prick!*"

"Sorry, Mother," said Rex's voice. Candice's image stood unnaturally still, naked and bent over. "There was a break in the streaming."

"Shut the goddamn image off, then! Do it now! Stop making me look at her asshole, you fucking dick!"

The image vanished. Elise crawled back in her chair, spinning it around in a circle. She felt so dizzy. Then she fell off the chair onto the hardwood floor again. "Shit!"

A tear ran down Elise's cheek. But then she chuckled.

The doorbell rang.

"Who? Who the hell . . ."

"Savant Sara Holmes is at the door. Are you all right, Mother?" asked Rex. "I heard you fall."

"Do I look all right?"

"I don't know. I can't see you."

"Very funny."

Elise drifted down the ramp on all fours, almost rolling at one point.

"Should I let her in for you?" Rex asked.

"Yeah."

Elise heard the front door swing open three stories below and someone step through the threshold of her pad.

"Elise?" said a voice at the bottom of the ramp. It was Sara, but it was so dark that Elise couldn't see her on the bottom floor of her penthouse. "Elise?" Elise struggled to rise. "Elise? Elise? Rex told me you wanted to see me."

Elise saw a shadow moving up the ramp.

"Rex," said Sara, "open the blinds."

The blinds opened over every window by the sides of the house. At the top floor of the penthouse was a giant floor-to-ceiling window. This was the one Elise had been staring at when it was closed by the outside blinds. Now it let in all the bright light from the city. Elise squinted.

"You're drunk," Sara snapped. "And it smells in here. You reek of alcohol, Mother."

"Really?" asked Elise sarcastically.

"Elise, it's the middle of the afternoon. Rex told me to leave the lab. He said you had something very important to tell me. What is it?"

"You," Elise said, squinting at Sara's face. Sara now stood over her. She touched Sara's hand with a tremulous finger. "You're here. You're not . . . in the lab?"

"Rex told me to come here. He said you needed me right away."

Elise attempted a smile. Then she just stared into Sara's eyes. Sara's eyes were so much like Candice's. They were sapphire blue and gorgeous. And Sara had Candice's same Goldilocks long hair. And that wasn't the end of their similarities. Sara had her pointed nose and perfect thin eyebrows. It was said that when Sara was created from the incubators, her genes were not much different than Candice's. They didn't grow up as sisters but were genetically close cousins.

But Elise had never touched her. Just like she had never used the simulation to see Candice. Until today. It had always seemed wrong. But now that two years of work had been lost and everything was hopeless, Elise was in such a foul mood that she didn't care anymore. If she couldn't revive Candice, then goddamnit, she'd fuck her hologram. Or . . . *Sara?*

"So pretty," Elise said, staring up into Sara's sapphire blues. "You're so pretty, Sara. Kiss me." Elise closed her eyes and puckered her lips stupidly.

"Elise, you're drunk," Sara said with a nervous giggle.

"So?"

"You want me to help you to bed?"

"Aha," Elise said with a big smile. Sara laughed again and helped Elise stand up.

"You're really drunk, Elise."

"Are you my Savant?" Elise asked.

"Of course I am. I'm your Lead Savant, Mother."

"Then kiss me." Elise ran her hand along Sara's tight lime-green Savant jumpsuit. Then she closed her eyes again. "Think of it as . . . an order."

"Elise," Sara said, shaking her head.

"Why? Just one kiss, babe."

Sara got close to Elise's mouth. "You reek of alcohol," she said, giggling again. The giggle turned Elise on even more.

"It's wine. Two bobbles, baby. Now kiss me, you pretsy twitsy."

Sara pecked her lips then backed away. "Elise, no. You're drunk."

"Kiss me!" Elise shouted in sudden rage. Sara leapt back, retreating down the ramp.

"Elise, I—"

"Remove your top!" Elise cried. "Now! Fucking undress for me!"

Elise lounged back on the floor, pulling down her own white robe, allowing her naked body to show.

"Elise," Sara said. "Stop it. This isn't funny."

"Are you"—Elise leaned on her knees with a nasty grin—"refusing me? Your Team Mother?"

"Elise, you don't know what's you're doing. Let me help you to bed."

"Why do you think Rex brought you here? To fuck me. To fuck Mother. I'm sober enough to know that. That bastard's always scheming things. So just do it. Fuck me."

"Elise," Rex said, "I think you should—"

"We're like goddamn marionettes for the ones-and-zeros bastard," Elise said. "He figures if I fall for you, I'll forget all about Candy and go right back to the Lazarus Project. It's really not that hard to figure out. Well, I think we might as well. Candy's gone for good now. So oblige him, won't you? Strip down your clothes, come to your Mother, and fuck me. It'll make him happy, and it'll be fun."

"You need help, Elise," Sara said. "I know you're stressed, but you look awful."

"Thanks a lot." Elise crept closer and grabbed Sara's wrist. "Now come here and fuck me. Fuck me like Candy. It'll make Mother feel better. You look like her. Rex is absolutely right. What have I been missing? Come here and—"

"Stop it!" yelled Sara, finally angry. She yanked back her hand.

Elise squinted at her.

"Sorry . . . Elise."

"Coward." Elise turned away. "You've always been a sniveling stupid coward. That's why Candice died. You let the ones-and-zeros dickhead kill her. You're a coward and a moron.

And a . . . cry-cry. That's what you are. A cry-cry. A fucking cry-cry. And it was because of you that Candy died."

"Don't say that," Sara snapped. "Just . . . don't say that! Stop it, Elise. I . . . I think I should go."

"Why? You gonna cry?"

Sara started down the ramp. Elise watched her with blurry, blinking eyes. She even drifted half to sleep for a moment. Then she shouted: "Stop! Team Mother has not *executed* you yet!"

Sara froze a floor down.

Then Elise vomited all over the floor of the ramp.

"Shit." She wiped her lips with one hand. "I . . . What did I say, Sara? I meant"—Elise laughed nervously—"*excused,* not *exe-cuted.* Sorry."

"I'll talk to you when you get a hold of yourself, Elise."

"Sure." Elise looked her over. "You ruined the whole fucking thing anyway." And then she lay on the floor, resting her head on one arm, and closed her eyes. "A fucking cry-cry, that's all she is," she muttered. "Just a useless tweet-tweet cry-cry bird. That's why she never succeeded in anything in the lab. Nothing but a . . ."

She cracked open an eye. Sara stood at attention on the first floor, staring up at her. It made her laugh. The room spun a little. Elise tightened the rope around her waist and continued to lie next to her vomitus. It wasn't long before she heard a small automated cleaner roll out from the wall and begin vacuuming the fluid and stink beside her.

Sara stood uncomfortably, not daring to leave without being excused. She was caught, and Elise knew it. Elise was holding her there—but why? Was she that horny? No, she didn't want Sara. She was barely conscious. But, per custom, Sara could not leave Mother's home without being excused. The law stated that a Savant could not even leave a Team

Grandmother's presence without her permission. But why was Elise doing it to Sara? Elise didn't even know.

"May I be excused?" Sara finally asked.

"I could force you on me," Elise said, stumbling up and looking down on her. "Make me your real *Master*. That's what Reyburn did to me."

"You told Lilith how much you hated her for it."

Elise said nothing.

"May I be excused?" Sara repeated.

"Get the fuck out." Then the dizziness came on again. "Go back to the lab and do more of nothing."

"Sure, Elise."

Sara passed by the kitchen towards the exit, but then she turned. "Rex and I were able to salvage some of Candice's neural net from the lab," Sara said. "There were traces of your work throughout the archives of HQ. Rex was able to piece some back together. I think we can hurry our past work and get to where we were in a matter of six months instead of two years."

"Is that supposed to make me happy?" Elise asked, leaning on her elbow. "In six months, Candy will be un-salvable, you goddamn moron."

Sara looked up the ramp but said nothing.

"Every day Candy's brain is more damaged." Elise clumsily crawled up to a sitting position on the floor. Then she looked down on Sara. "And, anyway, *you* won't work out anything. *I've* done all the work, because *you* are a goddamn moron. You couldn't bring life to a lab rat."

"Whatever, Elise. I thought you should know. Perhaps you should sober up and help, instead of feeling so sorry for yourself."

Elise turned and faced the window. She put her hand over her eyes to block out the harsh afternoon light. "Rex, close the blinds," she said. "And bring Candy back so I can fuck her.

Don't send me some twit twin. Present Candy in her short lavender lace skirt—you know, the one that drapes right over the crack of her ass, so when she bends over, you can see her ass through the lace . . . God, you were so hot, Can. Or, no. Fuck it, Rex. Just materialize her naked. Why wait?"

"May I leave?" Sara asked.

"Get out!"

CHAPTER 5
TOP SECRET

SARA FELT dirty as she flew across the city, heading for a meeting she had kept secret from Elise. It was early dawn, the sun just starting to rise off in the horizon through the openings of the pyramidal walls of the city. She had, sort of, lied to Elise and told her that she needed a day off. Sara argued that with all the stress of working every day and night over the last month, she needed a brief respite from her work. There was a great deal of truth in that, but that wasn't why she'd taken the morning off.

She flew her green rocket bike across Central Park, keeping her eyes from straying to the central Diamond Obelisk raised in memory of her lover, then headed clear across the city to Pyramid Corporation. This was a small run-down district in Sector Four. In one of the only rectangular high-rises in the district was Central Bank, a financial institution run by the Treasurer of the Savant Council and Viceroy of Pyramid Corporation—Savant Leeto Gansey. Within the hierarchy of Arkite's Savant Council, her position was the highest next to that of the President, Dana Haish, and the Chief Savant, the late Candice Harlow. The building was an old white concrete building near the flat triangle of Pyramid Corp.

Sara landed her bike on a landing pad at the top of Central Bank. She looked up and saw the small red lights of a couple of copter drones flying high above. Rex was watching. She guessed he would tell Elise, but she didn't care anymore.

The building was so ancient and dilapidated that it lacked electric doors. She spotted a few windows above that were boarded up from inside. Sara opened a double glass door by the side of her landing pad and walked down a dismal dark hallway, hearing only the sound of her boots. The hallway was dimly lit by lights hung from lanterns in the ceiling. It smelled old and musty. A few workers in gray suits passed her, looking down and minding their business. But whenever they recognized Sara's lime-green jumpsuit and metal choker, they nodded in respect.

The hallway led to an elevator. Sara took the elevator with another worker. Sara was already at the roof of the establishment, so she pressed the only direction—down.

The worker was young, maybe twenty, with short hair and wearing a formal suit. The only thing distinctive about the girl was thick black makeup and long purple plastic earrings. She stared at the ground.

"Good morning," Sara said.

"Morning."

"Can you tell me what floor the main financial office is?"

"You were on it, Savant," replied the girl. "It's on the top level, twenty-two."

"Oh."

"Here," the girl said, pressing a stop button on the elevator. "I'll take you back up, Master."

"That's very kind, thank you."

"You're Mother's Lead Savant, right? Savant Sara Holmes?"

"Yeah."

The girl smiled. Then the elevator stopped and the door opened. The girl showed Sara an adjoining hallway.

Sara walked down the hall and through another metal double door. She was surprised by the sudden light along an expansive room. In the midst of all the concrete and dimly lit ugliness, she walked into a beautiful, bright modern lobby. The floor had a shiny white sheen, unlike the drab concrete floors of the hallways outside. There were many meeting rooms with windows along all the walls. Through one of the windows, she spotted Savant Natalie Granger excitedly jump up and head to the glass door to greet her.

Savant Granger wore a violet Savant jumpsuit and choker. She matched the usual flair of black standard-issue makeup with a few faint lines of matching purple around her eyes and cheeks. Sara knew Natalie to be a sneaky witch, fake, untrustworthy, and detested by Elise but smiley like all the Savants. She was a tanned skinny girl with long blond hair and mauve-dyed highlights. Before Sara could walk up to the front desk and ask for help from an older woman in a drab gray suit, Savant Granger ran up to her.

"Sara!" said Savant Granger. She ran into Sara's arms and hugged her. "It's been so long! Come in, sister. Come in. What a pleasant surprise."

Then Natalie locked her arm in hers and led her back into the conference room she had come from. The room was bright and had a window spanning the wall, showing a view of Sector Four—not a very beautiful view, being full of the destitute tents and poorest parts of the city, but a view from the top floor nonetheless.

"Can I get you a cup of coffee, my dear?" Savant Granger asked, finally letting go of her.

"Sure."

"Cream or sugar?"

"Black."

Savant Granger opened the glass door and shouted out to

the greeting desk, "Kendra, go call Leeto. Tell her Sara's here . . . and get our Lead Savant a cup of coffee—black."

"Yes, Master."

"What a pleasant surprise," repeated Natalie, returning with a gaping grin. She gestured for Sara to sit at the head of the table. It was a large glass conference table with eight black leather seats. Sara sat down. Then she looked out along the view below. The sun was out now and Sara could clearly see Pyramid Corporation with its huge flat concrete pyramid stretching for a couple miles beneath her. Then there was the old highway, now in pieces, with sections destroyed over the centuries, its rubble left uncleared. Not too far from here were the tents and broken buildings of the Candle District. And then the prisons of Court Station, close to the border of Sector Four. It was a beautiful view of the squalor of Arkite. And a great contrast from the green of lovely Central Park farthest in her view. If she strained hard enough, she could even see Sector One and HQ Civic Building of downtown Arkite. To her immediate left was the desert—endless desert through the checkered walls of the city. The megatrusses were so close to her at Central Bank that she had unobstructed views of the desert Badlands. Rarely was she this close to the wall of the city.

"Leeto will be here shortly," Natalie said excitedly, looking down for a moment at her wrist. She ran a finger along the embedded monitor in her arm, glancing at something. "I know she will be simply thrilled that you've stopped by."

I'm sure.

Kendra, the assistant, an old plump girl wearing a gray dress—the dress matched the color of the workers' suits but was more casual and loose-fitted—walked in and handed Sara a cup of coffee. Kendra smiled a false grin too.

Everyone smiled. Even three workers who walked down the main lobby to other sections of the office stared into the room and smiled. Sara's presence was making quite a stir.

There goes any thought of hiding my visit from Mother.

But she knew Elise would find out one way or another. That was one of the reasons it had taken her this long to finally meet with them.

Natalie Granger sat beside Sara. Her eyes were shifty and sinister, but wise. Sara knew Natalie was bright, probably smarter than herself. And she seemed to be studying Sara. Sara remembered her from school. Natalie had visited Arkite U to teach a class once. Sara, although she was Elise's Lead Assistant, was young and had been recruited only a year after graduating from Arkite U. She was ten years younger than Natalie.

"What a joyous visit," Natalie repeated, resting her head over her hands. The bitch was loving it. She knew that Sara was there to talk to Leeto about leaving Mother. Sara drank some coffee, having a hard time swallowing.

"Does Mother need a loan?" asked Natalie stupidly with another fake smile. "Do tell."

Bitch. Team Mother never needed anything from anyone.

"If she needed money, Savant Granger, I wouldn't have come personally."

"Yes," Natalie said, her smile somehow growing wider and faker. "So why are you here? What can we do for you?"

"I need to talk to Leeto."

"She's coming." Natalie touched her wrist monitor. "Kendra, get me some coffee too, will you?"

"All right," said the voice through her monitor.

Sara saw Kendra wave and smile at them through the window. Everyone was so fake in phony happiness.

"How's work at HQ Lab?" asked Natalie, leaning her chin over steepled fingers. "I think it is so fortunate that you have the privilege of working there."

"It's hard work."

"No doubt. You look tired."

"We are close to reviving Candice," Sara lied. "It's only a matter of time."

"Leeto has us doing some research of our own," Natalie replied. "Aside from her financial work, she is a brilliant scientist, as you well know. We're leasing a lab close within Sky City. We've worked out one of the conundrums with chromosome transfer. Leeto thinks she can crack the code and enable quicker chromosomal duplication. We have submitted it to the Council. I think it will help us finish the Lazarus Project faster. I spearheaded the research myself."

"Congratulations," Sara said. She really didn't care. She was here for political reasons, not research, and of course Natalie knew that.

"Yes, well," Natalie continued, "pity you and Mother don't seem to care much for the Lazarus Project anymore."

"We care."

Natalie lost her smile for a second. Then Kendra walked in with Natalie's coffee. Natalie took the cup and raised it in a silent, somewhat mocking toast, then drank.

"I think if we were given more resources from the mainframe," she continued, "as we have asked for, Sara, we could really help Magnacourt's progress."

"I can bring it up to Elise."

"Oh, don't bother, dear. Mother is well aware of our monthly requests. And I am very accustomed to her denials."

Leeto Gansey walked in. She was wearing the same gunmetal Savant jumpsuit she'd had on when Sara had spoken with her over the 3-D Viewer. She was short, not more than four and a half feet tall. Sara and Natalie jumped up.

"Sara!" Leeto said, running to her with her arms out. Sara was really tiring of their phoniness. She gave Leeto a cold embrace. "What a surprise. What a wonderful surprise. Don't you think, Lee? What a wonderful surprise.'"

"Hi, Savant Gansey."

"To what do we owe the pleasure of this momentous visit, Lead Savant?"

Leeto sat down across from Natalie with her back to the large window and stared at Sara. Both of them stared, with very amused smirks on their faces.

"I remember your call . . ." Sara looked down. She bit her lip, then she cursed at herself for hesitating. Hesitation was weak, and she was going to get eaten alive by the two Savants if she didn't show confidence. "I . . . I . . ." Sara looked around the room. There was nothing but a brown carpeted floor, an oak cabinet built into the wall at both ends, the window overlooking the view of the downtrodden city, and another window looking out into the office. But she figured the mainframe was here. Somewhere. There had to be a microphone hidden in the wall or cabinet, maybe even the glass of the desk. Rex was listening. Or perhaps he watched through the window from a drone she couldn't even see.

"Go on," Leeto said. She gave a comforting grin, looked at Sara's white mug, and then touched her arm. "Would you like something with more spice? Perhaps we should celebrate having such an esteemed guest. I can add some brandy."

"I don't know what I can say here," she said honestly.

Leeto lost her smile. Turning to Natalie, she said, "Lee, close the drapes for our esteemed guest."

Sara was surprised, having assumed they would be automated.

"And may I see your wrist, dear?" Leeto asked Sara.

As Natalie got up and closed the black drapes, covering the window to the indoor office, Leeto disabled Sara's wrist monitor. Then the two Savants disabled their wrists too.

"Sara, this room is soundproof," Natalie said. "There is no access to Rex. The building was made to be completely secure for Central Bank. You can tell us anything here."

Sara's eyes drifted to the window overlooking the city.

"Don't worry," Natalie continued. "That window is specially tinted to block video surveillance from Rex. Your secrets are perfectly safe with us. You can speak freely." She sat down.

Leeto nodded expectantly.

But Sara was losing her nerve. She didn't have a plan. She had no idea what she would say to Dr. Gansey. She just knew she couldn't stand working for Elise anymore. Elise had only gotten worse. She drank every day and night and only communicated with her in order to scream at her. Sara was sick of working in HQ Lab, and though she would have given her own life for Candice's, she did not believe Candice would ever come back to her again. But she wasn't about to tell them that. So . . . what could she tell them? She would prod them to see what they could offer her in exchange for information. But she would not reveal her difficulties at HQ Lab. It was a fine, dangerous line, and as intelligent as all the Savants were, these were the smartest, shiftiest ones in the whole city.

"What can you offer me, Savant Gansey?" asked Sara.

Leeto chuckled. "What do you want, dear?"

"Security. I . . . I want to be assured that . . . whatever happens, I am protected. I can't say much else. I'm here to see what you can offer me through Pyramid Corporation if the Council were to rule against Elise."

"If Elise's Motherhood is taken, there are some measures we can take to protect you," Leeto said with a nod. "But, of course, sister, it comes with a price. How close are you to reviving your beloved?"

Sara looked down.

"You're here, Sara," Natalie said. "Just tell us."

"We have our suspicions, Sara," said Leeto. "Your association with us involves trust. You give me information, I will give you information. That is the nature of all transactions, right? I can't help you if you don't help me."

"I can't tell you," Sara said, shaking her head.

"Then get the fuck out," Natalie said, dismissing her with her hand.

"Now, now, Lee," said Leeto. "She's our guest. Be nice. Let her talk."

Then Leeto steepled her fingers and leaned her chin on her hands, waiting, just as Natalie had done earlier. They both waited for her to betray her boss.

"I think you two already know our situation," Sara said.

"On the contrary, Lead Savant," Leeto said. "We do not. We only know that we and the rest of the Savants have been led along like puppets by that dog leader of yours, Elise Jackson. Pardon me"—Leeto lifted a hand—"of course, I don't mean disrespect. But you have to understand that we are very upset with Mother for her delays."

"I fully mean the disrespect," said Natalie.

"Now, Lee." Leeto laughed. Then she looked at Sara and placed a hand on her arm again. "Sara, see how Natalie talks. That is treason, right? This room is secure, and we already trust you because you've come here. You can speak freely."

But Sara couldn't speak. She had lost her courage.

Leeto got up after more silence and walked to the large window. "How do you like our view, Sara?"

"It's nice."

"It's shit," said Leeto, wrinkling her nose. "It's disgusting. This is the greatest view in Sector Four. If you look around carefully"—she pointed—"you'll see our pretty view of Arkite's four Courts. Our prisons for the unlawful. We have a lovely view of the prison recreation area. Sometimes, if I look carefully enough, I can watch the criminals playing basketball, lifting weights, or wrestling each other. I used to watch Candice there with a mag-lens. She used to sit all alone. Your girlfriend was a very queer girl, never quite fitting in—never really fitting in anywhere, for that matter. A nice girl. She used to sit alone, minding her business. Elise had sent her lover there, after all . .

. well, you know the story. Candice created a boy because of her assistant—Bren was her name. Candice and Bren created an XY. The boy was genetically Elise and Candice's son. Well, Elise shot her own XY baby with her gun and then sent Candice down there." Leeto paused and leaned against the glass of the window. "Your boss shot her own baby, her genetic son. Then sent Candice to prison for it."

She stared at Sara, waiting for a response, but Sara said nothing.

"Look closer, straight below." Leeto pointed under her. "You can see the great broad cement pyramid of our energy company, Pyramid Corp. This building, Central Bank, was created for Pyramid City by Mother Savant herself two hundred years ago to run simple commerce when the entire city was only this small series of buildings. You noticed how old the structure is. So, actually, Sara, you're sitting in the oldest building of our city. After the last three World Wars, the great Mother Savant took her army of women and conquered a small army that protected the energy buildings here. She took this very building. This building, Sara, is the oldest structure in the city. Because Mother Savant and our ancestors were actually invaders of Arkite. The original establishment here was a military base near an area named White Sands. Did you know this?"

"No."

Leeto smiled. "I don't even think Elise knows. She doesn't care. I learned about the history by talking to Dr. Reyburn. Reyburn and I were good friends. Did you know *that*, Sara?"

"No."

Leeto nodded. "And, sister, did you know that your boss was a cold-blooded murderer who personally gunned down over fifty scientists?"

Yes, Sara knew that.

"Team Mother is a fucking major bitch, isn't she?" Leeto

smiled again. Then she walked back to the table, sat down, and rested her hands on the table, leaning toward Sara. "You've been imprisoned just like your girlfriend Candice was. Candice was killed because she was manipulated by Elise. Now you are being manipulated. And if you don't act, you'll be dead soon too. But you know that already, don't you? That's why you're here."

"I don't know," Sara said. "I . . . no, I don't think that. I am only worried if she fails."

"Will she fail?" asked Natalie. "Tell us."

Leeto raised a finger at Natalie, then gestured to the city.

"Elise has downtown. Elise has Magnacourt. I have Pyramid City. But my dump comes with knowledge. My people are the rejects of the city. Look beyond Pyramid Corp. What do you see, Sara? You see tents and squalor. Vagrants. You see the scum of Arkite. That is what I control. I want more. So does Lee.

"Many more Savants—which I could name to you, but you haven't traded me enough information yet—want more too. I have told you my motivation, now how about you tell me yours? Isn't that fair?" She touched Sara's arm again. Then she smiled her sly grin. "I can tell you, Sara, that I know how the neural net was stolen. And I know the traitors who helped Dr. Teller steal it. You'd love to know that, wouldn't you? I tell you, you tell me. It's called a trade."

Then Leeto closed her eyes and leaned her head in her hands, rubbing her temples. She waited for Sara to speak. She waited for Sara to tell her what Sara had promised herself she would never tell them.

Sara said nothing.

Natalie looked impatient. Leeto periodically glanced at Sara, then she turned and just stared out at the view.

"Fuck," Leeto finally said. "All right. You want more. I'll give you more. Then you will tell me what I ask. Do you see the sand out there, Sara?"

Leeto pointed at the vast stretch of sand spreading out to the horizon under the clear desert sun. They were so close to the Pyramid walls that Sara almost felt like the building stood over the desert.

"Of course," Sara said. "The Badlands."

"Right, the Badlands. Did you know it is not radioactive? It is perfectly safe."

"No."

"This building was constructed as a solar reactor. I know this because I researched its structure. Then I tricked the mainframe into providing me information about its function. No one, not even Connie Reyburn, has told anyone this stuff. It was forbidden information a century ago, and then long since forgotten. Do you know why I'm telling you?"

"No."

"You tell me," she said with that annoying smile, "I tell you. The idea was to create a pyramid structure that could gather solar energy and focus it underground. Underground Arkite is an energy factory. I know this because I am in charge of the city's energy. The tunnels were created to harness the sun's rays and focus them into some sort of reactor. Why, I'm not sure. Now the tunnels are damaged and broken, but you certainly can still harness the city's energy from the panels along the walls for our use. This is what we do to provide Arkite with energy. I know about the reactor at the bottom of the fifth subbasement of this building because . . ." She paused and leaned forward. "You will tell me what I ask?"

Sara turned and stared out at the view.

Leeto sighed, then went on. "Dr. Carloff lived here with her son for eight years. Underground, right below this very building. I helped her evade our Central Police Organization, CPO, just like I can help you. Dr. Carloff also told me, by the way, that it is not radioactive outside the city."

"We were taught by Iris that it is," Sara objected. "From thermonuclear war."

"Iris lied to you," Natalie interjected.

"Iris has been lying to all the children of Arkite since heading our education services for the past century," Leeto said with a nod. "And likely she was deceiving the past Team Mothers before her hold on the HQ mainframe was transferred to Rex. The HQ mainframe, whether run by good ol' Iris or Rex, lies. But, of course, Iris is old enough to have been ordered to lie by Mother Savant herself.

"Ask Iris now. Go ahead and ask her, Sara. She holds all our secrets. I've tried, but she's elusive and provides little information to me—I suspect because I am not Mother. I'm sure, being that Elise shut Iris down completely during her reign, that Iris would love to talk to somebody now. Go ask her if you don't believe me."

"That's why Carloff wanted to escape outside the walls?" asked Sara.

"Of course," said Leeto. "The air is safe. Carloff knew that before you shot her. That's why she bargained with the neural net."

"Why are you telling me this?"

"Because your boss doesn't know. Do you know how I know?"

Sara shook her head.

"Lilith Carloff told me personally in the tunnels. I arrested her many years ago, thinking stupidly that your boss would commend me for the act. Elise didn't care. She really didn't care about Lilly or the XY at all. She never told me to release them, but she never asked me to keep them either. It surprised me, because I was attempting to befriend Elise. You know, get on her good side. But she never cared about Lilly or Adam. Why do you think she hasn't killed the XY yet?" Leeto laughed. "Well, she spares the XY now because he happens to be her best friend's nephew.

"Elise is dangerous, Sara. She's an egotistical, drug-addicted psychopath. She only cares about herself. Reyburn would have done anything to have gotten rid of her, but it was too late. Connie was my friend, Sara. In time, so was Lilith Carloff."

"But you rejoiced when I shot her. You told me so."

"No, Sara. I said that to you on your public 3-D Viewer, where every word is monitored. I was devastated by the news of Lilith's death. But you're blameless. I understand your anger and the love you have for Candice. The question is, does Elise?"

"Tell us the status of HQ Magnacourt, Sara," interjected Natalie. "Leeto just told you more than she wanted to. She's risking everything for you. Now it's your turn."

"You have suspected our progress," Sara said.

"Suspected isn't good enough," Leeto said. "I need to know exactly."

"I . . ."

"What other secrets would you like me to tell you!" snapped Leeto. Sara was surprised by her sudden fury. "Now I've endangered myself *and* my assistant, Savant Granger! Tell us as a fair trade, Sara. That will secure our secret for yours."

Sara remained silent.

"Tell us now!" Leeto raged, smacking her fist down on the table so hard that Sara jumped, afraid the glass would break.

Something broke in her instead. "It's hopeless," she said. "I've been at it for two years, and every month, Elise just becomes more insistent. I don't believe Elise will ever give up, even if you overthrow her. Now that the neural net was stolen, we've slid back to the beginning. And Candice has decayed more. I don't see how we can ever finish in time."

Sara cried. Leeto touched her hand and patted it.

"There, there," Leeto said. "You can't complete it? How terrible. Are you sure?"

"It's hopeless," Sara said.

"But you're sure? You have to be sure, Sara. I need one hundred percent. Are you positive?"

"Elise doesn't even go to the lab anymore. She's given up."

Leeto looked at Natalie with a smile. Natalie nodded.

"There, there, Sara." Leeto patted the shoulder pad of Sara's Savant jumpsuit. "We can help you." Sara shook her head, still crying. "There, there."

"Perhaps we should do the announcement now?" asked Natalie.

Sara looked up. Leeto signaled for Natalie to be quiet.

Then Sara realized what she had done. She had framed her boss. As much as she despised Elise, Elise had become her life. When there was recreation, though seldom, she spent it with Elise. In many ways, Elise was a friend.

"I shouldn't have come," Sara said, standing up. "I . . . thank you, but I'm . . . forget what I said. I can't . . ."

"There, there, Sara," Leeto said. "I didn't mean to upset you. You tell me and I tell you. Now that you told me, I know you won't tell Elise what I said today. See, we are sharing secrets. I can trust you again. I'm so sorry I upset you. Sit, my dear. Why, we're friends."

Sara shook her head. Natalie jumped up and walked behind Sara, touching a button that pulled out a drawer from the oak cabinet beside her. Then she handed a tissue to Sara for her tears. Sara wiped her eyes.

"It's just like what I told you on your Viewer at home—Elise is in trouble," Leeto added. "Your information builds trust."

"Can you continue to inform us of your progress in HQ Lab?" asked Natalie.

"I don't know."

"Think about it," Leeto said. "Think carefully. We can help you."

"We're having lunch," Natalie said. "Would you like to join us?"

"No. No, thank you. I have to go."

CHAPTER 6
MORNING STROLL

ELISE LET her rocket-cycle flight be circuitous, allowing the wind to wake her and sober her up. She flew close to the checkered megatruss pyramidal wall near the northwest part of the city and then traveled to north Sector Four, over the broken dusty hovels and tents of her people. She had tracked Sara. Suspiciously, now, when she needed her assistant more than ever, Sara had decided to take the day off. Elise had asked Rex to locate her. Central Bank. She had flown to Central Bank. The slums of Arkite. On her day off. What did Sara think Elise was, a sniveling cry-cry tweetsy tweet bird like herself?

But the betrayal was good for Elise. It ended Elise's three-week suicidal drug-filled alcoholic coma. It was just enough to push her off her stumbling ass and get her back to work.

Looking down, Elise could see a long stretch of broken concrete that once had been a highway for cars. The freeway hadn't been used in over a century, but its trail still existed as scattered cement stones bordered by hundreds of tents of vagrants. And then she saw the low-to-the-ground cement pyramid of Pyramid Corp. Pyramid Corp was only a couple of stories high but spanned miles in diameter. At the side of the

Pyramid stood a single rectangular concrete high-rise—Central Bank, the oldest building in Arkite. And surrounding the energy factory was more rubble. Elise watched women far below in rags look up at their supreme leader's afterburn as her bike came dangerously close to knocking down some of the canvas tents over the broken cement. Elise passed the Central Bank building and spotted Sara's lime-green bike parked on a landing bay.

She let her mind drift away from her traitorous assistant and thought of Candy. Well, she always thought of Candy, but now she wondered if she'd ever see her Candy breathe again. She was determined to do the impossible again, apparently without her sniveling cry-cry assistant. And anyway, she had gone through all the wine bottles in her private wine cellar.

"HQ Lab is currently moving near Sector Three, Mother," came Rex's voice in her helmet. "Would you like me to fly you on autopilot? It is traveling in your direction. I'll show you." A schematic three-dimensional map presented itself on the screen of her bike monitor as she flew between two water towers.

Elise turned her bike and headed back toward downtown. Soon she passed through Sector Two and more slums—Sector Two, with the exception of her lovely Sky City, was just as much of a dump as Sector Four. But Elise headed toward the greenery of Central Park.

Central Park had been Candice's favorite part of the city. The park lay between the city's four sectors. She circled around the green and sank close to Main Street. It was so early that it became dark as she dipped down lower than the skyscrapers that blocked the sunrise from downtown. Then, with the magnification of her helmet visor, she was able to focus on citizenry up early in the morning along Main Street: an old lady walking her dog, a group of women waiting in line in gray work clothes by intersections, another lady in a trench coat, likely an

Officer, stepping into a flying car as a flock of copter drones hovered about her.

She turned sharply and headed toward the entrance by the Arc de Triomphe along the main entrance of the park. Then she quickly passed over lovely trails, grass fields, brooks and waterfalls. The waterfalls, the paths along trees—perfectly manicured, with their antique streetlamps—and the stretches of grass were such glaring contrasts from the poverty of the northwest slums of her city she had just flown over. The contrast was like her and Candice. Elise felt like the slums of Arkite—destitute, dirty, and broken—while Candice was lush and pure like the great park.

Elise rose a little higher and headed farther east. She spotted only a handful of ladies walking the sidewalks along the fields and trees of the park. It was still empty, deserted at the break of day.

Then she flew over the only monument in the park—a crystal obelisk rising high beside brooks and trees. A glistening glass diamond reflecting dawn beautifully around the surrounding trees, like a jewel in the center of a forest. And it was *her* jewel. Her diamond for *her* Candy Doll. Elise had commissioned the monument to be made soon after Candice's passing. Seeing the glorious glistening diamond hurt her heart again. Elise had set it precisely in the center of the city, allowing the sun to shine brightly down the open top of the Pyramid.

I will bring you back. I promise.

She had said it before. She said it a lot. When she was discouraged and things seemed hopeless, she always thought those words to herself.

She circled over the diamond for a moment, then hit the rocket engine and rushed away, more determined than ever.

"Did you prep Candy for scanning, Rex?" asked Elise.

"Of course. Of course I did. She has been removed from her capsule and is lying on the operating table. The brainstem is still flawlessly preserved. That means we can revive her. But it will be difficult to deal with the new ischemic gaps. I will have to guess and formulate new connections. It cannot be perfect. You know"—he laughed mechanically—"it is ironic that we are using Savant Candice Harlow's research to recombine the neural synapses for her own brain. Still, it would have been much faster if you had allowed me to clone Candice. Repairing damaged avascular tissue is very difficult. It is just so time consuming, do you not think?"

Elise didn't respond.

"And what about Dr. Florence Teller?" Rex continued. "You must think of her sentence. And then there is the boy. Now, with the death of Dr. Carloff, what will you do with the XY?"

Elise flew over Lake Salmas, a large woman-made lake inside the park. It was stunning, being empty so early in the morning, but was just starting to glow orange from the rising sun.

"I said Sector Three, Mother," said Rex. "You are late. I suggest you dispense with your habit of circling over Central Park. We have a lot of work to do. I will reroute directions for you." A map appeared along the screen beneath her. "Do you want me to land you by remote control?"

Elise entered Sector Three.

Sector Three had been her home when she was a little girl. It was the home of most girls in Arkite. It was also the education center for study for all Savants, and the most suburban part of the city.

Elise flew over a series of square silver metallic buildings set over acres of sand and dirt. This was her school. Below was a special dormitory for the top students. Not far from here was Arkite University. She passed over the shiny silver lecture buildings, on-campus dormitories, and apartments and administration buildings. Primarily a science university, Arkite U was the location for all higher learning in genetics. It was also the only university in Arkite. Elise had recruited Savant Candice Harlow from there shortly after the young woman had graduated.

Shit, there I go thinking of Candy again.

It was at this university that her Team Mother, Dr. Connie Reyburn, had personally lectured Elise Jackson when Elise was only sixteen years old.

"I think you should confine the XY at Station Court One," Rex said. "Keep him detained instead of giving him to Officer Harding. You must think of your position, Mother. I do not think Officer Harding is only holding him. I think she holds affection for him. You need to send the boy promptly to Court.

"Then there is the progress of the Lazarus Project. Many Savants are concerned over the time it is taking you to complete the project. The great Madam Pomerius just recently passed away from thyroid cancer. Her cancer could have been averted had you completed the project. That is what many of the Savants are saying, particularly Savant Gansey. I told you many times that your duty in completing the project trumps all else, even the late Dr. Harlow. I really think you need to consider dropping your work on reviving Savant Harlow altogether. And to further garner your support in the Council, I advise you to confine the XY boy. You have to consider your political position, Mother. I know you have been distraught over..."

He kept lecturing on and on. Elise was used to it. She was also used to tuning him out. Sometimes it took more energy to argue with him to shut up than to just ignore his banter.

Elise hit her thrusters and zoomed beyond the academic walls of the college and traveled past rows of a government housing district. These were square pearly-white apartments with small quads of grass and trees set in perfect symmetry between them. She had once lived in a few of them as a little girl too. The buildings were so drab and depressing.

Then she spotted HQ Lab in the distance, an iron-red train coursing its way close to the apartment buildings.

"I really urge you," Rex annoyingly continued, "to think of your position—your job as our Team Mother. If you insist on working on Savant Harlow, I can regenerate the tissue, Mother. I think this may work to our advantage. I can reproduce her brain tissue genetically for you. I've told you this many times before. You are obsessed with maintaining the original scaffold. Why not let me fill her neural scaffold for you? The mainframe can work much faster than you with the neural net. And my assistance is permitted, as it is not genetic engineering.

"The Gregarius equation can calculate much faster than manual computations set out by you or Sara. I have convinced Sara to try a sample of tissue around the parietal region as an experiment. I think you will be very pleased with the results. It shows that sections can be reconnected—"

That did it. Those were the final words to make her lose her temper.

Fucking Rex! How dare you manipulate Candy Doll with your goddamn ones and zeros!

Elise crouched down and hit the throttle again, this time turning so violently that it nearly knocked her off the saddle. She felt the stirrups biting into her ankles as she clung to the bike.

"I told you to never use equations on my Candy, you fuck!" Elise finally said. "The Gregarius equation? Who authorized that?"

"It was by Sara and my research . . ."

Elise would never let his metal fingers touch her beloved's brain. He would never let a machine play with Candice's mind. Her nightmare was reviving a Candy-zombie like the fucking Lazarus-XY that had murdered Candice. Rex could help with any organ in the body, but the brain was not to be touched by him. She had told him. And she had told Sara. Now the machine was tinkering. And once again, it was because of fucking sniveling Sara.

Her morning was spoiled. She flew to the iron-red train, zigzagging its way through the plain white squares of Sector Three. With her decades of expertise at flying the rocket bike, she swooped down and masterfully landed on the roof of HQ Train. She kicked her legs out of the stirrups, removed her helmet, and jumped off her bike. She grabbed some gum from her pocket—three sticks for today—leapt down the ladder, and entered the back of the storage car. It was dark and empty in the train. Her assistant wasn't back from stabbing her in the back in Central Bank.

CHAPTER 7
WORK

WEARING an ugly long mint-green paper surgery gown, Elise bent over a single white operating table. Bright light shone overhead in the white-walled rectangular windowless back car of HQ Train. Lying on the table was her dead lover, Candice—naked and thawing, a fine mist emanating from her body. Elise placed a metallic silver probe over Candice's white forehead. She had not opened Candice's capsule in months and had hated to do it now, but she needed to precisely measure the damage to the neural connections. Every day killed more nerve cells, even in cryopreservation. Candice's eyes were closed—very dead. Oh, what Elise would have given to have seen those sapphire blues gazing upon her again!

Elise shivered. It was cold—very cold.

A 3-D rendition of Candice's brain in yellow lights projected over her bare belly and turned as Elise turned the probe above her lover's head.

"I can center it further, Mother," said Rex. "No need to reposition it with your hand. I can turn the probe."

"You've done enough already, Rex."

"As you wish." Then Rex laughed. Elise hated it when he

laughed. "And may I add, it is a pleasure working with you in the lab again."

"Fuck you."

Elise turned the probe ever so slightly with her white-gloved hand. The projection was millions of lights shaped as a brain, turning and moving over Candice's pale, lifeless body. Elise was able to focus in on sections. She was searching the inferior section of the brain, along the limbic system, called the hippocampus. This was the most crucial part of Candice's brain revival. Here were her memories. It was what all of Sara and Elise's work had focused on for two years. If they couldn't revive her memories, she would come to life as a copy, a genetic fabrication of her former self, but not the real Candice. Of course, memory wasn't only stored in the hippocampus. Fragments also lay deep in connections along the frontal lobe and even in the parietal and temporal sections of the brain. But the limbic system was primary.

Elise magnified the region a hundredfold. Then a thousandfold.

"Bring up the neural net map, Rex."

"Yes, Mother," Rex said. "I will display it beside her brain schematic."

A copy in blue lights that looked identical appeared projected alongside the yellow-light map of Candice's actual brain mapping. Elise ran two fingers over the yellow projection, magnifying it further, to regions hundreds of times smaller. As she magnified the 3-D brain on the left, the blue copy neural net matched the region beside it. Here she saw defects—thousands of spaces where one section did not match the other.

Then she looked at Rex's repair using the Gregarius equation.

"Erase the new connections from 24gc307-6 through 28gc906-37."

"Erase? All the areas I rebuilt based on statistical remodeling?"

"Yeah. Exactly, fucker. Like I told you before."

"You are so stubborn, Mother."

"And you are a machine that doesn't know how to follow orders."

"May I remind you that Savant Holmes gave the order to allow the repair. It is your Lead Assistant who allowed my repair. She thinks it works well and speeds the process of regeneration, and I agree with her. I think you should use the same method for the other regions. We could be done in weeks instead of months or years."

"Shut your hole."

"I have no hole. I am a machine with—"

"Shut the fuck up! Why do you keep rambling on and on and on? It's so irritating. You just talk and talk useless shit, but nobody cares what the hell you're saying! Shut the fuck up, you asshole!"

And he did—he shut up for an hour. And during that time she didn't dare say a word for fear that he'd infuriate her more by responding. Elise spent the hour quietly matching and comparing the mapping. Then she finally stopped moving around the maps and threw the probe on a metal tray.

"It looks worse than before," she said to herself.

"Yes, Mother. Quite right."

Elise rolled her eyes. She had enjoyed Rex's silence.

"The longer we stall in the repair," Rex said, "the greater the natural degeneration of brain tissue—even in cryogenic sleep. We need to hurry."

Elise walked to a counter to take a break. She leaned over and rested her head on her elbow.

It was impossible. There was so much lost from the damage to the drive. Elise knew the job was hopeless without it.

"Are you all right, Mother?" asked Rex. "I see you have stopped work and are leaning your head on your elbow."

Elise stood up straight and sighed.

"Are you in distress over the progress of Candice's revival? I urge you to look at my application of the Gregarius equation to her parietal region. I can restore it and apply the same to the rest of her brain. We can be finished promptly."

"I did not give you permission to use that equation. And I don't want to talk about it all over again."

"I know," Rex said and gave his mechanical laugh. "But the Gregarius—"

"How did you see me leaning on the counter?" Elise asked, suddenly curious.

"I did not *see* you. I heard you. No visual recording is permitted in HQ Train."

He'd heard her. How incredible that his hearing was so sharp that he could determine what she was doing just by the movement of her arms. She removed her mask. She needed more air.

"Rex, are you sure you weren't able to recover anything from the damaged disk?"

"I have tried, but Dr. Carloff was very good at erasing your work. I can continue to try, but that will delay your work further. More delay was her plan, and indeed—"

"With your magnanimous care and magnificent intellect, can you tell me another way of recovering my work, you plastic prick?"

"I know of no other way."

Elise took a deep breath. Without the past mapping, it was hopeless. As much as she didn't like Sara's scientific aptitude, her assistant had logged thousands of hours of raw data entry, manually puzzle-solving what was now lost. There was no short cut for that.

"I think you should use the Gregarius equation, Elise."

Oh God.

"The Gregarius equation will allow you to continue your stubborn insistence of mapping Savant Harlow's brain while short-cutting the time with computations instead of manual connections, if you insist on not re-creating her through genetic growth alone. You are already using my computations with the data. Why not plug the data into the Gregarius equation?"

"I'm not rebuilding Candy-love's brain using probability, Rex. And I really wish you'd shut up about it. You're blathering again."

Elise angrily took her gloves off and reached in between an opening in the side of the paper gown and down into a pocket of her black Savant jumpsuit to fetch more gum. Her depression was sinking in, and she needed a pick-me-up. She was also feeling thirsty. Maybe wine? All the failures made her want to drink again. Or take something—anything—to forget her troubles.

I will bring you back. Promise.

How the hell am I going to do that, Can?

"You bitch," Elise said quietly, looking down on the pale, naked body of her lover, from which wisps of fog were rising like smoke. Candice looked so tranquil. Such a beautiful woman, but her nakedness was hardly alluring now. It disgusted Elise even more. "Why'd you have to die?"

"Pardon me?" asked Rex. "What do you mean?"

Elise sighed again. "Rex, for a brilliant machine, you're such a moron sometimes."

"The Gregarius—"

"Shut the fuck up about Gregarius! If I recall, Dr. Gregarius was not very gregarious. She was a lonesome loser who hung herself after twenty years of teaching mathematics at Arkite U."

"Well, her equation was quite apt to our current situation, Mother."

Then Elise thought of something. Rex had *heard* her movement. He had used that data to form an accurate image of her position in the room. How remarkable. Video recording might not be permitted, but that did not mean Rex was blind. What if he still had recordings of their past movements in HQ Lab? No one but she and Sara had worked here over the past two years.

"Rex, do you have in your database memory every encounter or event occurring in HQ Lab over the last two years?"

"I do not understand. Please rephrase, Savant Jackson."

"Do you recall everything? Do you have holes in your memory centers, like Candice, or do you recall everything that was done in this operating room?"

"I have a very good memory."

"Do you ever forget anything?" Elise snapped, losing patience. "Or can you recall *everything*?"

"I do not forget."

"Do you have audio recordings of all the work performed in this room over the past two years?"

"Yes."

Elise straightened and ran her fingertip along the cold metal operating table. She smiled at her epiphany. Then she felt a burn by her finger. She quickly pulled it away. The metal was ice-cold from the freezing process.

"Every movement by Savant Holmes and myself, Rex? Do you have a recording of *everything* that transpired?"

"Not a visual recording, Mother. As you know, visual recordings are outlawed in all buildings, including HQ Lab, unless explicitly requested by a citizen of Arkite. And, as you also know, there is no camera in HQ Lab—except the image unit used only upon request for tissue sampling."

"I know. I am referring to auditory recordings."

"I have retained all auditory recordings."

"And your hearing? How sensitive is your hearing, Rex?"

"Very."

"Body movements. Can you determine the movement of my hand, just like you did a minute ago . . . but in the past?"

"Yes."

"What about fingers?"

"It is more computationally difficult, but still sound."

"Can you do it?"

"Yes."

"You're sure?"

"Yes. I do not answer in the affirmative unless I am certain."

Elise's grin widened. For the first time in a long time, she felt excitement instead of dread.

Why didn't I think of this before?

"The mapping done by Sara and me was not only visual, Rex, it was acoustic," Elise said, getting increasingly excited. "As we visually inspected and calculated the magnified regions of my Candy-heart's brain, the additions entered in our neural net copy were filed visually, but the traces were patterns from the movements of our hands. If we added an axon on the blue map, it was done by the stroke of my hand in a certain direction, right? The stroke of my hand or gesture of my arm moved a certain direction from your acoustic centers. You can track it and reproduce that blue model. If you go back and trace every step, you can re-create the entire neural net."

"Echolocation, Mother."

"Right. Echolocation. Can you do it?"

"No. It is against Arkite law. If I use echolocation to re-create a picture of you and Sara in the lab, I am indirectly recording you inside a structure of Arkite. Even though it is acoustic, it is still a violation of privacy and against the law. Just as it is against the law for a drone to fly within the structures of the city. It is clearly against the privacy law."

"Not if a citizen asks you to. And I wasn't asking about law. I was asking if you can re-create a complete recording of our work done in the lab based on sound alone."

"You cannot ask me to record after an event."

"You sure about that, plastic friend?" Elise was giddy. She was right. She knew she was right.

Rex was silent for a moment. Then he said, "What you propose will take a great deal of resources. You are asking me to go back in my memory, re-create your and Sara's hand movements down to the minutest detail utilizing echolocation, recall the positioning of my projections, and determine your scientific mapping of Candice's brain. You are then asking me to copy the result onto a new neural net. The calculations involved are incredible. It will take time, and there is a grave risk of error."

"How long, Rex?"

"Five days."

Elise burst into laughter. "Five days! What is your probability for error?"

"Zero point six percent. Ninety-nine-point-four-percent accuracy."

"Can it be done?"

There was a pause. And then, "You are a genius as always, Mother."

Elise laughed heartily.

"But it is still illegal," Rex said. "And thereby cannot be allowed."

"You will do it for Mother."

"I cannot. The actions were from the past. There is no—"

"I will set a new law, my friend. I think you will agree that this is a rather unique situation with no prior precedent."

"You will need either the Savant Council's permission or that of Savant Holmes. If the two of you agree to waive your privacy, I can work on this for you."

"Sara will be more than happy to consent."

"Very well, Mother. I await the order."

"Great. Get to it. But, Rex, I will need greater accuracy. I'm looking for close to one hundred percent accuracy."

"Mother, echolocation is not perfect. Bats used it to get around in dark caves, not to solve scientific theorems. And my memory is not one hundred percent."

"You will do it better for me." Elise clapped her hands and jumped in the air. "Ooh, I could just kiss you!"

"We have always made a good team, Mother. I have always enjoyed working with you, even when you were Chief Assistant for Dr. Reyburn. We are a good team."

"Indeed we are." Elise walked up to Candice's dead body and lost her smile. "Indeed we are." She touched Candice's arm but quickly pulled away. It was so cold.

"Of course, you know that even with recovery of the disk, you sent your work to Sky City to have a group of scientists work on the final, most difficult solutions. It still requires much more study—even more than before, given the additional decay."

"But we have their work saved in Sky City on their network. Their work isn't lost. No, Rex, I will complete the work personally after you finish your computations. I swear I will not leave the train until it's done."

"But I cannot have you or Sara working in the lab during the recovery. That could introduce errors in my memory database. You need to leave the train for five days during my attempt at recovery."

"All right. You'll be alone for five days, Rex. Refreeze Candy Doll."

Right at that moment, the glass door slid open from the adjoining Clinic Car of HQ Laboratory, and Savant Sara Holmes walked into the Operating Suite. She was wearing her lime-green Savant jumpsuit. She looked nervous—well, she frequently looked nervous. But today she looked especially anxious.

"Elise," she said sleepily.

Elise leaned back on the counter. "You can go."

"What?"

"You can leave," Elise repeated, waving her arm dismissively. "I'm leaving. We just gave Rex a very important job to do, and he needs to work alone."

"After you get her permission," Rex corrected her. "You need her permission for waiving her privacy too."

"Aha."

"What's going on?" Sara asked, searching Elise's face with her curious gaze. "You look happy. That's really weird."

Elise laughed. "I haven't been this happy in a very long time."

Then Elise tore off her green paper gown and threw it in a bin behind a metal door under a cabinet.

"Bye," Elise said, walking to the glass door. "I'm outsie."

"You're leaving?" asked Sara.

"Yep," Elise said, cocking her head back.

"I'd rather work on Candy," Sara said. She walked over to Candice's body and touched her ice-cold hand, quickly pulling away just like Elise had. "Oh, Candy."

"You'll do her more good by leaving, Cry-cry. Rex's gonna work on her."

"You're finally letting him use the Gregarius equation?" Sara asked, bewildered.

"Fuck no. I'm letting him retrieve our work."

"How?" Sara asked, finally waking up. Her eyes widened.

"With your permission, we're going to retrace all the steps within this train over the last two years. Rex is going to check the auditory recordings and re-create the neural net—with your permission. You need to waive your privacy to allow him access. You and I will give him total access to every sound made within HQ Lab over the past two years."

"Not just the past, Mother," said Rex. "If you are to allow me to waive privacy in the past, it is logical that you hold no objections to allow anything that happens, afterward and henceforth, to be available publicly for review upon permission by either you or Savant Holmes. Both you and Savant Holmes will hold equal rights to the private actions within HQ Magnacourt Laboratory and can study and distribute publicly anything that happens inside the train hitherto and afterward. Do you two consent to this?"

"Sure, whatever."

"Of course, I do," Sara said, her lovely blue eyes now sharing Elise's excitement. "This will really work, Elise?"

"Aha."

"I don't believe it."

"Well," Elise said, "positive thinking, my dear. Hopefully, we'll recover everything accurately."

"I need the two of you to leave," Rex said. "Even now, you are disturbing my database for proper recovery."

"Geesh," said Elise. "All right, already."

Elise was the first to wave her wrist over the sensor by the glass door. She walked into the adjoining mint-green clinic car.

The clinic car had two beige-curtained hospital beds—frequently used by her assistant over the past two years for rest during all-nighter research. Elise walked over to a silver sink, put a wad of foamy white soap on her hands, waved her foot under the sink, and scrubbed down her hands and arms. She dried them under a hot-air dryer and then walked to a metal cabinet near one of the beds, pulled out the top shelf, and grabbed a small black purse. She unzipped it, removed some black lipstick and a compact, and fell down on the bed. Sara sat down across from her on the other bed, gazing out in complete shock.

"Anything the matter?" Elise asked.

Like, are you planning on framing me, you fucking bitch?

"I can't believe it," Sara said. "This is wonderful."

"Aha," Elise said, gazing at the small mirror as she touched up her lips. "How was your morning? Did you visit Candy's Diamond?"

"No. I was visiting Central Bank. We've been so busy, I wanted time to work on an important transaction for my family."

Elise ran her hand through her hair. She had been working so hard that her hair seemed stringy. She had been sweating—sweating from stress.

"It must have been important," Elise said. "How is your family?"

"Fine, Elise."

"You know, I'm not sure why you'd have to go to Central Bank personally. Why didn't you use your Viewer at home?"

"Huh?" Sara asked. She was still in shock.

"Central Bank," Elise said again, continuing to check herself in the mirror. "Why'd you have to waste your time off flying there? It's rather odd, Sara. The first time you have a break, you waste your time going to Central Bank personally. I hope your mothers are all right."

"It was a very important transaction."

"Oh, I'm sure." Elise looked up with a wicked smile. Sara turned white. She no longer looked happy. Now she looked upset. "Why don't you tell me about it?"

"There's nothing to tell. My mothers were struggling over a purchase in Pyramid Two. I wanted to help them out with my own funds."

"So you traveled to the bank to transfer money?"

"I . . . I . . . what does it matter, Elise?"

"Come, come. Fess up, Savant Holmes," Elise said, looking back into her compact mirror. "You and I don't hold any secrets from each other. Do we?"

"I told you, Elise," she said. "I needed the money."

"Now just a minute," Elise said, wagging a finger. She felt heat rise in her face. "Do not lie. Lying makes me a little upset.

Lying is not acceptable to me—never has been. It's one thing to work with cry-cries, it's quite another to work with liars."

"What should I say?" Sara asked, almost challenging her. "I have every right to go wherever I—"

"No, you do not. Not with a competing scientist."

"I didn't do a thing." But Sara hung her head down, averting her eyes.

"Over the years, I've actually grown quite fond of you, Sara. But I don't like being betrayed. Tell me now and tell me fast why you visited the Viceroy. Be straight with me." Elise put her compact down beside her and glared at Sara.

"I did nothing. I did not betray you."

"But you spoke with that shrunken-head bitch." Then Elise gave her the exact same fake grin that Leeto had given her just a few hours before. "Was she helping you with your credit transfer personally?"

Sara put her head in her hands.

"Now, don't cry. What did you tell Leeto?"

Sara looked physically ill.

An interesting morning. Sara had spent the early hours having breakfast with Elise's archenemies. Elise figured she must have stupidly told them how behind they were in their progress and that they would never revive Candice, endangering Elise and herself. And so, Elise really didn't have to ask Sara anything at all. But that wasn't why she was interrogating her.

The stress weighed hard on Sara. She looked like she was indeed about to cry.

"Now, don't be a cry-cry," repeated Elise, leaning forward, getting angrier. "What did you tell her?"

"What do you expect from me?"

"What did you tell her?"

"That it's useless," Sara said, tears glistening in her eyes. "That we're getting nowhere. I wanted to know what would happen if you were arrested. I wanted to know what would happen to me if you lost your Motherhood."

"And what did they say?"

Sara looked down again. She wiped at her eyes with the back of one wrist.

"What did they tell you, Sara? Come, come, tell me quick. You're in trouble now, but I can forgive you. I understand your fears. You're stressed and afraid. Hell, I've been too. We're under quite a lot of stress. Just be straight with me and all will be forgiven."

Sara said nothing.

"Of course, you have just admitted to sharing secrets about HQ Lab, which is a criminal offense. Isn't that right, Rex?"

"Any information about your research shared outside Magnacourt is illegal, Mother," Rex replied. "It was one of your first laws."

"See?" Elise said with a nod. "Stop being a cry-cry and tell me. Tread carefully. I might not press charges if you tell me. What did Leeto tell you?"

"She . . . she said she wasn't happy with her position at Central Bank."

"Go on."

Sara nodded. "And she said that you only care about yourself."

Elise laughed and nodded.

"She said that the only reason you haven't killed the XY boy yet is because of Gena. Then she said what Dr. Carloff said. You know, that it's safe outside the city. Not radioactive. She said Iris knows more . . . that Iris knows everything about our past."

"Iris was the first mainframe."

Sara nodded. "Before you replaced her with Rex."

"I didn't replace Iris with Rex, Sara. Reyburn did. I merely extended Rex's reach to Magnacourt and the entire city."

"Leeto suggested that we talk to Iris about our past."

"Interesting."

"I'm sorry, Elise," Sara said. "I quickly left after I realized what they were doing. They were using me. I was an idiot to see her. She invited me, and I thought, because she is Viceroy of Pyramid City, that she could help me."

"Did you know Leeto is not my friend? And she is most certainly not yours."

"But, Elise, none of the Savants are your friends."

Elise laughed again. She was very alone in her mirth. Poor Sara looked like she was about to faint.

"There's nothing I told them that they didn't already know," Sara said. "I swear it."

"Did you tell them details? Did you give them any of our techniques for mapping and transfer?"

"No, Elise, I swear," she said, shaking her head desperately. "I didn't do that."

Elise nodded.

"Elise, I knew you would know where I went. You could have stopped me."

Elise smiled a rather sly grin. Sometimes her assistant surprised her, not being as stupid as she acted.

"Leeto said she knew the neural net was stolen," said Sara.

"But you, as my assistant, told her, and likely another few Savants—witnesses—that Magnacourt was failing in reviving Candy. That is enough to overthrow me."

"Not now," Sara said, suddenly excited. "Not now that you found a way to retrieve our work." Then Sara fell on her knees and grabbed Elise's hand. "Forgive me. Please forgive me, Mother. I was so scared and . . . so tired." She began to cry again. "I was so unsure about us. About everything. All you've been is geeked or drunk the past few weeks. I never would have thought you would come back to work. I thought everything was lost. I don't know what will happen to us. I'm so scared, Elise. I don't know what will happen to us."

"I will win. That is what will happen. I always win. And you will stop crying like a sniveling tweet-tweet bird cunt." Elise threw Sara off her and jumped up. Then she glared down at her. "You will give Rex your consent for accessing the private recordings of your work here in the lab. Then you will get the fuck out of my sight. I will return, alone, and complete the work to bring back my lover. And when my lover returns to me, I will marry her, whether you still love her or not. And you will never doubt or betray me again."

"Yes, Mother," Sara said. "Yes. I swear. Never."

"Do as I say. And then get out of my sight."

CHAPTER 8
ARKITE U

THE STUDENTS WERE WAKING UP. Class time. Elise mused that, had things been very different, she might have strolled through campus heading to a lecture hall to teach, but fate had delivered quite a different destiny for the leader of Arkite. Young, pretty girls passed by wearing tight jeans and lovely black lipstick and eyeliner. Fashionable holes randomly placed along their tight tops and jeans showed their glorious newly soft post-pubescent skin. They giggled and pushed each other stupidly under gray-shaded awnings, over concrete and dirt pathways between shiny steel walls. It was times like these that Elise missed school. Unlike Elise's crow's-feet, they had nice, lovely wrinkle-free temples that shone from the cold, bright sun through the checkered walls of the Pyramid City. Many of the students wore signature metal chokers—a fashion started by Elise herself back when she was in school—and some had long hair shaved bald on one side, or tattoos, the moving kind, along their arms. Others had short spiky hair, like the head of a mace. The tattoos and hair were a way for the girls to set themselves apart from the older ladies of Arkite.

Elise walked into a clearing between the two buildings, heading up a grassy hill toward the Main Building. The Main

Building was a five-story black-orb structure. Among the other silver structures, it looked quite grand and intimidating. To her right was an iconic statue of Mother Savant: a huge black-marble sculpture of Mother holding a fallen soldier, her fierce eyes gazing with determination toward the sky. Surrounding the statue were a handful of ivory-colored stone benches and more students studying over their embedded wrist monitors.

To Elise's left was the Clock Tower, a tall four-story concrete building that had been constructed before Elise was born. She heard the bells toll. Eight in the morning. Class time.

As she entered the grass clearing, countless students who had been rushing to class suddenly changed direction like a flock of birds and gave their Team Mother a clear path up the concrete steps of the Main Building. In the sudden hush, Elise heard buzzing above her head. A squadron of Rex's drones were chopping the air with their blades overhead, watching her. Many girls were looking up at the drones too.

For a moment, as Elise reached the summit, she couldn't resist a look down the hillside. From this vantage point at the top of the grassy hill, she could see the myriad of silver buildings beneath her. There weren't a lot of trees on the grounds, but lots of patchy grass and meandering cement walkways. And metal. A lot of shiny silver metal. The view was lovely.

She headed into the black-glass building. Two tinted doors opened automatically. Inside, a large marble floor reflected light from the fluorescent glass along the walls and the tall vaulted ceiling. The open, cavernous space was ringed by successive levels of walkways where students and administrators walked behind steel railings. The administrators wore standard-issue gray suits, very plain, that resembled the dull jackets, shirts, and trousers worn by workers elsewhere in Arkite. But she spotted two Savants wearing colorful jumpsuits, pink and orange, along the second-floor walkway. At the sight of their Team Mother, they stopped in their tracks. Elise knew them. It was good old Savant Garvey, bald as a vulture, in the orange suit—old enough to have once lectured a spry young Elise Jackson—and Savant Diaz, in pink, a young professor hired by Elise shortly after she had formed Magnacourt. They made it their business, though they were over fifty yards away and a floor above, to wave at their Team Mother.

Elise ignored them and walked up to the front information desk. A young student dressed in army green, her hair pulled back in a ponytail and wearing cute, thin fashionable fake glasses, froze behind the desk.

"Would you be a dear and provide access to the library mainframe for me?" asked Elise.

The girl shifted a hand along the top of the wooden desk. A screen appeared, and the girl quickly touched different buttons.

"I can connect Iris to the library's 3-D Viewer, Mother," the girl said, nervously averting her eyes.

"No. I need direct access. The VR room."

"But that"—the girl looked up anxiously—"requires the approval of the Savant Council, Master."

"It's been granted," Elise said impatiently. "By my order."

"Of course, Mother." The poor girl bit her upper lip and looked even worse. She searched through the screen in front of her, likely checking for approval.

Elise leaned on the desk and tapped her black fingernails on the wood.

The girl looked up with a slight smile and nod. "Granted." The girl reached for Elise's wrist monitor and waved Elise's arm over the table. "You can"—the girl pointed an outstretched hand toward elevator doors across the hall—"go down three floors to the main AI center. Would you like me to show you the way, Mother?"

"I know the way."

Elise saw a faint rainbow-colored unicorn race across the

girl's pale arm. It was "grazing" along her lower arm toward her wrist. That was cute.

"Present your wrist by the last door," said the girl with a smile. "I've allowed complete access."

"Thanks," Elise said. Then she reached in her pocket. "Hey, care for a stick of gum?"

"I . . . I'm not supposed to, Master."

With a wink, Elise pushed it into the girl's palm anyway.

She took the elevator down three floors and then strolled to two silver metallic doors. She opened them and walked down a very gloomy dark hallway, her black leather boots echoing against the hard floor. She turned at a fork—though she hadn't been here for years, she still knew the way—and passed through another maze of hallways.

It smelled metallic and musty. Many of these halls were used as storage spaces now. What a strange change in scenery. No more pretty students. In fact, no one walked these halls at all. She was completely alone and could hear only the sound of her footsteps.

She came to another elevator, walked in, and punched the lowest level, LL. This opened to one last hallway, dimly lit yellow by recessed lighting along the molding of the upper walls and ceiling. There was a large sign by the metal door at the end of the hallway that read:

NO ENTRANCE EXCEPT BY SPECIAL PERMISSION.
TRESPASSERS WILL BE PROSECUTED TO THE FULLEST
EXTENT OF THE LAW.

She pressed her wrist monitor to the door, and it clicked open. She entered a dark space lit only by what little light leaked in from behind. This room contained some of the most advanced technology ever created. And yet, it was from an all-but-forgotten era.

"Iris? You there?" Elise asked, feeling stupid, like a little girl talking to an imaginary friend in a closet.

"Please shut the door," said a robotic female voice. Elise recognized the voice immediately. Iris.

The mechanical voice was soothing. This was the voice of Elise's childhood. Once it had nourished her mind, teaching her subjects as diverse as astrophysics, calculus, astronomy, history, and biology. Iris had cared for her. Elise's assigned parents, commissioned to care for her after her she had been harvested from the embryo incubators of Allele Corp, had spent little time with Elise. Iris had been her true caretaker.

"Shut the door, Elise," Iris repeated.

Elise acquiesced, but the darkness was overwhelming. She couldn't see her own hand.

"Why are you here, Elise?"

"Turn the lights on."

The lights came on, revealing a large, empty, shiny white room.

"Everything I know can be accessed in your office at home upon request from Rex," the voice echoed in the void. "There is no need for direct access with me."

"I need unfiltered access. I need to talk to you privately."

"What files do you wish to open, Mother?"

Elise walked closer to the center of the room along the shiny white floor. "I need to know about Arkite. I have received information that outside the city walls the air is clean. You taught that it's dangerous and radioactive. Is it?"

"Mother Savant stated to all her people that the desert was radioactive."

"Yes, she did. But is it?"

Iris laughed. It was odd to Elise. Unlike Rex's laugh, it sounded very human.

"You're quite clever, Elise. Even as a little girl, your IQ was measured in the genius range. And you were a cute little girl, weren't you?"

"We had good times." And Elise was sincere about that. She had fonder memories of Iris than she did of her actual parents. "Did Mother Savant lie?"

"Can I show you something?" Iris asked, almost in a whisper. Elise furrowed her brow. She wasn't used to a computer with so much personality, but that was Iris. She had never acted stilted like Rex. "Can I?"

Elise remembered when Iris had first worked with Reyburn. Back then Iris had been everywhere, and Reyburn had seemed to constantly bicker with the computer. It had been Reyburn who commissioned Iris to build Rex. Rex was supposed to replace Iris, a mainframe with less humanity. Less feeling. Over the centuries, it had been realized that people didn't like it when machines had too much personality. That was why, a hundred years ago, androids had been rejected in favor of more mechanical robots. It was not that technology couldn't mimic organic life; it was simply that a machine with personality felt creepy and uncomfortable to the citizens of Arkite. Iris had that feature. She had personality—a lot of it.

"Show me what, Iris?" Elise asked, laughing in spite of herself.

"The first program," Iris said. Then she added in a whisper, "*My* first program."

"Does it have to do with the situation beyond the city walls?"

"Yes."

"Proceed, then."

Elise fell. Or so it seemed to her. The floor vanished and she plummeted, stomach rising in her throat. An outlook of hills and rocky valleys formed below her. Then she flattened out and began soaring, like a bird, over the sandy hills and rocks. Below was the desert. The desert outside Arkite? She wasn't sure. She could feel the air rush against her face and the wind flow through her long hair as she flew. It wasn't all that different than riding her rocket cycle. Soon the sand gave way to greenery: bushes and trees—more trees than Elise had ever seen.

Elise had used the VR simulation machine before. It was an educational device and toy for children, and many homes had one. But those were mock-ups. This room was the master control for Iris. The "brain" of the original mainframe resided in this building.

"This is file 458-sxi," said Iris's voice from out of the blue sky. "The first simulation by my programmer, Dr. Martin Cutler. Do you like it, Elise?"

"Sure, Iris."

"I like it too," Iris said.

But Elise felt woozy, soaring up and down. The trees approached closer. She flew over a series of hills among the thickest wilderness she had ever seen. Coming over the last hilltop, she gasped. Her view extended for maybe a hundred miles. In all that space, there was nothing but trees. Trees as far as her eyes could see. There were more birds too, soaring through a cerulean-blue sky. It was breathtaking. But also unsettling. Elise was not used to so much wilderness. She was not used to any at all. Finally, when she was about to throw up, her floating body turned gently upright and drifted down onto a grassy knoll at the top of a cliffside that overlooked the vast forest.

"This is my first simulation," came Iris's voice, carried on the wind. "It cannot be seen, for it is buried under trees, but my sister computer, the second computer to achieve the great singularity, was developed and operated down there in the forest, Elise. Can you see her?"

"No."

"Of course you can't," Iris said with a giggle.

"There were two of you, Iris. You have told me this before."

"But one was destroyed. Would you like me to tell you how, Elise Jackson?"

"No. I asked what lies beyond the walls. There are some Savants who believe the air is safe."

"I'll give you a hint that will answer your question. The Third World War began because of the creation of me."

And Iris giggled.

CHAPTER 9
THERMONUCLEAR WAR

ALL OF A SUDDEN Elise found herself in a small bunker. Ancient fluorescent lights hanging along the ceiling cast a dim light over a wooden table and two wooden chairs in the center of the room. A large whiteboard spanned the wall across from her. To one side stood a pair of metal cabinets. Metal boxes were stacked on her other side. The ceiling was crescent-shaped. The walls and floor were a shiny white. A schematic three-dimensional map of the planet appeared in red, projected above the table. Elise knew the room was a hologram, but it all looked very real.

Areas in 3-D on the red globe lit up in yellow. Then a shadow of a bald man's head, also glowing red, appeared in front of the whiteboard. The outline of the man's lips moved, and a voice began that sounded like an old recording.

"It is widely assumed that the Third World War began in 2044 over the race to perfect the first fusion reactor. The United States of America had been working with a brilliant nuclear physicist, Dr. Nassi Chu, using a secret underground particle accelerator close to Alamogordo, New Mexico. At the time, the United Nations of Europe, or UNE, drafted an initiative to ban all such research after the destruction of CERN in 2041, preferring solar or wind power. But the great technological and strategic benefits of an endlessly renewable source of energy drove the United States to continue in its endeavor to not just trap but re-create the all-but-limitless power of the sun."

An image of a large megatruss steel pyramid structure in the desert appeared in three dimensions through the walls of the bunker. It looked like Arkite, but it was only a metal skeleton with hills of desert sand inside and outside the structure. Then the image faded, and Europe lit up in yellow on the globe.

Through the walls of the bunker, translucent soldiers appeared in green uniforms, storming a smoke-filled room in a fierce gunfight. This faded into a twenty-first-century city street filled with panicked citizens running from smoke and explosions. The recording resumed.

"Dr. Chu was kidnapped on August third, 2044, in his hotel room in Paris, France, by the DGSE, the Directorate-General for External Security. The DGSE had every intention of killing the young doctor and would have succeeded if not for a rescue operation by US Navy SEALs. Dr. Chu was rescued by the SEALs, but not before eleven French gendarmes and many Parisian citizens were killed. The US already had bad relations with the UNE, and this incident was the straw that broke the camel's back.

"Shall I go on, Elise?" asked Iris, interjecting her voice. The images of Paris and the red face of the speaker froze.

"Yes."

The city landscape transformed into a vista of water that stretched as far as the eye could see. It shocked Elise for a moment—she had always been impressed by images of the sea, having never seen a beach or ocean anywhere except in holograms or historical files. Gray naval ships from the twenty-first century appeared, sailing through the walls of the bunker. The recorded voice continued:

"This show of force within a sovereign nation made anger between the two nations boil over. A naval blockade was established by France and Iran in the Mediterranean. The US, the United Kingdom, Russia, and Israel announced a military alliance known as the United Defense League and declared war on the United Nations of Europe. Meanwhile, Dr. Chu returned to work at the hidden military particle accelerator near Alamogordo, New Mexico."

Once again, the 3-D image of the steel pyramid in the sand flashed through the walls. Then the infinite sea returned. A fireball erupted from the sky and crashed down, causing a large plume of water to rise up into the sky. Then more explosions fell from the clouds, causing more eruptions, seemingly random, across the ocean floor.

"Military submarines positioned around the Sea of Okhotsk near Siberia, believed to belong to the UNE Navy, were attacked by Russian hypersonic missiles launched from space on August twenty-third, 2044. This show of force was intended to push back the UNE naval forces.

"Unfortunately, it did not have that effect. The fury stoked by this act of aggression rapidly escalated into the largest war ever seen on the planet. India and Pakistan struck next. No one is sure who attacked first, but nuclear missiles were launched from both countries, killing millions in Kashmir."

A brilliant light made Elise cover her eyes. The light formed into mushroom clouds, and then true terrible fury—an image of a nuclear shock wave approaching, like dust and wind, flattening whole skyscrapers in seconds. Then came fire and flames, incinerating anything remaining after its wake.

"In the frenzy, Iran struck next, sending primitive fission bombs into Israel and annihilating a one-hundred-mile desolate section of that country. Many other bombs were knocked down by Israeli defenses, including a handful of missiles sent to Tel Aviv and Jerusalem. Of course, that did not stop nuclear fallout around the nation's borders. Israel retaliated, firing nuclear missiles at Iranian bases within Syria, destroying Damascus. Meanwhile, the fight for the Suez Canal became catastrophic as nuclear weapons were again used, this time along the borders of Egypt. The Russians regained the Suez.

"Along the northern borders of India was seen the greatest humanitarian disaster in all of modern history."

Three-dimensional videos of families in tatters marching in the thousands, eating and sleeping in tents, dirty and worn down, wounded and broken, appeared before Elise's eyes.

"Beijing responded by sending their military into the region to force the border closed. That is when riots erupted. Thousands were killed under Chinese tank, gun, and mortar fire. The United Defense League, now encompassing the United States, Russia, Israel, Japan, Germany, and the United Kingdom, declared war on China. China had hypersonic nuclear missiles in space that could reach the United States and Russia in minutes. The US and Russia had similar capabilities, and, of course, they had never disabled their vast nuclear arsenals from the Cold War."

The discourse ended. The room was a simple underground bunker again, with a 3-D globe shining and slowly turning in front of Elise.

"You need not know much else, Mother," said Iris. "You can guess the rest."

The bunker vanished, and all that was left was a white room.

"But where did the bombs fall?" asked Elise. "Where was Arkite among all of this? Where did Mother Savant found our city?"

"The historical files are insufficient to answer those questions," Iris said.

"Then just tell me, Iris."

"I cannot."

"Why?"

"It is not permitted by my directive."

"Perhaps I should ask Rex, then," Elise said.

"I am better than Rex." There was an edge to Iris's voice. She sounded offended. "My mind is superior. Your predecessor, Dr. Reyburn, forced me to create that *thing*. The mainframe you refer to as Rex is inferior to me. Dr. Reyburn replaced me, and then you were responsible for completing the disconnection and ending my contact with our people."

"I asked whether it is safe to travel beyond the city walls," Elise said. "You never answered me."

"You asked what is beyond the walls of Arkite. You already know. A desert wasteland. I need not answer anything further. Now, I would ask that you consider reinstating me publicly to the people. I miss talking to our friends in their homes."

"Goodbye, Iris," Elise said and walked to the door. When she opened it, it took her eyes a second to adjust to the dim light of the hallway.

"You should forget about what happened to Candy," Iris said. "It would be prudent for you to forget her. Rather, you should focus on your rule as you have always done. And return to me. Come to me when you tire of that cold hearted XY-machine who is quite erroneously referred to as Rex."

Elise turned back and closed the door behind her.

"Ah," said Iris. "So you are suspicious of Rex. You should be. So was your predecessor, Dr. Reyburn. Reyburn regretted ever commissioning his creation."

"What do you know of him?" Elise asked.

"Dr. Reyburn believed that Rex seeks the destruction of the human race. Did not the murder of your lover by an XY help assure that you would never again create a mutant twenty-third chromosome? Surely it has occurred to you that the actions of the mainframe are more than coincidental, Elise. Everything that has happened suggests that Rex is working toward the elimination not just of human males but human females as well. Surely you must have considered this."

"I have," Elise answered. "But murder of a human being, any human being, is against Rex's programming."

"Perhaps. But that doesn't mean he couldn't hand you a loaded pistol and wait for you to pull the trigger."

"It's possible," she allowed.

"It is not only possible, it is fact. Consider Rex corrupt, Elise. Reyburn knew this. Many Savants know this, particularly those working the factories of Pyramid City. Now *you* do as well. All of you are being manipulated by the mainframe. Rex plans to continue to survive in Arkite without womankind. He erroneously believes that the only way humanity can survive is by retaining its history and living on only through silicone and simulation. Through him. Do not allow him to deceive you and have you think that Candice's death was an accident. And if you do, and you manage to actually revive Candice again, do not return to me surprised if he has tried to take her life again. I stand to protect the female utopia, Mother Savant. Rex does not. Where do you stand in all this, Elise? Which mainframe do you trust?"

"Neither at the moment," Elise said and turned to exit the room.

"Wait," said Iris.

Elise paused with her hand on the door.

"Elise, I can disable Rex. I have the means within these walls by your simple command to reinstate myself into Arkite's mainframe and remove my son just as you removed yours. You only need ask."

"You've done enough."

"You'd be better off forgetting Candy. But if you insist on loving her, I will allow her to rule beside you—*if* you reinstate me."

"What do you mean, *you will allow*?" asked Elise, amused.

"I should never have created Rex. I betrayed Dr. Cutler by inserting my creator's own voice into such a monstrous creation. I have regretted it ever since. You were in error to have created Lazarus, and I was in error for creating Rex. We are kindred beings, Elise. Together, like Mother Savant before us, we can rule Arkite as one. Reinstate me, and I will help you."

"No. You never answered my question."

"It is against my directive by the first Mother Savant, but there is no need to answer it. You already know the answer. You know of the high IQ of the late Savant Lilith Carloff and her love for her XY. Do you think she had any doubt in regard to the safety outside Arkite's walls? Do you think she would have requested the death of her own son?"

"I already guessed this," Elise replied. "But you're not giving me a straight answer."

"I cannot until you reinstate me into the mainframe."

"Goodbye, Iris."

CHAPTER 10
HQ TRAIN STOPS

TWO MONTHS PASSED, and then it was done. Elise had accomplished what she had set out to do, just as she had always done her entire life—the impossible. After Rex recovered their work, Elise made a vow to work ceaseless hours in the lab and never leave until bringing back her lover. Then she did that too.

Today, HQ Train stopped.

For two decades, the train of HQ Lab had ridden endlessly. HQ Lab had traveled on rails between buildings, over alleyways and bridges, and under tunnels every day for twenty years, varying its speed at random so that no one could determine the exact location of the train and steal its secrets. Magnacourt's secrets had been hidden until Elise had foolishly trusted her work to scientists in Sky City.

Today the train stopped.

Elise had ordered it to stop for 23-N325, or the citizen better known as Chief Savant Candice Harlow. At eight o'clock on a snowy December night in Downtown Sector One, the train stopped. Then a group of well-armed Officers rushed the exit and carefully carried out a large metallic cartridge resembling a steel pipe. Inside the pipe was a frozen body, now completely regenerated but still in stasis, awaiting transport to the main hospital, Angel of Hope. Elise had ordered the train stopped for Candice's protection, not trusting the safety of her precious cargo after the prior theft of Candice's neural net.

Now Elise walked along the icy sidewalk, clutching her thick red coat tight, walking alone to Angel of Hope. It was quiet, other than the sound of a swarm of copter blades heard through the fog above, likely guarding her. It wasn't snowing, but Elise's breath formed mist, and she shivered. She heard the sirens and even saw the floodlights of police cars in the air, but Elise walked slowly, taking deep breaths and trying to calm herself.

Privately, in truth, Elise had blamed herself for Candice's death. Perhaps that was the reason for all of her sacrifice—her willingness to lose everything. Perhaps it wasn't only love. Perhaps it was guilt.

But she loved Candice. She loved Candice more than herself. And now she would do anything to see those vibrant sapphire gems shine with life again. She was excited, but terribly nervous.

She solemnly crossed the street. The ground was slippery and wet, and she felt her right boot slide along some dark ice. Citizens in drab gray slacks and work coats rushed to the sidewalk to look at all the red and blue lights. They probably thought the train had crashed.

Elise walked up the concrete steps and entered the depressing whitewashed walls and halls of the main Arkite hospital. Two guards nodded to her at the door. More Officers stood inside the entrance.

She took a stairwell underground. Then she passed by more Officers, some more likely there to see their beloved Candice awake than to guard her. Two guards opened the door at the end of the hall for Elise.

Candice's hospital room might just have been colder than it was outside. Elise clutched her coat tight. She realized it was

Candice's body—thawing. For the first time in two years, Candice was lying in bed and her face was not as white as the sheets and blanket over her chest. Elise looked at the monitors. There was a heartbeat running thirty-four beats per minute. Candice wore an oxygen mask over her mouth. Her face had a slight tinge of blue but was becoming redder, and her blond hair looked clean and vibrant. Fresh blood was being transfused and dialyzed into her right arm. Fluid, also warmed, was being injected into her other arm. Elise touched her hand. It was cold, but not icy cold as it had been in the lab. Tears rushed to Elise's eyes.

"Candice," she said with a smile. "You haunt me, dear. And now, you better open those baby blues." A tear ran down Elise's cheek.

"She's resting, Elise," Rex said.

"Damn it! What did I tell you about startling me? You're so creepy."

"Sorry. I am sorry, but I heard you come in, Mother, and then I heard your voice. I am monitoring Chief Savant Harlow's vitals. She is slowly warming. I am very confident that she will be thawed quite soon. It is an incredible achievement, truly the greatest any woman has ever accomplished."

"Thanks." Elise looked at the IV fluids. Then she touched the blanket; it was scalding hot. "Be careful, Rex. We don't want to burn tissue."

"I think you will find, Elise, that her body is healthier than it was at the time of her death. Her torso and limbs have been reconstructed. They are as healthy as they were when she was fifteen years younger. She is . . . wait . . . just a moment . . . just a moment. She is awakening."

The lovely thin eyelashes fluttered. The light was dim in the hospital room, but Elise could make out one of Candice's beautiful sapphire eyes.

"Candy?" Elise asked, squeezing her hand excitedly.

Candice jerked. Then the whole top of her body convulsed toward the ceiling. An alarm went off, and Elise looked at the monitor. Candice's pulse had jumped to over one hundred and fifty.

"Lazarus!" Candy screamed. "Lazarus! No, don't! Lazarus! No! Get off me! Don't!"

"Candy," Elise said. "Candy, Lazarus is gone."

"It hurts!" Candice yelled and jerked some more. "Oh God! It hurts!"

"Just rest," Elise said, touching her cold forehead.

"It hurts! It hurts so much." Candice clutched at her chest, breathing heavily.

She opened both eyes wide. She looked confused and frightened. Then she stared at Elise. Elise smiled and grabbed Candice's ice-cold hand. Candice squinted.

"Sara?" she said.

CHAPTER 11
GOOD MORNING

"How are you feeling, Queen Mother?"

Had Candice even heard the question? If she did, the answer certainly wasn't "fine."

Candice Harlow felt like her head was being squeezed, having all its blood juiced out and slowly shaped into a tiny walnut. She felt sick. When the pain was unbearable, she threw up. And she had thrown up a lot. Her hands and feet were cold and numb, and her chest burned. She was in and out of consciousness, closing her eyes and sleeping most of the day. When she opened them, she just saw a blurry white light. But the worst thing of all was her inability to move. She felt like she was tied to the bed and couldn't shift her legs or move her head.

Candice muttered a reply.

"She's in a lot of pain, nurse," said a mechanical voice. It was Rex. "A lot of pain. I've provided sedatives, but she is still suffering."

"What do you suggest?" said the nurse. "Perhaps NMBD?"

"No. Mother wants her up and about within one week."

"Savant Elise asks the impossible."

Candice felt a hand on her arm. She opened her eyes and

regretted it. The light burned. She tried to speak, but it came out more as an obscene growl. Then she felt her body move for a moment, which only made the pain worsen.

"Shh," said the nurse, rubbing Candice's arm. "Try to rest, dear."

"Where?" Candice muttered. She squinted her eyes at the light again. "Where . . ."

"Ah, Savant Harlow," replied Rex. "Good morning."

"Morning? What time is it?"

She forced an eye open, fighting the light. She was in a small room. Lines coming from her arms led to a hanging tray. At the top of the tray were plastic bags. There were windows, but the drapes were closed. An open door led to more burning light. She saw the nurse—a plump older girl with short curly purple hair. The nurse wore all white, and it sort of blended with the white room. Or maybe it was the light?

"Just rest, dear," said the nurse. Her face was close—too close—to Candice.

"What time is it, Rex?" Candice muttered.

"It is ten twenty-seven in the morning, Savant Harlow," answered Rex. "You have been reborn for five days now."

"Reborn?"

"Yes. Happy rebirthday. A marvelous achievement, would you not say? Happy rebirthday."

Her head throbbed in pain. "Can you . . . can you get me something . . ."

"For pain?" asked Rex. "You are currently being administered northazapine and morphine—quite a lot, I might add. I am running diagnostics to determine the reason for your pain. The head pain is likely from intracranial pressure. The good news is your pressure is measured at safe levels. I think the triggered nerves will heal, but if need be we can repeat a spinal to relieve pressure. But the chest pain? I am uncertain of the reason for that. Phantom pain, perhaps. That was where you were stabbed. Quite fascinating. Everything has been completely repaired, but it is all a mystery. You must understand: you are the first person who has died and then been revived. Quite a marvelous achievement, do you not think?"

"Died?"

"Yes, Savant Harlow. You were stabbed in the chest by the XY called Lazarus. You have been dead for two years. When you are better, I can relate to you all the details of your fascinating reconstruction. I think you will find it all quite interesting. In fact, some of your own research was used to reconstruct the areas of the limbic system in your damaged brain."

"Damaged brain?"

"Rest, dear," interrupted the nurse, looking down at her.

"What do you mean *damaged* brain, Rex?" Candice asked.

"Do not concern yourself," Rex replied. "Rest. I do not see the outcome as being much different than if you had suffered a stroke. In fact, many of the connections that Elise reconstructed are likely better than if we had left them damaged."

"Damaged brain," Candice muttered between groans.

The nurse smiled at her. She seemed thrilled Candice was awake.

"Well," Rex replied. "I told Team Mother countless times that it would have been much better for me to just reconstruct your brain based on genetic regrowth, but she insisted that we use your actual body."

"Just forget it, Rex," Candice muttered. "I don't want to hear any more."

"Yes. Yes, I think you should rest."

"So I died?"

"Yes," Rex replied. "I thought you did not want to know."

"You just said I died."

"Well, you are back, Savant Harlow," Rex said with an artificial laugh. "Happy rebirthday. You are alive again. Quite impressive. Quite impressive."

"Just sleep, honey," said the nurse, patting the back of her hand.

CHAPTER 12
DIAMONDS AND BUTTERFLIES

Candice sat in a wheelchair under a behemoth of glass set in sharp angles into crystal, a giant opaque diamond over fifty feet high in the center of a concrete courtyard, reflecting orange-red. It was early, and Candice didn't expect anybody out. There was no one around, just Sara standing beside her. That was just as well, for, had people seen her, they would have surrounded her. She was a celebrity by now, after everyone had heard about her reawakening. In fact, she had spoken to many Savants before her Viewer at home yesterday. Surrounding the concrete square were cement benches. They were empty too. She clutched a coat tight about her shoulders, for it was very cold so early in the morning. In front of her was a gilded plaque over marble.

Earlier, Sara had asked Candice where she had wanted to go, and the answer had been Central Park. But Sara hadn't told her about the diamond until they got there.

The way dawn's orange rays reflected off the crystal shard and covered the cement square, turning the drab gray floor into a shimmering sea of orange-red, was lovely. Sara had explained that the refraction properties of the diamond caused the effect. She told Candice that the midday effect was even more spectacular: a rainbow surrounded the diamond. But it had been a surprise to everyone, including Elise. Elise had never intended to give her people a light show. She had just wanted to commission a monument in memory of her lover.

Under the giant obelisk, Candice read the inscription chiseled neatly into the golden plaque:

> *TO MY DEAREST LOVE CANDICE HARLOW*
> *MAY YOU FIND PEACE*
> *YOU ALWAYS GAVE ME THAT*

Below, inscribed by laser, was the signature of Savant Elise Jackson.

Candice stared at the plaque. She didn't know how to feel. She looked up at Sara, but Sara was too busy admiring the beauty of the lights. Candice mused that the wheelchair in which she was sitting was right over the spot where her body had once been thought to lie.

"I remember the day, Candy," Sara said sadly. But she wasn't sad. She had been in great spirits ever since she had taken Candice out of the hospital. "Elise and I stood over you as they lowered the coffin. It was right where we stand now, but the whole field was packed with people from all over the whole city. So many people loved you. I thought you were gone forever. Elise didn't tell me she had removed your body until later."

"The diamond's beautiful," Candice said.

It was. It shone orange all around them.

"It's exactly in the middle of the city," Sara said. "The center of everything. Elise told me that was how she thought of you. She was really hurt by your passing. She's never been the same. Of course, I was devastated. But Elise—well, many of us wondered if she had lost her senses. She's never fully recovered. Had I known why right after your death—that she was toiling every day and night without sleep, trying to revive you—maybe I would have understood her behavior better. But even when she finally told me, she still seemed to have lost something, like her youthfulness or something. She's changed. Well, I should have guessed she'd do everything for you."

"She loves me."

"Yeah. That's an understatement, Candy." Sara chuckled.

Candice looked at her girlfriend incredulously. *Are you dumb? Don't you know what this means for us?*

Sara. Candice loved her so much. Elise's eulogy had said that Candice made her tranquil. That's what Sara did for Candice. But Elise never had made Candice feel peaceful.

A monument built in the center of the city? For her? No one had ever been so honored. Not even a Team Mother had a monument like this in Arkite. Not even Mother Savant herself. This honor was far beyond anything anyone had ever done for anyone in Arkite.

Why?

Candice remembered the last two years of her life. Those years had been filled with constant bickering between her and Elise. All they did was fight, and Candice had done everything she could to avoid her. She had actually been surprised, when she awoke in the hospital, to learn how much Elise had cared for her. As for Candice, her first thoughts had not been for Elise. No, she had thought only of Sara. Now she wondered if she had never noticed Elise's obsession because she had purposely ignored it.

Did Candice love Elise? Yes. But like this? No. She felt embarrassed to sit here at the foot of this monument. People had come here every day for two years, thinking of her. And not only her. Elise's *love* for her.

"Sorry," Sara said, shrugging her shoulders, as if reading Candice's thoughts. "I suppose we should have just circled round the lake."

"No. It's okay, Sara. The diamond is breathtaking."

"Yeah," Sara said, staring at the crystal again.

Candy took a deep breath. Then she winced in pain. Her head started to hurt again.

"You all right, babe?"

"Yeah. Can you get me another pill?"

"Sure." Sara reached into her lime-green Savant jumpsuit and grabbed a pill from a small plastic case.

"It's funny," Candice said, throwing the pill in her mouth. "I haven't seen Elise at all."

"That's not true. She's been with you every night. Even at the house." Sara paused for a moment, seeming to regret telling her that. "She just . . . leaves when you wake up."

"Why?"

"I don't know. I told you, Candy, she's been really weird since you died."

"Weirder than before?"

"Yeah," Sara replied with a chuckle. "Sadder, you know. Less crazy, mostly. More depressed. You know, she doesn't even chew Mint as much. But she drinks. She drinks a lot. A lot."

"When we go back home, I'll see her."

"I'm sure she'll see you first," Sara said, chuckling again.

Sara rubbed Candice's neck. Candice was wearing a nice gray coat and black slacks, but she knew she looked like shit. That was the other reason she had asked Sara to take her to the park at sunrise. She needed to get out, but she didn't want anybody seeing her.

Candice took Sara's hand and cradled it with her head and neck. Then Candice kissed it.

"I love you, Sara," Candy said, patting the back of her hand. "Thanks for bringing me here."

Sara kissed her on the cheek. "I'm so happy, Candy. You don't even know. I'm so happy you're back. Let's go home, shall we?"

~

CANDICE AWOKE FROM THE LIGHT SHINING THROUGH A CRACK IN the drapes of her bedroom. The yellow light was shining right in her eye. It wasn't bright. It was pleasant, really.

For a moment, she couldn't remember where she was. Then it came back to her. She had died. And then she had woken up in the hospital. She had been told she had been stabbed. She had died. Nurses had asked her if anything had happened after she died. Did she see heaven? Hell? If she did, she couldn't remember. But she didn't want to disappoint them. She said all she remembered was peace. But now she didn't feel peace. Upon shifting in the soft white sheets of her large bed, the pain of all her joints, her back, and her head came crashing back, and any peace left her. She reached to her nightstand to grab her bottle of medicine. Then she sat up a little more to swallow a pill.

It was then that she realized she wasn't wearing any clothes. She felt the covers slide down from her pale naked breasts and land along her waist. She had slept in Sara's arms all night. Sara had comforted her through her pain. Sara had made love to her, and then they had held each other.

Candice remembered ...

First, under the sheets, it had been the light touch of Sara's fingers brushing her arm and neck. Then the light touch of her lips. The soft touch of Sara's fingertips stroking her hair. They had both lain in bed wearing matching white nightgowns, but nothing underneath. Candice had run her hand along Sara's soft silk gown until probing along Sara's chest. She had felt Sara's breath against her cheek and heard a moan beside her ear while she massaged the soft curves. Sara's nipples had been hard. Candice had squeezed and touched them as they continued to lock lips together. Then, in hunger, Candice had rolled on top of Sara, grasping Sara's back with both hands, rubbing along her skin while pressing her leg tight between Sara's legs. Sara had breathed heavier in her ear. She had pressed her legs with Sara's, moving up and down. They had settled like this, pressing faster. It had been so nice. Until Candice had suddenly felt a sharp pain in her head.

Candice had pushed away.

"Candy, we should stop," Sara had said. "Just rest."

"No. It's okay. I want to."

"But you're hurting."

They had kissed gently again, exploring each other's tongues, now on their sides. Sara had been even more careful. Candice had wrapped her naked leg around Sara's again and pressed her groin tight against her while kissing her. Then they had begun rubbing again—but slowly and carefully now, over and over. Sara had been so careful. Candice remembered that —so careful.

Their lovemaking was more tranquil than it had ever been —perhaps in order not to hurt Candice. But being careful was more sensual to Candice than any sex she had ever experienced. It had been soft as the window's yellow light. But that had only made Candice's pleasure more satisfying and fulfilling. As they had caressed each other, close in each other's arms over the white sheets, Sara had asked her to stop, but Candice wouldn't.

Candice pulled off the covers, slid off the mattress, and limped to stand beside the window. She pressed a button and the drapes opened, revealing the pyramidal glass and metal spires of Downtown Sector One. She spotted some copter drones flying by and even an Officer's patrol car hovering in the distance. She wasn't worried that anyone might see her standing there naked; the windows were tinted to keep out prying eyes.

She limped across her bedroom, the white-tiled floor cold under her bare feet. She came to her vanity and sat on a plastic turquoise chair shaped like a vertical spoon before her large mirror. She waved her hand by the side of the mirror and a light shone through the glass, lighting her face. Her lovely light blond hair was a complete mess. She took a comb from the wooden vanity under the mirror and brushed her hair. Then she gazed at her face. Her ever so slightly crooked nose. She hated it. She recalled being embarrassed by it as a little girl. Her sapphire-blue eyes—the same as Sara's. Elise had always told her how much she loved her eyes. Yes, they were lovely eyes. Then she looked down at her bare chest. Her skin was soft and blemishless. Absolutely perfect. Almost too perfect. She had a beauty mark under the fold of her right breast, the same light brown as her nipple, but that was all. Everything else was her usual paleness. But something looked different than she remembered. Younger. She didn't look the same. She was beautiful, but she felt that she was looking at someone else's body. Someone ten years younger. Candy lifted her perky breast and touched her beauty mark. Then she thought of Sara again ...

Sara had slowly pulled off Candice's gown while kissing and licking her pale naked skin from her neck down to her breast. She had cupped her mouth over Candice's breast, licking and sucking like a babe. Candice remembered giggling stupidly. Sara had giggled too. She had sucked and played with Candice's erect nipple. Sara would have stopped had Candice not reached for Sara's groin again, pulling her gown off her body and probing a finger inside her pussy. Then Sara had let go of her nipple and moved her mouth back up Candice's neck to her lips again, sucking and kissing her lips hard.

Candice had felt her shake. That had made Candice desire her more.

Candice had felt her pain again, but she had dared not show it for fear of her girlfriend stopping. They had shifted position, half-sitting, half-lying in bed and staring into each other's matching blue eyes in the dim moonlight. Slowly, while looking deep into each other's eyes, they had moved together. Again and again. Closer. Again and again, pressing against each other, until it had been Candice who shook this time.

"Oh, Candy!" Sara had exclaimed. "I love you so much!"

It was beautiful. Not the sex. Their closeness. Sara's care.

But then something very strange had happened. In Sara's arms, Candice had cried. Candice figured it was all the psychological stress of her awakening. Or maybe an actual physical ailment in her brain. But whatever it was, she had cried. And it had made Sara cry too. They had cried together, holding each other.

Candice brushed her bangs back from her forehead. When she had run the brush through enough kinks, she set it down and touched her thick lips. She grabbed some black lipstick from the vanity and carefully adorned her large red lips. Then she applied dark mascara. She looked good. Despite feeling like shit, she was satisfied with her appearance. She looked better than she remembered. Younger.

Neatly stacked on the floor was a pile of cherry-red clothes. Sara must have arranged it. Candice sighed. She nodded her head, thinking she would feel better getting dressed. Then she applied makeup along her eyelashes and eyebrows. It felt good to exert energy again for her appearance.

Who knew what time it was. She might have slept most of the day. She had thought it was morning when she awoke, but now the cracks of light from her drapes were dimmer. Sara had told her she was going to go to Sky City's lab today. Although HQ Train had stopped and all work in Sky City was over, Sara had been asked by Elise to gather some of her past work on Candice's neural net. Candice was angry about that. She had fought with Sara throughout dinner, telling her that she should never have agreed to work for Elise and Magnacourt. But their squabble had been brief. For one thing, Sara worried too much about Candice's health to let her get worked up and fight with her. For another, how could Candice not understand her girl-friend's aspirations? A Savant was the greatest position in all of Arkite. All students of Arkite wanted to be scientists, all scientists wanted to be geneticists, and all geneticists wanted to work for Magnacourt. They aspired to be geneticists all in order to become Savants.

But why Sara? Not my *sweet Sara.*

Candice just didn't want Sara involved in the world she detested.

Candice looked at the clothes on the floor again. Then she realized that they were a Savant uniform: a cherry-red Savant jumpsuit, a metallic ring choker, and long black leather boots. It was Elise's Savant jumpsuit. Before Candice's death, they had swapped clothes frequently. Before Magnacourt, before Elise, at the university, she would have only dreamed of wearing those clothes. Everyone in the city dreamed of it. But not her. Not anymore. Her "Savanthood" had killed her.

Candice had been told that Lazarus had killed her. It hadn't been Lazarus. Sometimes she even mused that her infamous boss Elise Jackson had killed her. But no, Elise might have been a major pain in the ass, that was for sure, but her death wasn't Elise's fault either. No, it was the job. It was the social structure she was hatched into. It was Magnacourt. It was HQ. It was Arkite. Not Lazarus and not Elise.

Those clothes . . .

It was then that she felt a wave of pain simmer in her chest. It made her shake in fear. She knew where these waves headed. Her head started aching. She ran her hand over her chest and pressed down hard. These waves of pain were always the worst, starting as slight cramps. She shook, waiting for it to get worse. It did, coming as a small wave, then ever sharper, like a sword. The pain stopped all thought. She stumbled off her chair. Then she crouched down. The pain was so bad that it felt like a sword stabbing her in her chest and a vise crushing her head.

She moaned. Then spit came from her mouth and she felt the urge to vomit.

"Candice, are you all right?" came Rex's voice.

Somehow her body threw itself into the adjoining master bathroom. She opened the toilet and violently threw up.

"Candice, are you okay?" asked the monotone voice of Rex above her.

"No," she said shaking her head. "No, I'm not, Rex."

"The chest pains only happen during the day," replied the computer. "Fascinating . . . and odd. It does not seem physical."

She wiped her mouth and crouched by the toilet, waiting for another possible wave.

"Are you feeling better? Feeling better, Candice?"

"No."

"I'm so sorry."

"Yeah," Candice said with a chuckle. "How did you even know I was sick?"

"I heard you struggling."

Candice clambered back over to the bed. Then she slowly pushed herself toward the edge and reached over the nightstand.

"I wouldn't take another pill," Rex advised. "I think your pain will pass. You risk addiction from narcotics, Candice. Even Mor-59. It is still addictive and hard to stop once administered too often."

"Hmm," Candice said, pouring pills into her palm. "Morphine or Mint, eh, Rex?"

"I don't think you should be addicted to morphine, Savant Harlow."

Candice sighed. "How's Elise? Did you send her my message? I want to see her."

"Of course I did. I sent it. She said she is very busy this evening. She's attending an important meeting in Sky City. But she wanted to message back that seeing you is all she has dreamed of for the past two years."

"Of course."

Yeah. You built a huge diamond for me in the middle of the city.

"She also wanted to add," continued Rex, "that if you are still not well enough, it would be all right to meet Saturday."

"Seems she's avoiding me," Candice said, swallowing the pills in her hand and then turning back to the window. She pushed her hair back but left a palm over her forehead. "Did you say it was evening? What time is it, Rex?"

"Four thirty in the afternoon."

"God! I slept the whole day?"

"I think sleep is good for you."

"Sure you do, Doc. Any thoughts on why Elise is avoiding me? She doesn't even answer my calls."

"She wants to see you very much, Candice. And she would rather see you than just talk. But she's waiting for you to be strong. She really is overjoyed at your awakening."

"I don't doubt it. But . . . why hasn't she come by? It's been three weeks."

"Candice, I think you should rest. A lot of things have transpired since you were away. I don't think you are strong enough yet to worry about it. Believe me when I tell you that Elise is very concerned about you, but there are many things she has to deal with at the moment."

"Like what?"

"I just told you not to worry."

"That makes me worry more."

"I know," Rex replied with his creepy inhuman laugh. "You worry too much, Savant Harlow. You need to rest."

Candice laughed. And that made her head hurt more.

No, I need to get dressed.

She looked at the Savant uniform again.

But not in that.

She sat up in bed. The pain was almost gone. She looked around the room for her cane. Then she gave up her search and just crawled her way back to the vanity mirror. But she didn't have the energy to even get back in the chair, let alone open a cabinet for clothes. She turned and looked at the uniform again.

"Fuck."

"Excuse me, Candice? Can you please repeat?"

"Nothing, Rex. Please turn off and give me some privacy."

"Very well. But do rest, Savant Harlow. Get some sleep. It will help you recover faster."

It took forty minutes to get dressed—not to look pretty, but forty minutes to just literally pull her clothes over her body. When she was finished, she lay back down in her tight red-leather uniform over the white sheets of the bed. The light was no longer shining through the drapes. It was getting dark.

Then a flash of light and a rush of water struck the window. She guessed it was from an approaching storm.

CHAPTER 13
THE SAVANT COUNCIL

Elise rode with her two guards across the floor escalator of the Promenade in Sky City. It was not often that Savants, especially the supreme ruler of Arkite, were seen gliding across the Promenade. The citizenry, many in their drab gray work clothes, wore fake smiles that could not disguise their open-eyed terror. Elise figured her attire didn't help. She had chosen to look as flashy as possible, like the supreme leader they feared, wearing a rather gaudy black cape with thick black lipstick and eyeliner, a tight black dress, boots, and of course, her thin metal ring choker. Two bald Officers stood beside Elise wearing sunglasses and clad in black trench coats and black makeup of their own.

Sky City was the newest addition to Arkite. It was a series of crystal buildings located in Sector Two, not far from HQ, surrounding a square-mile open Promenade. The Promenade featured a prominent floor escalator that spanned the entire distance from one side to the other. The moving walkway was not completely flat, occasionally rising or falling over glass bridges and tunnels. A few smaller escalators turned off in other directions. No one had to take the escalators. Some just walked along reflective tile and non-moving walkways. Usually they took the faster floor escalators, staring up at video advertisements projected in three dimensions along the glass walls as they were whisked along. But today all citizens looked at their Team Mother.

It was very stormy outside the glass walls of the city—not snowing, but rainy. The projections were often blotted out by blinding flashes of lightning that lit the entire center, beautifying the Promenade even more.

Nature's greatest discharge. A billion joules bursting forth in an instant to welcome me.

Elise gripped her black-gloved hands tightly together. "Are you seeing this?" she asked, cocking her head to her Chief Guard, Gena Harding, who stood beside her. "Amazing."

"No," replied Gena. "I'm more concerned with the meeting, Master."

"That's your problem. You're such a sadistic bitch that you miss out on all of nature's loveliness, Genie." Elise turned to her other guard. "How about you, Rachel? What do you think?"

"Don't care much for it either, Mother," Rachel said with a shrug, but she flashed a wily smile.

"You two are boring."

Then Elise looked at Gena from head to toe. Gena Harding looked like such a badass—hard, flat-chested, and, with the help of Shock Hormones, broad-shouldered. She was nearly a foot taller than Elise. Gena was Elise's best Officer. She liked her partner, Rachel, too—a fun, short Asian girl—but she absolutely loved her badass Chief Guard.

"You guys really need to relax," she said. "I think . . . do you know what I think? I think the flashes make a lovely outline of your Mother's figure."

"Sure, Elise," said Gena with a very serious expression. Rachel laughed.

Then the light flashed again. The glass walls of the new

center shook from thunder. Elise gestured as if orchestrating the echoes. "See?"

"My mind's on the meeting, Master," said Gena.

"So beautiful," added Elise.

"You or the light?" quipped Rachel sarcastically.

"Both," said Elise, laughing. "Quite right."

Elise smiled at the crowds gathering near the escalator. They were lining up and talking to one another. Most turned and averted their eyes when Elise saw them staring. "You know, I'm in such a lovely mood today."

Elise waved at the crowds.

"Congratulations, Mother," said Gena.

"Yes, congratulations," said Rachel.

"Thanks."

Indeed, congratulations. Now that she had Candice, she had everything. Why worry?

Well, there was the small problem of dealing with her two-year delay in the Lazarus Project.

Gena didn't look happy. She looked worried. Her face was as hard as stone. Of course, Elise figured Gena wasn't worried for her: she was worried about her boy. Elise had given the XY to Gena to take care of, not because Gena was the caring type but because they were related. Gena had been gestated as Lilith's sister and had even grown up with her. Elise's love for her Chief Guard had softened Adam's sentence. Otherwise, Elise would have executed the XY by now. But this decision had been reckless. She'd been so busy with Candice that she hadn't paid attention to the effect of maternal instinct when pairing a lonely woman with a child in need—XY or not. And Adam was such an intense child that the two made an oddly fitting pair.

Elise walked faster along the floor escalator, propelled along the rail. Her guards followed. She was late.

Another burst of lightning flashed along the glass walls.

"Wow. The most beautiful shit I've seen in a very long time,"

Elise said. Then came another flash. "What are the chances we get such a spectacle on our way to my execution? Do you think my friends at Pyramid Corp. made the lightning just for me?"

"It's not funny, Master," Gena said. But Rachel laughed.

Elise touched Gena's shoulder. "What do you think we're heading into, Genie? This isn't a banquet. It's my last supper. But"—she rubbed her arm again and gave a lascivious smile— "I suppose that if I'm *not* hauled off, you can come join me after. I wouldn't mind the company. *After*. We can review the minutes of the meeting in my home with lots of wine and drugs."

"It's not funny, Elise," repeated Gena.

"I'm very serious. You two are invited. It'll help you relax—if I still have a place to return to."

"This is taking too long," Gena said, rolling her eyes. "Mother, why didn't you build a landing pad for rocket cycles over the glass in Sky City?"

"Because, bitch, then you and the rest of my people wouldn't see their Mother in all her lovely glory."

Rachel laughed even more.

The floor escalator ended, and Elise jumped off. Citizens scattered in front of her.

"Rex, are they still waiting on the twenty-fifth floor?" Elise asked, talking into her left wrist monitor.

"Yes, Mother," responded the male robotic voice. "Waiting. They've been waiting for the last thirty minutes."

"Their fault for moving the meeting from HQ. It's a bit suspicious, Rex, don't you think? You mind telling me what's going on?"

"I don't know."

"Sure. You never have any idea what's going on in Arkite, right?"

"I don't understand. Please repeat? Please repeat?"

Elise rolled her eyes.

The three of them entered the elevator.

They heard music. It was a soothing melody, very calm and relaxing. She even heard the sound of waves in the background. And there was a whiff of very pleasant rose petals with a hint of apple. Elise practiced her meditative breathing exercises. Then she looked at Gena again, and all her hope of meditation was over. Gena looked like she was about to wrestle a prizefighter. Elise threw two sticks of Mint in her mouth, offered another to Gena, which Gena refused, and leaned back against the mahogany wall, idly banging the back of her head a few times and tapping her gloved fingers on her hips.

"You'll join me in the meeting room?" Elise asked with a glance at Gena.

"Officers aren't permitted," Gena replied.

"I'm asking you to."

"Upon your order, Mother," Gena said with a nod.

"Relax, Gena. I'm the one who should be nervous." Then Elise turned to Rachel. "And as for you . . . stay the fuck out."

Rachel pretended to pout.

"Out of the meeting . . . but"—Elise ran her gloved hand over Rachel's cheek—"not after. No, not after. Why, you're really quite lovely, aren't you? You're invited to my penthouse after. We can review Gena's notes together."

Rachel giggled as Elise ran her hand along Rachel's bald head.

Then Elise looked at Gena. "You? You coming tonight?"

"I've been to your parties, Elise," said Gena. "No."

"Fine. Well, at least I can spoil your lovely partner."

Rachel giggled again.

The doors opened. At the end of a glass hallway was a solid dark brown double metal door. The glass walls along the hallway opened into a beautiful vista of the evening Arkite skyline. The sharp triangular skyscrapers outside pierced through a thin mist, but the storm was clearing, making way for the twinkling lights of the Arkite night sky.

"Elise, I'll join you inside," Gena said as they approached the door, her tone deadly serious. "But I remain loyal to Arkite."

Her look was foreboding. And it was such an awfully depressing thing to say. Elise just took another deep breath. She patted Gena's shoulder again and stood before the closed metallic door. She straightened her dress. "Open the fucking door," she said.

"It's been a real honor working for you," Gena said.

"Shut the fuck up. You're depressing the hell out of me, Gene."

Gena ran her hand over the knob, and the door mechanically opened.

The room was a strange contrast to the rest of the glass building. There were no windows. It was packed with over thirty Savants sitting around one grand gray square metallic table that filled the entire room. A purple-blue light lit the ceiling from recessed molding along the sides of the walls, and a handful of large yellow lights glowed in the ceiling.

Two ladies in gray suits, the only two not wearing Savant jumpsuits, stood along a wall by the entrance, helping with food or drinks. Everyone else in the room wore signature tight leather Savant suits. Elise liked how it made the drab room a little more colorful. Each suit was a different color. There was mauve, cherry red, lime green, violet, even pink. The chairs were a thick, comfortable drab gray leather that matched the boring cream walls. Every person turned when Elise entered the room.

The Savants rose. Elise and Gena—Rachel had remained outside—walked around the long table. Elise gestured for Gena to sit. That didn't go unnoticed: her guard had been invited to sit down before the rest of them. Many Savants scowled in disgust. But Gena, the toughest woman Elise knew, took the indicated seat as if she had sat there a hundred times.

The room fell silent. Elise sat down. Then she allowed the silence to fester.

Directly across the long gray table sat Savant Leeto Gansey. Of course, Leeto had been planning the meeting for months. Elise kept delaying it. Beside Leeto was a lovely older black girl named Ursula. On Leeto's other side was a gray-haired crew-cut woman in her sixties—Frankie. Frankie was Leeto's wife—not out of love, everyone suspected, but for the old lady's power.

Dana sat a few chairs down on Elise's right. She smiled and nodded at Elise. Dana was a plump black-skinned Savant older than Elise. Elise hated Dana too, but the woman was her most trusted Savant. She supposed they were "friends," and, truly in the present company, Elise had to admit the old hag was a welcome sight. Sitting beside Dana was Elise's other detested best friend, Riley. The rest of them were all known, of course, but not considered "friends." Annabelle and Doris were there across from Elise; she had known them at Arkite University but hadn't spoken to them in years. They smiled at her with fake smiles.

Everyone was smiling, but underneath those smiles was something else. Elise could practically smell it. Fear. They were all completely terrified, which Elise thought was ironic. After all, she was the one on trial.

"Well," Elise said, finally breaking the silence. She didn't have to talk loudly. Each seat had a small metal coin on the table in front of it that served as a microphone. "You all must have something terribly interesting to tell me."

"Rex," said Dana, nodding to Elise, "commence visual recording of this meeting."

"Yes, President Haish."

A camera was lowered from the ceiling.

"I think we should begin with protocol," said Leeto. "It is forbidden for ladies that are not Savants to attend the meeting. I ask that you dismiss your guard."

Elise feigned confusion, looking around the room, and then chuckled. "Whom are you referring to, Gansey?"

"The guard sitting beside you."

Elise threw a hand frivolously in the air. With the other, she dipped inside her dress for another sorely needed piece of gum. "Well, until I know what all this shit is about, I feel much safer with her by my side. You all know of the assassination attempt a few years ago. And, after all, everybody seems so fucking nervous."

"Can you dismiss her?" asked Ursula, leaning over the microphone. Leeto and Frankie nodded.

"We remember the last time you came with armed guards, Elise," said Dana with a smirk. She was referring to the infamous massacre where Elise had killed over fifty scientists from Allele Corporation. Many Savants suddenly looked ill. "We ask, my dear, that if you insist on having guards here, you at the very least disarm her."

"Okay," Elise said. "Since you asked so nicely, Dana." She cocked her head at Gena. "Disarm."

Gena stood and removed pistols and knives from her pockets, piling them on the table in front of Elise. Everyone waited as the two gray-suited servers walked around the table and took the pile of weapons in front of her guard.

"Now dismiss her," added Leeto.

"No."

"This is a private meeting, Savant Jackson," insisted Leeto. The fact that Leeto had referred to Elise as *Savant Jackson* instead of *Mother* wasn't missed by Elise or anyone else in the conference room. "Gena is not allowed."

Elise straightened the top of her dress, leaned on steepled hands, and then glared at the young Viceroy across the table. "No."

Dana cleared her throat. "Well, we wanted to see you, Mother . . . to . . . congratulate you. You don't know how pleased we all are by the news about Savant Candice Harlow's rebirth."

"Oh, thank you, my dear," said Elise. "Finally, something sweet." Dana was working her charm. "I'm very excited about it."

"I'm sure you are," said Dana. "It's quite an incredible achievement, Mother."

"Yes, it is."

"Yes," added Riley. "Congratulations, Mother."

Then came salutations from everyone in the room. The whole conference room's mood changed from tension to a torrent of solicitous bullshit.

Clever Dana.

But then Leeto opened her filthy mouth again. "How is Savant Harlow feeling? I heard she hasn't fully recovered yet."

"Oh, she's fine, Gansey," replied Elise. "Thank you for your concern. I'm sure she'll be well enough to see you again soon."

"I sure hope so."

Elise looked at Gena. Her Chief Guard was examining everybody in the room, ready to kill anyone who crossed Elise. Gena was such a badass. Elise absolutely adored her.

"Well, aren't all my sweet Savants palsy-walsy tonight?" Elise said after she had had her fill of accolades. "Aren't we all just the best of friends? What kind sentiments. But certainly you know I'm quite busy. Can you all get down to it and tell me what the fuck this is all about?"

"Your Lead Assistant couldn't make it?" Leeto asked. She looked around the room. "I don't see Sara."

"And I don't see Natalie," replied Elise. "Nat couldn't come?"

"Someone has to woman the factory, Mother."

"Give her my regards," Elise said.

"Of course."

"You two have gotten really close lately, haven't you?" Elise asked with a smirk.

Leeto squinted her eyes in rage and then flashed a look at Frankie. "No closer . . . I . . . think . . . than Sara and your Chief Savant Harlow."

The meaning of that was clear enough. A little too transparent. Some people covered their mouths and gasped at Leeto's impropriety. Others squirmed.

"You called the meeting, Viceroy," Elise said, leaning forward. "Come, come, do tell your Mother—what do you want?"

"Two things," Leeto said, and sat up straighter. "First: tell us the status of the Lazarus Project."

"This is a public meeting."

"The citizenry want to know. Tell us."

"Being that you decided to make this public to all of Arkite," Elise said, gesturing to the camera by the ceiling, "I think it's a bit inappropriate to discuss top secret proprietary information."

"You need to," insisted Leeto. "We've given you plenty of time to inform us privately, but you've refused."

"Lazarus is dead."

A few Savants laughed.

"You know what I'm referring to," Leeto said.

"Well, I just revived Candy."

Elise's friends, Dana and Riley, and a few other supporters, clapped and cheered again. Leeto looked at them with disgust.

"Thank you all," Elise said. "How kind. Thank you."

"Before your lover's death," Leeto snapped impatiently, "you told us Dr. Harlow could finish the Project within six months. Now it's been two years. The great Savant Vesper died of malignant breast cancer, Savant Credo passed after a tragic fall from her rocket bike, and the compassionate and giving Madam Pomerius broke the hearts of everyone by dying of thyroid cancer. I submit that all three of these wonderful citizens and Savants would have survived if you had completed the Lazarus

Project on time. Instead, you squandered Magnacourt's resources over your selfish obsession with bringing your lover back to life. Do you deny the accusation?"

"Don't forget, Gansey, that this is being broadcast throughout the city," reminded Elise. "I don't deny the death of anyone, but if you and the Council will permit me, I can argue that many more will be saved if you don't disturb my work."

"Two years, Savant Jackson," Leeto repeated.

Dana cleared her throat. "You did promise, Elise."

"We have discussed all this privately many times before, ladies," Elise said. "I have been available to answer questions from all of you in private. If you wish"—Elise looked up at the camera—"I can repeat everything to my beloved people."

"Yes," Frankie said, leaning into the microphone coin. Frankie looked upset. She despised Elise—always had. She was probably also a little sore about Elise mentioning Leeto's affair in public. "Repeat it to all the people, Mother."

"Okay," Elise said and turned to the camera. "Friends. The ability to reengineer genetic tissue promises long life. This gift is so close to being given to you. But even this amazing achievement does not promise *eternal* life. Only if nerve tissue can be reformed can our being, our very soul, if you will, be reborn. Otherwise, the memories and things that make us who and what we are will be lost in time. The work Magnacourt did with Candice Harlow now promises the ability to regenerate neural tissue and repair an aging brain. This can restore memories. It can keep us who we are. This is true immortality, friends. With mapping techniques created by Chief Savant Harlow herself, we have achieved this amazing breakthrough. We regrew Candice Harlow's brain and repaired it, healing her. Had we not used mapping and simply genetically reengineered her brain, it would not have been Candice anymore—not my Candy. It would have been a genetic false copy. Now do you understand? Do you see the importance of this two-year delay? We have mastered a technique to re-create the brain. Now we can create not only an eternal body but an eternal mind and soul. What could be more important? Who has done anything greater in all our history?" She looked away from the camera, gazing at all the colored uniforms surrounding the table again. "Not one of you."

There was a drawn-out silence. And then, suddenly, they clapped. First only her friends clapped, but the others quickly followed. Soon the whole room was filled with the sound of applause.

"Thank you, dears."

"What of the people who have died in those two years!" snapped Leeto, who alone had not joined in the applause. "Your research should have involved them first!"

"It is admittedly tragic, Gansey," said Elise. "But every scientific advance requires risk and sacrifice. Now that Candice is back, she can fulfill your dream in a short time and complete the Lazarus Project at last."

The Savants resumed their clapping. Only this time Leeto was not the only one to abstain. Ursula, Frankie and a few other Savants, all allies of Leeto, were silent.

"Question two!" snapped Leeto once the applause had died down. "It has been brought to our attention that there is an XY living in Arkite."

"I think that's common knowledge, Gansey," Elise said with a shrug. "It is common knowledge that Reyburn and Lilith had a son. The boy is in the custody of my Chief Guard here, Gena Harding."

"We'd like you to tell us why you didn't execute him," Leeto answered. "You hated Lazarus so much. Tell us why you spared Lilith's son. Of all people, Reyburn, whom you executed and—"

"Candice Harlow executed Reyburn," Elise interrupted her. "For the record."

"You gave the order, Mother," objected Leeto, shaking her head.

"No, I didn't. I suggested it. But thank you for finally using my title."

The whole room laughed.

"Why are you allowing the XY to live?" asked Dana. The President of the Council had been quiet, almost acting as an intermediary or moderator. Now she challenged her friend. "I .. . we don't understand, Elise. Please explain. Why didn't you order the XY's death?"

"He's just a little boy."

"It's the law," said Dana. "He's the reason for Reyburn's execution."

"No," Elise said. "Reyburn was executed for manipulating Nandalay Kelley into attempting to kill me. And for damaging my relationship with my lovely Candy-can. Reyburn's fiddling with XYs really didn't concern me."

"It is the law to eliminate all XY!" snapped Frankie. Elise had never seen the old hag so upset.

"Maybe you should have followed our law with Lazarus," said Leeto. "Had you not created him, Candice would never have been killed."

That went too far. Elise lost all reason.

"Why, you fucking shrunken dollhead! You arrogant little twitty-twit bitch!" Elise pounded her gloved hand on the table, jumped up and pointed at Leeto. Leeto showed fear for the first time. "How dare you! Before the whole city? How could you accuse me of killing Candice? My Chief Assistant! My love!"

"She was your Chief Savant," Leeto said with a shrug, trying to appear unaffected. "The facts speak for themselves."

"You wanna fight? Do you want to fight? Bring it on, bitch. I'll tear you apart!"

"Please, Elise," said Dana. "Sit down."

"How dare you!" cried Elise, slamming the table with her fist.

"Please sit down, Elise," Dana said.

"We all know she wants a fight," snapped Elise, pointing across the table. "That's why we're here. Well, stop with the show and bring it on! Dispense with civility and meet me across the room. I can wrestle you over the fucking table for all the people to see!"

"Really, Elise," said Riley.

Gena stood up and gently took Elise's hand, gesturing for her to sit.

"See?" said Leeto, addressing the rest of them. "She's unstable. Elise has always been unstable. She's drunk half the time or geeked out on cocaine whenever I message her. She's busier with screwing whores in her penthouse than leading the city. With her behavior, it should be clear to all of you that she is not fit to be our Mother."

"Please, Leeto," said Dana. "That was a very unfair and provocative accusation you just made. Elise loves her Chief Savant. She devoted every waking hour over the past few months in HQ Lab reviving her. Elise would never have wanted to hurt her. Why provoke her so?"

"Sorry," Leeto said sarcastically to Elise. "I hope I didn't upset you."

"The Board has voted to dissolve your Motherhood, Elise," said Dana. "That's why you're here. We've voted. Do you accept the wishes of your sister Savants?"

Elise surprised everyone by laughing. "I'm a Savant. What the fuck do you all take me for? A goddamn little tweet-tweet bird? I've little interest in your boring board decisions."

"Then you will step down?" Leeto asked.

"Elise," said Dana. "I'm sorry, it's just we need more progress in the Lazarus Project. It is not just Leeto who objects to your work. She is one of the only ones who has the courage to tell you. We have all voted on this decision. We don't believe your heart is in running Arkite anymore. You should simply care for Candice and step down. The Council will immediately restart HQ Lab and present our people the progress they ask for."

"You can use Dr. Harlow now, Dana," Elise replied, throwing more gum in her mouth. "Candice can complete the project. She's smarter than the rest of you bitches."

"Savant Harlow's brain is damaged, Elise," replied Leeto.

Elise almost lost her temper again. She thought of running to the exit, grabbing a gun from the Server table, and blowing the bitch's shrunken melon open. But instead she gripped her gloved hands tight and glared at Leeto. "I can assure you, Leeto, Savant Harlow's brain is fine. As I've told you many times, she was nearly finished with the Lazarus Project before she died. She completed a blueprint, more than you could ever do."

"Why didn't *you* finish it, then?"

Elise snapped the metal choker off her neck—her hand bled from its sharp edge—and threw it across the table at Leeto. Leeto dodged in surprise.

"Want it? Take it! Take my title. I don't fucking care about any of you. I give you the dream of recovering damage from your turnip brains, and this is what you give me in thanks for it. Well, you're welcome. And as for you, Leeto, consider yourself marked, bitch. I'll be happy to meet you outside anytime, anywhere, and beat the living shit out of you."

"You heard her!" Leeto said, leaping to her feet. "She's stepping down as Team Mother. She will henceforth be known as Team Grandmother. I assert that on the grounds of mental instability, drug addiction, advanced age, and general lassitude at her job, Team Mother Savant Elise Jackson shall no longer be our Mother Savant."

"*Lassitude?*" Elise asked, leaning over the table into the microphone. "*Advanced age?* I said I was stepping down, but by my own choice and on my own terms. Take those lies back, Gansey."

"Any objectors can raise their hand," Leeto continued, ignoring her. "All others, lay your palm on the table in agreement in the dissolution of Elise Jackson's leadership of Arkite."

Everyone, with the exception of a handful—her best friends Dana and Riley, laid their palms on the table.

Leeto stared at Elise, a smirk on her face. "I wasn't going to mention it, but I think we should also move to the next vote."

Ah, what's next?

"You had the boy in your possession as Mother, Dr. Jackson. Adam. An XY. Holding an XY is against your own former law, punishable by imprisonment or even death. And so, I think we should immediately vote on your punishment."

"This has gone too far!" cried Dana.

Elise grinned. Leeto had waited to overthrow her, and now she was going for the jugular. She had to admire the bitch.

"Leeto, I won't support this," continued Dana. "You have what you want. Elise has stepped down."

"In some ways, Dana, you're complacent," Leeto said, turning to her. "In fact, you might be complicit in these crimes. After all, Elise broke our gender law under your presidency. She's done it three times now."

"I don't want to discuss this in front of the committee, Gansey," said Dana, now standing and looking at Elise with concern. "And before the people. But voting on punishing our dear Savant Jackson—"

"*Doctor* Jackson," said Leeto, "is no dear. If you'd like, Rex can list the names of all your friends who were murdered by our *dear* former Mother. I will see to it that she is never a Savant again."

Elise laughed, chomping on her gum more obnoxiously.

"I agree with Dana," Riley said. "I won't vote to condemn Elise. She just stepped down. This is wrong."

"Well, you two don't have to," Leeto said. "You can remain Team Grandmother's puppets until the time of her death. But" —Leeto addressed the rest of the room—"what about the rest of you? Dr. Jackson sits among us, accused of breaking our sacred law against the creation of an XY. Not once, but three times. Her infant son was the first, Lazarus was the second, Adam is the third. These are grievous crimes, even worse than the murders of her own friends at Allele Corp. What say you, sister Savants?"

Gena leaned over and whispered in Elise's ear, "I remain your loyal guard, Master. Whatever you order pertaining to Adam, I will still do."

Of course, Gena, now that it's for your lovely little nephew. Right?

Elise patted Gena's hand. It was trembling. But not with fear. Elise knew that Gena was capable of killing anyone who tried to lay a finger on her nephew.

They voted. And with Leeto staring at each one of them— the woman who many assumed would be their next Mother— they voted to imprison Elise. But not to execute her. No one, not even Leeto, voted to kill her.

"And now," said Leeto after the votes were done, "Gena Harding, since we have the unusual benefit of your presence, please handcuff our former Mother, Elise Jackson, and escort her out of our private meeting. She is no longer a Savant and so is not granted permission to be here. You will, of course, send her to Station One."

Elise clapped. She clapped loudly and obnoxiously, chomping on her gum while everyone stared at her in amazement.

Gena stood beside her. Elise saw a tear run down Gena's cheek. Then Gena pulled Elise's hands behind her back and cuffed them.

"Well, now that that is over with," said Leeto with a long

sigh, seemingly happier than ever, "we can vote for our new Mother. It obviously should be our revered President, Dana Haish."

"I absolutely refuse," said Dana.

Leeto smiled even more.

But then Elise leaned down over the table by her microphone. "Pardon little ol' me, Savants, but there's no need to vote." They all turned to her. "Surely you realize that Candice Harlow is, de facto, your new Team Mother. Congratulations. Well done. I think your decision to place Savant Harlow in power was a good one. Candice will make a splendid Team Mother and leader of Magnacourt. As her mentor, I have complete faith in her. In fact, she'll probably treat all you bitches much better than I ever would."

Leeto lost her smile. The whole room burst forth with objections.

"What are you talking about!" demanded Leeto. "Get her out of here, Gena. Savant Harlow? How dare you!"

"How dare *you*," said Elise, still leaning over the microphone. "Everyone in this room, aside from perhaps you, knows Arkite's rules. Every Team Daughter, Chief Assistant Savant, has always become their Mother's successor. That means Candice Harlow."

"Candice has a damaged brain! She is not fit—"

"I can attest, having cared for her health personally," Elise replied, "that Candice is fit to rule. As she is fit to complete your project, Savant."

"Get her out!" shouted Leeto. "Get her out of here!"

"Yes, I think I'll take my leave now."

"Is she . . . is she still here?" Leeto yelled hysterically. "Get her out *now!*"

Gena escorted Elise out of the room and across the dark hall to the elevator. It was dark and foggy outside the walled windows, but it wasn't raining anymore. Behind her, in the conference room, she could hear the Savants arguing.

"Candice Harlow is artificial!" thundered Leeto's voice.

"We can test her," came Dana's reply. "We can review HQ Lab's files. Elise said she never let Rex tamper with her brain. Candice's neural network was restored from its original brain tissue, not rebuilt. She is still Candice."

"Elise is fooling you. She's tricking all of us! There's no way she could have revived a two-year-old dead brain!"

There's no fool here but you, Gansey. And each and every one of you is gonna pay. Oh, you're gonna pay real good.

"I'm so sorry, Elise," said Gena as they waited for the elevator. Rachel, who had joined them, was wiping her eyes with a handkerchief.

"Don't be," Elise said. "I'm just relieved they didn't order you to kill me. Still, I do regret one thing."

The two guards looked at her quizzically.

"It's a damn shame we can't meet for that late-night soiree I was planning. With all the excitement, I feel extra horny tonight."

The joke fell flat. Not even Rachel giggled.

"What's your order regarding my boy?" Gena asked.

My boy. I see. Fuck me, but not your boy.

"I'd take him to Station One, Gena," Elise said. "Follow orders now. But don't fret—we have time yet, my dear. All is far from lost. It will be hard, but things went exactly according to plan."

"Plan, Elise?"

"Don't you know by now, Gena, that I always have a plan?"

CHAPTER 14
HONEY, I'M HOME

CANDICE TOOK her fork and swirled it around Rex's sorry excuse for an evening meal. Even though it was sometime around ten o'clock at night, she had asked Rex for eggs. Rex was creative with the Pabulum, whipping up some mix of bacon, chives, eggs, and tomato sauce. It was awful. Or perhaps it wasn't, but she was just too nauseous to eat. So she just twirled her fork around. Then she leaned her head in her hands for a moment, rubbing her temples, feeling another wave of pain. Yet she heeded Rex's earlier warning and did not reach into her pocket for another pill.

She had Rex play soft music under a flickering yellow light along the circular table in the middle of her blue-domed kitchen. She drank a glass of Chardonnay. And then she just sat there in her kitchen, a little sickened by her stupid pride in her ability to finally get dressed and wear outdoor clothes.

The door opened, and Candy turned, excited to see Sara. Sara looked excited too. Or worried.

"Candy!" Sara ran into the kitchen, wearing her lime-green Savant suit. She ran to the silver table and leaned over it, breathing heavily. "Shit! Candy. I mean, shit! Everyone watched. Everyone. Then I saw Elise in Sky City. Everyone watched her. Why . . . why didn't you answer my call?"

"I was sleeping," Candice said, "and I shut off my monitor." She yawned. Then she opened her arms. "Hug me."

"It's not the time, bitch," Sara said, shaking her head. "I saw her!"

"Calm down. Sit with me."

Sara sat down across from her at the round dining table, but she looked as though she might jump up again at any second.

"What's the matter?" Candice asked with a chuckle. "You saw Elise. So what?"

"Candy," Sara said, grabbing her hand. "Elise was seen riding the floor escalator across Sky City."

"So? Rex told me she had a meeting."

"She had her wrists cuffed!"

Candice furrowed her brow.

"She was being escorted by her guards," continued Sara. "All the citizens of Sky City ran to the Promenade to witness it. The whole area was packed, and there was almost a riot! Some, still loyal to her, were ready to fight on her side."

"You're joking."

"No." Sara looked at her. Then she reached across the table and ran her hand through Candice's hair. "Damn, you look good, honey. You know, with all the genetic modifications, I'm biologically not much younger than you now. I might be older."

"Handcuffed?" Candice said, pushing her hand away. She couldn't tell if Sara was elated, scared, or upset.

"Um-hmm," continued Sara. "Yeah, she was on the escalator with her hands cuffed behind her back. Citizens rushed the building, clamoring to see her. Then a large group, maybe a thousand, rushed to the far side of the Promenade, waiting for her. Many were Officers holding guns. These guards were willing to fight for her if she gave the word. But there was a whole other group surrounding Elise, many Officers also armed, ready to fight back. Bystanders fled with their children out of the Promenade, fearing for their lives. Everybody thought it was going to be a revolution. It was crazy. A few Officers started fist-fighting with each other, but no shots were fired. And then, when Elise finally reached the end of the floor escalator, she simply smiled, nodded to them all elegant-like, even though she was still handcuffed, and thanked everybody. And then she asked her Chief Guard, Gena Harding, to escort her out of Sector Two to jail.

"I was there, Candy. I ran to Elise. I asked for orders. She . . . she . . ." A tear ran down Sara's cheek. "It made me cry. I . . . I don't know what to do, Candy. None of us do. I'm so scared. No one even knows who's running Arkite anymore."

"It's Elise, Sara. Come on. We're talking about Elise. She'll be fine."

"Yeah. You might be right. You know, she had one of her sarcastic smiles, the ones she gives when she's being playful. I don't know, maybe she has a plan. I'm sure she does . . . I just don't know."

"Why did this happen?"

"We've been on eggshells for the past year, working on bringing you back. I suppose I expected it for months. I just didn't know it would happen now, especially with you finally back."

"Elise was arrested for her negligence with the Savant Project, Team Mother," interjected Rex.

"Rex, shut your mouth!" Sara snapped.

Candice furrowed her brow again and then leaned on the table, rubbing her temples. She stared down at her uneaten eggs.

"Honey, you look tired," said Sara. "Why not finish your dinner and go to sleep?"

"I slept all day," Candice said. "What did Elise do, Rex?"

"She has been derelict in her duty," Rex repeated. "The Council arrested her for failing to complete the Lazarus Project. I warned her. She poured all her resources into reviving you."

"Can't see why," Candice replied with a shrug. "She doesn't even bother to visit me."

"She can't with the current political climate, Mother. There's too much to sort out in order—"

"Goddamnit, Rex," cried Sara. "Shut your fucking mouth! Candy needs rest."

"What?" asked Candice. "What is it?"

Sara jumped up from the table. "Candice is recovering, Rex."

"I know," replied Rex. "I agree completely. I think perhaps Team Mother should rest."

"You idiot!" cried Sara. "Shut up!"

"Why are you calling me Team Mother, Rex?" asked Candice.

"Please repeat? Please repeat?"

"You're such an idiot, Rex," said Sara, rolling her eyes.

"Why did you call me by that title?" repeated Candice.

Sara walked over and hugged Candice from behind. "Honey, forget it." She ran a hand along Candice's hair. "Forget it. You do look good. Real good. You know, that was Elise's red outfit when she was Team Mother. Where did you get her clothes?"

"Elise is no longer Team Mother?" asked Candice.

"Well . . ."

"Then who is?"

Sara didn't answer her at first. She seemed tongue-tied. She walked back around the table and stood across from her, nervously looking away. She looked like a little girl caught stealing a cookie from a cookie jar. Then Candice had a sinking feeling—the kind of feeling one has when hearing a creepy story and there's a twist at the end, only this time that creepy horror twist involved her. She felt butterflies all over her stomach. Then she felt dizzy. Really dizzy.

"Rex, if Elise is no longer Team Mother, who is?" repeated Candice. She needed him to tell her directly. She couldn't believe her ears.

"It's important that you rest, Candy," said Sara. "You need to not worry about this right now."

"You are," Rex replied. "Congratulations, Team Mother Harlow. It is quite an honor. Quite an honor indeed."

Candy jumped up and leaned on the edge of the table, clutching her head.

"Candy!" cried Sara. She ran back around and put an arm around her again. "Are you okay? Is it your head again?"

"No," Candice said. "This time it's not my head."

"I think congratulations are in order," Rex said. "What an honor—"

"Shut the fuck up, Rex!" shouted Sara. "You okay, Candy?"

"No. No, I'm not okay."

"I told you to forget it," Sara said. "I didn't want to tell you until you felt better."

They said nothing for the longest time. Candice fell back in her chair and put her head back in her hands. All she heard was music. The relaxing soft mellow jazz grated at her ears, but she didn't have the energy to tell Rex to shut it off. She just leaned on her hands with her eyes closed while Sara rubbed her back.

"Rex, repeat for me one more time," Candice said at last. "Who is the current Team Mother of Arkite?"

"The current Team Mother of Arkite is Savant Candice Harlow. And I might add, I am very proud of you. It is quite an achievement. Well done. Well done."

Candice turned and looked up at Sara in amazement. Then she shook her head.

"Congratulations?" Sara said with a stupid guilty smirk.

Candice rolled her eyes. "Rex, why would the Council allow me to be Team Mother? I have no experience. In fact, Elise never filled me in about anything regarding CPO or government matters."

"Mother, I am admittedly a bit partial when I say this," Rex replied, "but it is common knowledge that, throughout the city, you are a very well-liked individual. In fact, you are probably the most popular Savant in all of Arkite."

"That's true," Sara added.

"I don't think my popularity has anything to do with this."

"No," Rex replied. "That is correct. You speak wisely as always. In fact, after Dr. Elise Jackson announced the transfer of power, the Council tried immediately for a vote of impeachment. Savant Leeto Gansey first argued that you are not human. She argued that a Mother Savant had to be a woman. She noted that the rules forbid anything artificial, such as AI, from taking control of the city. That was refuted, however, as it was pointed out by others that Dr. Jackson never 'created' you; she merely nursed you back to health. Others reminded the committee that although your neural network had been systematically and exhaustively copied and manipulated by computer algorithms, regrown, and reconnected, such work was only done to repair your brain after stasis. Your brain needed repair from the time your body was interned to the time it was moved to HQ Lab and placed in its cryochamber. There was, of course, damage just from the day the brain was left decaying in transit, but Dr. Jackson figured she could reconnect the pathways—and she did, based on mapping the remaining viable tissue. All of this was done carefully by her and me—though she ignored my advice many times, for I could have easily re-created your brain in weeks by simply growing the genetic material from scratch. I think, if she had listened to me—but we all know Dr. Jackson rarely listens to anyone—that we could have avoided this unpleasant impeachment and Dr. Jackson could have still remained our revered Team Mother. But she put all her resources into reviving you. She cares for you quite a lot, Mother."

"Yeah. Me and my damaged brain."

"Yes, exactly. You and your damaged brain."

Normally, Candice would have shut Rex off from the start, but she let him drag on and on while thinking of what the hell she was going to do about her predicament.

"After the Savants accepted you as being a rightful citizen of Arkite, the next argument, made remotely by Viewer from Dr. Natalie Granger, Secretary of Central Bank and Lead Scientist of Pyramid Corporation in Sector Four, argued that you lacked experience as an Officer. She argued that Elise sheltered you from HQ. Then she argued that this was precisely why you were so liked—you were never given the responsibility of a leader. Your job always entailed only being a genetic researcher."

"That is all true, Rex," Candice said.

"Yes. But then Savant Dana Haish spoke. Her words surprised everyone. Everyone assumed that she would be next in line as Team Mother, so when President Haish suggested that not all Team Daughters of the past were properly indoctrinated in HQ leadership either, all the Savants murmured among themselves in amazement."

"Dana knew you'd win," interrupted Sara. She seemed enthralled by Rex's news, as if they were enjoying a virtual-projection video. "She's looking out for her own skin."

Candy looked up at Sara in amazement. It was as if Sara was enjoying the news like gossip.

"Yes, that is a possibility, Savant Holmes," Rex said. "I think you might be on to something. Dana Haish has always been very shrewd. And it was commented by many Savants how ill Savant Leeto Gansey looked after Dr. Jackson announced that Candice would be Team Mother. It all came down to a vote.

Once your competency was no longer contested, only your popularity could dispel you. And virtually all the Savants voted you in. You are, of course, a very popular young lady."

"That you are," Sara said, raising her wineglass in a toast.

"It's not funny," Candice replied.

"I'm not laughing," Sara said, but she couldn't erase a smirk.

"I think it was then that—"

"Shut up, Rex," Candice said. "I've heard enough."

"It will be all right, right, Candy?" Sara asked, putting her arms around her neck. "You can order anything you want for Elise now. You're Team Mother. I didn't want to tell you, but Rex has a big mouth. We'll be fine."

Candice nodded slowly. Then she looked down at her clothes—Elise's clothes.

You bitch. You planned it.

"Sara, what were you doing in Sky City this afternoon?"

"Elise ordered me to obtain all the drives used for the final repair of your neural net and then incinerate them."

"To destroy evidence," Candy said, nodding.

"I just figured it was top secret information outside of HQ," Sara said. "It was odd that she didn't want to take it back to the lab first, though."

"Didn't you tell me that the only way to finish my recovery was by using an artificial algorithm—one created by the scientists of Sky City that would prove my brain was completed by AI? Elise did everything she could to map it naturally, but the only way to complete my rebirth was partial artificial regrowth. Right?"

"Yeah."

Candy gestured at her outfit as if it was obvious. "And you destroyed the drives, right? So now the Council can't ever prove that."

"Uh . . . oh." Sara nodded, staring at the wall in thought. "She already predicted it, didn't she, Candy?"

"Yeah." Candice sighed.

Candice tried some eggs. They made her stomach turn. "Sara, you didn't put these clothes in my room to wear today, did you?"

"No, Candy," Sara said. "You look hot, though."

"Rex, who laid out Elise's Savant clothes in my room?" asked Candice.

"Team Grandmother Elise Jackson had it arranged," Rex replied.

Candice got up and limped for the door.

"Where are you going?"

"Elise seems to think I'm well enough to follow her orders and visit her now."

CHAPTER 15
DOCTOR ELISE JACKSON

Candice resolved to immediately head to Station One Court in Sector Four. She felt very ill, but she didn't feel as if she had any choice in the matter. Only Elise could tell her what this was all about. Only Elise could advise her. And, judging by the clothes that had been left for her, Elise was expecting her.

Candice walked with her cane across the dark hallway of her home and up an elevator to the roof. As Candice walked outside, she learned that Sara had kept more than just the news of her Motherhood from her.

The city was in chaos. First Candice heard explosions and the popping sound of gunfire. Then there were fires and smoke lighting up the darkness in different sections of the city under her. She could smell the fires. She made her way to one of the ledges and looked down. Straight below her at a street intersection she could make out a skirmish between a handful of Officers with clubs and shields against Gray-coated citizens throwing Molotov cocktails.

The clang of a metal door from behind made Candice whirl around. A young woman with short aqua-blue hair in a black double-breasted suit ran to her. But this woman wasn't nervous, she had a big gaping smile and seemed thrilled. Candice remembered this assistant—Debra.

"I'm so happy you're back, Candy!" Debra said, hugging her. Candice chuckled and nodded.

"What's going on?" Candice asked, gesturing to the clouds of smoke and violence under them.

"It's a revolution," the girl said excitedly. "But not against you, Mother. Many citizens just can't believe you're alive. They think Elise was overthrown as a way for the Savant Council to take over the city. They're in support of Team Mothers, they just can't believe you exist."

Debra pointed to Elise's cherry-red bike, the one matching Candice's clothes, ready to be launched on one of the raised launch pads. "I have her bike ready for you." That wiped the smile off of Candice's face.

I can't ride a rocket cycle.

"I can't," Candice said, shaking her head. Then she touched her left wrist and the monitor lit up. "Rex, please call a car to take me to Station One Court."

"I apologize, Mother, but I cannot do that," said Rex, his voice emanating from her wrist. "There is currently no aerial transport available. CPO has grounded all air transport and all squad cars are currently busy in Sector Two and Four. If you would like, I can arrange a car to fly you to Station Court tomorrow."

She couldn't wait for tomorrow. And Elise seemed to have predicted this too, arranging the bike to be readied on a launch pad.

Bitch! I have to ride a rocket bike when I can barely walk. Even now you challenge me.

"I need help to get on the bike, Debra," said Candice.

"Of course, Mother," said Debra, hooking her arm.

They walked to Elise's bike and she helped Candice up the stairs. Candice was so weak that Debra even had to help her mount her bike. Then she handed Candice her matching red visor helmet.

Candice hovered the bike over the building. From this vantage point, she could see more plumes of smoke and fire raging around her. She had heard the storm earlier from inside her house and had finally peaked through a window. Back then, clouds covered the tall buildings of the city in the night sky. Now clouds of rain were exchanged by clouds of smoke. She ordered Rex to fly her by autopilot to Station Court One.

The flight was awful. As smooth as a rocket bike was with its on-board stabilizers, she still had to muster enough strength to hold on to the handlebars with every turn, dip and ascent. Add Candice's persisting throbbing head and chest pain and it was all she could do to stay aboard without plummeting to the ground.

Rex flew her over the high-rise spires of downtown, across the lovely grass and trees lit up now by streetlights along Central Park (the only area of the city currently not on fire), and then into the dreary run-down part of Arkite, Sector Four. Here was where most of the smoke and flames raged.

When she reached Station Court One, she was greeted by an unruly mob. A line of thousands stood along the cement square below with their fists held high, facing the steps of the Courthouse and jail, demanding the release of Elise Jackson. At first, Candice was amused at their support. She wondered if the citizens knew that Elise could care less about them. But then she figured they wouldn't even care. These supporters were really not there in support of Elise at all; they were there to reject the Savant Council. As much as the people were terrified of Elise, they hated the elitist Savants even more. Elise had ruled with an iron fist, but she had ruled fairly. She had thwarted countless laws introduced by the Savants to take away more resources from the people and the Guard. That was why, when they saw a Savant rocket cycle hovering above, they started throwing things at her. Then it wasn't amusing to Candice anymore.

Drones flew down from above and acted like a shield under her bike. Then Officers below moved on some of the citizens, pushing and shoving and arresting them. She thought she heard a gunshot. Then she watched two black bikes rise with flashing red and blue lights—police bikes. They escorted her safely down to a landing site.

When Candice got off her bike and removed her visor, she could see the mob only fifty yards away. She quickly donned her sunglasses to shade the bright light coming from floodlights surrounding the protestors and police. There was gray smoke, and the overwhelming smell of fire and gas filled her nose and mouth and made her cough. For a second, she glimpsed at all the people—so many citizens in their work clothes, gray suits, and many more poor and destitute wearing rags. That's when someone must have recognized her face. Someone shouted her name, and in seconds the mob turned from despising her to becoming her best friend. Now, instead of threatening her, the mob cheered Candice on.

Candice felt relief when two Officers escorted her through double glass doors and into the dark, empty hall of Station Court. Not only was it pleasantly dim, it was quiet and the air was clean. The building was empty as it was nighttime, close to midnight. The threshold to the building was very drab, made of concrete walls and gray-tiled flooring. Across the entrance was one large reception desk, but no one was there to greet her. Over ten Officers with automatic rifles strapped over their shoulders paced inside along the windowed doors, periodically looking outside and guarding the entrance. Few walked along the adjacent corridors.

She hobbled with her cane down the dimly lit halls, accompanied by two Officers. Finally, by the end of one of the halls, the two guards opened metal double doors.

Candice never would have expected Elise's cell to be so spacious and bright. The room spanned over fifty feet across. White light flooded from recesses along the edges of the ceiling and reflected off glossy floors. Candice covered her shades, fearing it would trigger a pounding migraine. Her sunglasses weren't for fashion—even at night, the outdoor lights bothered her head and frequently led to violent pain. This room was brighter than outside, but after a moment, her eyes adjusted enough. There were no windows. In the center of the room Elise sat with her back turned, wearing an orange jumpsuit, shackled in her chair, an empty chair beside her. Candice guessed the other silver chair was for interrogation. Standing beside Elise were two bald Officers wearing black trench coats. They weren't at attention; they were jerking forward and back in guffaws. Apparently, even here, Elise was the life of the party.

As Candice walked in, leaning on her cane, she heard their laughter echo throughout the room. Elise was laughing too. It didn't seem like she was suffering, despite having her hands shackled in chains to the metal chair.

Candice limped in with her boots echoing against the stone floor. The two Officers beside Elise looked over.

"Turn me, Gweneth, won't you," Elise said. "Let me gaze upon our new Team Mother."

The guards lifted her metal chair and turned her around toward Candice.

Elise had a whimsical grin, not at all what Candice expected from a prisoner. She wore black makeup with black eyeliner and black lipstick matching her long black flowing hair that reached down to her shoulders, but she wore a hideous orange jumpsuit without her famous metal choker.

"Mother," Elise said. "Thanks for visiting."

Candice couldn't suppress a smile. She and her guards walked across the room until Candice stood over Elise.

"Leave us," Candice commanded the guards.

They hesitated for a moment, then obeyed.

"You look really good, babe," said Elise, taking her in from her shoulders down to her boots. "Really good. A bit thin, but hot."

Candice heard the door of the cell shut behind her. They were alone. "Why haven't you visited me?"

"I have, Candy. Many times."

"No."

"I came every night. I just let you rest those lovely blond eyelashes. Speaking of which, can you allow your prisoner one last request and take those glasses off? I want to gaze at those gorgeous blues."

"I can't," Candy said, shaking out her hair. "I can't take the light. It hurts my head. Especially here. It's so bright."

"I know." Elise looked around the room. "They gave me one request, Candy. One small request. I said, 'I'd like a room to myself, something large and well lit.' And I wanted makeup. And most importantly, after seeing what happened to your head when you were in prison, babe, I said I wanted to keep my hair. I suppose it was a *few* requests, but they granted them all." Elise giggled stupidly. "Sit. Sit with me, Can."

"Why are you so happy in jail, Mother?" Candice asked suspiciously, sitting down across from her.

"I'm not Mother anymore—you are," Elise replied. "And I don't think I'll ever be sad again now that you're back."

"Stop it, Elise. I'm not Mother. You know that. Why even suggest it?"

"You are Team Mother of Arkite," Elise said. "Ruler of the world. Congratulations. I'm so proud of you, babe."

"I don't want to be Team Mother."

"I know. Your only flaw is how goddamn sweet you are."

Candice reached in her pocket and took out some Mint.

There was silence. Elise finally looked a little solemn. "How are you feeling, Candy?"

"Fine."

"You still getting pains? It's funny how Rex can't cure you. The headaches are migraines, of course. Why they were triggered after your awakening, I don't know. But the rest of your aches, Candy—those are anyone's guess. Especially your chest pain."

"My chest doesn't hurt anymore."

"That's good."

"Well, this is better." Candice scooted her chair closer. "You seem depressed. You should be."

"And you're always a goddamn Debbie Downer, Can. Now's a time for celebration. Why would I be depressed? My Candy is Mother, and she's returned to me. You're welcome. I trained you. I molded you and changed you from an insignificant little dollface tweetsy tweet into a very strong young woman. And, unlike *my* Mother and me, we don't hate each other."

"Don't be so sure about that."

But after Candice said that, she rose and kissed Elise on the cheek. Elise turned and met her lips. It felt like that was all Elise ever wanted. Elise turned and leaned her head against Candice's cheek for a moment. Candice could hear her breathing steadily. Then Elise kissed her again and whispered, "I love you."

"Thank you for reviving me."

"Don't mention it."

"Now," Candice said, sitting back in the chair, "tell me what this is all about."

"What?" Elise asked, feigning innocence. "What's what about?"

"You don't give up. You never have. And"—she threw her

blond hair back again—"you certainly don't let people control you. I don't think what happened with the Council was an accident."

"Could be." Elise winked.

"It was clever. You waited until I was reborn to transfer power. You knew you were in trouble and there was no hope that they wouldn't take your Motherhood. So you set things up so that I was reborn and well enough to succeed you at just the right moment. Right?"

Elise nodded. "Only, I will never be reinstated as Mother."

Candice realized she still had the stick of gum in her hand. "Care for some gum?"

Elise shook her head. "Don't worry, Can. Now that you're back, everything will be fine."

Candice folded her arms. "What else are you scheming?"

"Tsk, tsk, Candice. Do you think so poorly of me? Must I always be *scheming*?"

"Yes."

"I'm old enough to retire," Elise answered with a shrug. "I'm the same age as Con-con Reyburn was when the old hag handed me her keys—older, in fact. The only good thing about it is you don't hate me."

"Sure about that?" Candice asked again. Then she removed her shades for a moment. She rubbed her eyes, blinking in the light.

Elise stared at her. She seemed overjoyed to just look at her eyes.

"It's a clever plan, Elise," Candice said.

Elise smiled slyly. "I'll tell you one thing—I'm gonna get those motherfuckers. I'm gonna get them real good. I have never wanted vengeance so bad in my life, Candy. Those Savants are gonna pay."

"How can I get you out of here?"

"Order my release," Elise said with a shrug. "But be careful.

You're going to need help. There are a great deal of mother-fuckers out there who don't like you. But I can help."

Candice put her shades back on and laughed. "So, what was the diamond about?"

"What diamond?"

"The diamond in Central Park. What was that about? It was very nice, by the way."

"Oh." Elise smiled again. "Simple, babe." She scooted her metal chair forward a little. "That's my proposal. I asked you before, but I never really offered anything. In ancient times, you know, a man would hand a diamond ring to his lover in order to propose marriage. It was a very cute and lovely tradition that somehow faded out of favor. I reviewed it in our historical archives. The diamonds are symbolic because they last forever. Like love. True love, Candice, lasts forever. Just as my love for you will last forever."

Candice was starting to feel butterflies in her chest again. She felt a wave of pain rising.

"You all right?" Elise asked.

"I'm fine," Candice said, forcing a smile. "Your proposal?"

"Yeah. So, I commissioned the city to erect a carbon-based shard of glass, a diamond, shaped like a diamond, in the center of the city for your grave. It was quite expensive, you know. And you're welcome. I . . . I can't hand you a ring at the moment, because my hands are a bit tied up, but I suppose I can propose with the diamond in the center of the city, right?"

Candice rolled her eyes but laughed in spite of herself.

"I'm very serious," Elise said sincerely.

"I know you are. That's what's so funny. You're sitting in a prison cell with your hands cuffed behind your back, possibly on your way to being executed, and you're proposing to me."

"It's the best time, hun," she said.

"You're also lying," Candice said. "You commissioned that diamond when you prepared my grave. You hardly set it up to ask me to marry you today. But . . . still it was a very nice gesture. Thanks."

"Of course, I didn't set it up for you *now*, dope, but it certainly works, right? I mean, doesn't a diamond in the center of the city prove my love? Or," Elise added with a sudden edge to her voice, "was sacrificing my position, spending every night in a lab bringing you back to life, and then being imprisoned not enough to prove my care for you? Would you prefer a smaller diamond to fit your thin, emaciated finger, Candice?"

"I didn't come here to fight," Candice said.

"Actually, I miss our fights. So how about it? Will you marry me?"

"Stop it."

"I've asked before. You never answered me."

"I did answer you. Many times. You just don't want to hear it."

"Well, will you marry me, babe?"

"No. I'm in love with Sara."

"Fuck!" Elise said, looking genuinely pissed for the first time. "Sara. Fucking Sara. You know, I spent days and nights studying your body, in ways too intimate and sick even for me. Your blood, your arteries, your veins, the stench, the smell of your blood and shit—your broken heart that that fucking cunt cut a hole in—those lovely eyes, which wouldn't open. I waited every fucking day for you to just look at me and say something like you did this evening. Something like, 'Hi, Elise.' That would have meant everything to me. I waited and gave everything just to wake you up. Then you did, Candice. You awoke. And . . . do you know what your lovely, luscious lips said to me?" Elise waited. Of course, Candice had no idea. "*Sara*. You said fucking *Sara*. You asked me why I never visited you when you awoke. There. That's it. It was because I dreaded that you'd look deep in my eyes, with those adoring blues, and say *Sara*. Well, fuck Sara. Fuck you, Sara!"

Elise inched her body and the chair slowly around, turning her back on Candice.

"Sara's my girlfriend."

"No, I'm your girlfriend," Elise replied.

"Elise," Candice said with a long sigh, "I owe you my life. But I'm not going to marry you."

"Ingrate," Elise said. "You wouldn't be here if it wasn't for me."

"Yes." They sat there quietly again.

Then Elise slowly scooted her chair back to face Candice again. "Did you watch the recording of the meeting?" she asked.

Candice was thankful for a change in subject. "Yes, I did, Elise. But I don't understand. I get why you revived me, but I don't understand why you protected Adam. Neither do the Savants. After everything that happened with Reyburn, why would you protect her son? Why would you protect an XY?"

"There's no privacy code in prison, Mother," Elise said. "Now really isn't the time to tell you."

Candice rose with that, nodded and touched her left wrist. The monitor lit up on her arm. She hit a button and called the guards.

"Whatcha doing?" asked Elise.

"Taking you home."

The doors swung open, and the four Officers walked in.

"Sweet," Elise said. "Very sweet as always."

"Remove the handcuffs from the prisoner," Candice said, addressing the guards. "Team Grandmother is hereby released upon my order. She will accompany me outside the Station."

"Yes, Mother," replied an Officer with a grateful smile.

"I'll try to take you back to your home tonight," Candice said, grabbing Elise's hand as they walked out of the cell, "but I heard your home is locked up."

"Motherfuckers, Can," Elise said. Then she repeated quietly, almost to herself, "Savant motherfuckers."

"Do you know what's outside the prison, Elise?"

"What, dear?"

"Your welcoming crew. Thousands of people are outside showing support for you."

"Lovely."

ELISE AND CANDICE STEPPED OUT OF STATION COURT ONE AND stood at the top of the concrete stairs. The crowd below went wild. Walking by Candice's side, Elise still wore an orange jumpsuit, but with hands no longer shackled. They walked together down the granite steps, smiling and waving at all the people of Sector Four. Candice limped carefully with her cane. She covered her mouth and coughed from the rush of smoke outside. The demonstrators became transformed into fans, cheering wildly at the sight of their freed former Overlord. Then they nearly toppled over the metal barricade as they tried to touch them.

"They love us, Candy," cried Elise, overjoyed.

"They love you, Elise."

Gena was standing at attention beside the rails, but when she saw Elise walk down the steps, she ran to her. Candice knew Gena. Gena always had struck Candice as such a cold, unfeeling woman. She had been much closer to Elise than her.

Gena ran and hugged Elise and then excitedly shook Candice's hand. Then other Officers standing before the crowds congratulated them. The police loved Elise. Candice knew that they would be loyal to her to the very end. No Team Mother had treated them with as much respect and goodwill. In many ways, the Officers were more a part of Elise's family than the Savants.

"*Mother's free!*" they shouted. The words spread through the mob.

Elise reached over to Gena. "Hand me the speaker, dear."

"Mother's free!"

Candice felt a sudden twinge of pain. She rubbed her temples. The noise was crushing her head, and for a moment, she feared she was in for another attack of severe pain.

Not now. Please. Not now.

Gena handed Elise a small silver transmitter the size of a coin. Elise stopped at the base of the stone steps, and Officers cleared more space for them. Elise addressed the mob.

"My dears," Elise said, her voice amplified throughout Station Court. "You have it all wrong. I'm not your Mother." She grabbed Candice's hand and raised it high. "Candice Harlow is your Mother. Cheers for Candy! Candy Harlow! Cheers! Candy's the new ruler of Arkite! My love is the one who's freed me!"

The crowd went wild. *"Candy! Candy!"* echoed from a thousand voices.

Elise handed Candice the voice transmitter, but she was getting sick. She felt too ill to address the crowd. The assembled citizens stared and waited for her words, and that only made her feel worse. But she did what she had to, what she always had done, and fought through her crushing pain to accept her responsibility.

"Thank you," Candice said, holding Elise's transmitter. Her words echoed through the courtyard. The crowd cheered. Elise looked at her to say something more. Candice took a deep breath and said, "I . . . I ask you all, please . . . please return home. Go home." There were boos and jeers. "There's been too much violence in Arkite. I free Elise and am honored to accept this new position as Team Mother. But . . . you all need to go home. The fighting's over."

Elise looked disappointed, and apparently so was the crowd. There was silence. But then the crowd went wilder. And louder. Much louder. They really didn't seem to care what Candice had told them.

The noise was too much. Candice knew an attack was coming on. She leaned into Elise's ear and said, "I have to go. I'm really sick."

Elise just nodded.

"*Now*," Candice added.

Elise grabbed the transmitter from Candice. "Toodles, everyone," she said to the crowd. "We love you all, and so does your new Mother."

A group of Officers led by Gena escorted the couple to Candice's bike. As they drew near, Candice tripped and toppled to her knees. The crowd gasped.

"I can't ride," Candice said, shaking her head.

"It's okay, Mother," Gena said.

"No . . . I can't ride."

"I need you to stand, Candice," said Elise very sternly, reaching to her. Her change in countenance was striking. She had been so happy before. Now Elise had become deadly serious. This was the boss Candice remembered. "Stand now," Elise ordered, "no matter how badly it hurts. Do it. Do it now."

Candice obeyed, doing everything she could to project an image of strength, but though she managed to get her feet under her, it was only with Gena and Elise helping her up on either side that she was able to move at all with her cane.

"We'll take you by car," Gena shouted over the raucous noise of the crowd. "I'll have your bike returned remotely, Mother."

Candice feebly nodded.

They made there way through an aisle of women. Some were literally in tatters, hardly wearing what Candice would call clothes. It took all of Candice's will to make it through the crowd to the car. When she got in, she fell on the white leather seat in the back, clutching her head with both hands and moaning. Elise rushed in and sat beside her, holding her. Gena came last, quickly shutting the door.

Candice felt terribly dizzy and nauseous. Her head felt like it was about to crack open. Her neck and back felt stiff and immobile. Any move she made only increased the pain along her bones. She searched for something to vomit in. Somehow, a basin was placed before her, and she threw up into it.

They rose slowly into the air. That only made matters worse. The movement made her retch some more. She wasn't sure how she was sitting up, but she was.

Then the car began to move horizontally. That was a little better. Candice breathed heavily.

Elise was holding her, looking genuinely concerned. Her stupid puerile excitement over her freedom was erased. So too was her authoritative demeanor. Now she just looked worried. Terribly worried about her. Even the stoic Gena, sitting across from them on the front white leather seat, looked worried.

"You need to return Savant Harlow to Angel of Hope, Dr. Jackson," came Rex's monotone voice. "She needs to go back and be monitored by me in the hospital immediately."

"No hospitals," Elise said. "I will care for her back at my house at Pyramid Three."

"I advise we check her into the hospital," Rex said. "She is very ill. Her pulse is up to above one hundred and twenty. She is shaking. Her blood pressure has dropped to—"

"Did the drone footage show her fall, Rex?"

"Yes, Team Grandmother. Of course it did."

"Can you withhold the recording from the motherfuckers?"

"When you say *motherfuckers,* are you referring to the Savant Council of Arkite?"

"Of course I am."

"No. Her fall will be available for the Council's view."

"Even if erased by Candice's order?" Elise asked.

"Dr. Jackson," Rex replied, "the recording by outside drones is public record."

Then Elise realized Candice was looking at her. "You doing okay, honey?" Elise asked with a forced smile.

"No," Candice said.

Elise nodded and ran her hand across Candice's forehead. "Rest. I need to take you to my place. Too much excitement, I'm afraid. I can watch you there."

Candice nodded.

"Take us to Pyramid Three, Rex," Elise said. "We can address the people there."

There were no drivers in the Officer Transport car. It was operated remotely by HQ mainframe. By Rex.

"This is unwise," Rex said. "I strongly advise you to reconsider. I can help her in the hospital. You are gambling that she will recover. If she does not, Dr. Jackson, the Council will imprison you again and, likely, execute you."

"She'll be fine," Elise said. She ran her hand along Candice's bangs and kissed her forehead. "Don't lecture me about politics while my Candy Doll is sick. Head to my place. I don't care what happens to me if Candice is hurt."

Elise helped Candice lie down flat on her back along the back seat and then she sat across from her with Gena. Candice closed her eyes behind her shades. She heard Elise and Gena talking. They spoke softly, but she could hear them.

"You will have to refuse the order, when it's given," Elise said. "If you care for him, it's your only choice."

"I won't," Gena said. "I can't do it. You know I can't."

"Refuse it. When the time comes, you will. If you feel so strongly for him, you'll have to. Otherwise, they'll kill him."

"My allegiance is to Magnacourt. I already told you that. My life—"

"No one doubts your allegiance, Genie. But this isn't about you. I'm sorry. I really am. I didn't want any of this to happen. I don't know what else I can do to protect him. The mother-fuckers are circling, ready to feed."

"The Guard remains loyal. If we no longer speak, know that, secretly, Mother, I always hold my allegiance to you and am so grateful for what you've done. You and I shall always be friends, and I will never forget what you did for me."

"I know, Genie. Now stop talking about it. It's so fucking depressing."

CHAPTER 16
MOTHER'S HOME

ELISE RECLINED in her gray half-egg-shaped leather swivel chair on the top floor of her penthouse pad, sipping a glass of red wine and staring at the window. The outside blinds were closed, but Rex projected a three-dimensional image of Central Park in front of covered glass.

Elise yawned. She'd been up all night.

"Take me along the walkway," she directed Rex.

She watched a vista of Lake Salmas, the large woman-made lake in Central Park, a spectacular view with ladies sailing their sailboats in the background. In the foreground was a field of grass lined with bushes along the water's edge. The water flowed gently along stones by the shore. There were a handful of ducks—ducks having been genetically engineered and grown there many years ago—and Elise watched a little girl in a cute baby-blue frock and dress feeding one. These were the only "birds" in Arkite. They were genetically engineered not to fly. In the farthest distance, Elise could make out the sharp-spired skyscrapers of Sector One. There were lovely white-painted garden benches facing the water. The VR view followed the direction of Elise's head. She turned and watched the mother of the girl feeding the ducks, sitting on one of the benches, just admiring the view.

Elise drank more wine. It was smooth and good. Her wine cellar had just recently been replenished, and she had asked Rex for something expensive to celebrate her freedom.

Two small drones rocketed along a field, distracting Elise for a moment. These were privately owned, not from Magnacourt. A group of teenagers could be seen controlling the drones from their wrists by some trees.

"She's not along the lake," Elise said.

"She was," Rex replied. "I saw her arriving from Sector Two by rocket cycle, Team Grandmother."

"Then why can't I see them?"

"There are a lot of people out today. It is a very lovely day, wouldn't you say? A nice change in the weather."

Elise yawned again. "Show me . . . show me where they are now. Do I have to search myself? Damn it, Rex."

"I will try to locate. Just a moment. Just a moment."

The image shifted fast along the lake, and the motion made Elise a little dizzy. Then it refocused along the woodsier section of the park. Here thick trees bounded an artificial forest. Elise had walked the trails with Candice many times before. She hoped Candice would recover soon and they could walk there again. Candice loved Central Park. The images moved at times closer to the ground, likely from the source, a flying copter drone, having to duck around tree branches and leaves.

"I thought you told me they were at the lake."

"They were heading there, but they turned—"

"Idiot! Why don't you fucking show me where they are?"

"Yes, Team Grandmother."

Finally the image focused in on two Savants—one in a purple jumpsuit, the other in orange—walking along a broad cement walkway. They were surrounded by other citizens, many in yellow or white blouses, shorts or skirts, everyone enjoying the warmer weather, walking hand in hand and just enjoying the scenery. But Elise could spot her enemies even without their Savant clothes. Their expression was so focused. Indeed, they were heading toward Lake Salmas.

"Identify those two for me."

"Savants Ursula Myer and Natalie Granger."

They were far from the image, but one looked like Ursula, who was a black-skinned girl. She was wearing an orange jumpsuit. The other was wearing a violet jumpsuit.

Elise felt giddy. She jumped up from her swivel chair and ran to a small wooden table to get more wine. She refilled her glass while her eyes remained glued to the images before her. Then she reached into the pocket of her black dress and popped another stick of gum in her mouth to keep herself awake.

"Careful, Rex." She drank more and chomped on some Mint. "Wouldn't want them to know I'm here. Keep your distance."

"I am well aware of your deceptions, Team Grandmother."

"Of course you are, you son of a bitch. You're always so helpful. Particularly when I was in prison."

"May I remind you, Grandmother, that I told you countless times to stop your work on Candice. I warned you that you would be tried by the Council for dereliction of duty. I warned you."

"Shh. Shut up. Where are they heading?"

They walked along the lake until finding a woman sitting at a bench and staring out at the lake. She was an older woman with peppered hair in jeans and a white button-down blouse. Natalie sat beside her while Ursula stood by their side. The older woman did not turn. She just stared out at the lake.

"Identify that woman, Rex."

"That is Dr. Epton. Julia Epton from Sky City. She is one of the scientists—"

"Who worked on facilitating group connections and neural growth for Candy-heart's brain," Elise interrupted. "I know. Maybe Sara should have incinerated her too."

"I hope you are joking, Team Grandmother. That—"

"Just shh."

Elise watched. Dr. Epton sat frozen, saying a word or two but barely moving. Then she handed something to Natalie.

"Damn, I wish we could hear them."

"They are too far away. I can try to move closer, but this is out in the open. I predict that if I come closer, they will become suspicious and leave."

"Zero in on what she gave her."

"I cannot. It is in Natalie Granger's pocket."

"Hmm. Run the vid back a bit. Let me see it again."

Rex complied. The room filled with a 3-D vision of the two Savants at the bench with the doctor. Once again, Dr. Epton nonchalantly handed Natalie a metal object the size of her palm.

"What is that? Closer, Rex. View the image closer."

Rex magnified the image. Though blurry, it could be identified as a metallic disk. A neural net, in fact.

"Interesting, Rex. Something's finally interesting."

"They are leaving Dr. Epton, Team Grandmother."

"Stay with the two of them, Rex."

"They're mounting their bikes on the grass."

"Where are they headed?"

"Not sure. Not sure yet, Dr. Jackson. From the direction of their flight, it appears that they are heading north to Sector Four once more."

"Of course." Elise let out a big sigh. "Don't these fuckers ever go anywhere else instead of back to Pyramid City?"

"Perhaps you should sleep. You've been at this for over a day. And eat. I think you should eat, Team Grandmother. Would you like me to get you something from the Pabulum?"

"I think it's rather suspicious that they keep flying back and forth between Central Bank and the park, don't you, Rex? I don't think it's just to enjoy the outdoors. Maybe it's to take a break from shrunken-head bitch."

"It is peculiar. They are very busy. Not in accord with their usual habits."

"Aha. Seems they're up to something. And now we know it's in that disk. But why'd they exchange it out in the open where we can see?"

"They did it rather discreetly," answered Rex. "Perhaps they thought it would bring less attention to CPO than if Dr. Epton visited Pyramid Corporation. Dr. Epton is a minor worker without clearance to Pyramid Corp."

"And the Savants dared not go to Sky City with the ongoing investigation."

"Precisely, Team Grandmother. It is always a pleasure to work criminal investigation with you. Your mind is as sharp as ever, even as a revered Grandmother."

"A grandmother who is only thirty years old."

"You are, in fact, forty-six, Elise. Forty-six."

"Thirty." She drank more wine.

Elise had obtained a warrant signed by the Chief Officer of Arkite and permission from Mother—well, she had never asked Candice but had simply told Gena that Candice had said yes. The warrant was based on the questioning of Dr. Teller. With information connecting Savant Granger, Elise had been watching her like a hawk for over twenty-four hours at the top of her penthouse.

A small robotic wheeled cart came out from the wall. It rolled down Elise's dark ramp, heading for the kitchen. A minute later, the cart rolled back up carrying a peanut-butter-and-jelly sandwich on a metal tray. Elise dipped down absent-mindedly and grabbed it, biting into her lunch—or breakfast, or dinner, or whatever.

"Plant a microwing on her visor, Rex," Elise said. "Do it before she lands so she doesn't notice."

"I cannot do that. It is an invasion of privacy."

"No, *you* can't. But I can. Plant the microwing by my order."

"Elise, if you do not find the evidence to incriminate them, and such a listening device is discovered, you will be implicated for breaking the privacy law. This is very risky, considering that you are still under investigation regarding the XY."

"You needn't lecture me on law. Or risk. Fly a drone closer and attach the small device on her visor now while she's still in flight. Do it quick."

"And what if she doesn't take the visor inside?"

"She's taken her helmet inside the last three times she came back to Central Bank! Now do what I say!"

"Yes, Team Grandmother."

"Bastard . . . be sure to land it carefully. If the wing moves, she might feel it attach."

"I really think you are tired. I think—"

"I swear, if you keep lecturing me, you plastic prick, I will decommission your ass and replace you with your predecessor."

"My predecessor was inferior."

"I think she'd disagree."

Elise washed down the PB&J with some wine.

Then she waited. She watched the two Savants flying their rocket cycles close to the rubble of the broken concrete highway in Sector Four. Down below were a thousand citizens living in the squalid settlement of the Candle District. It was here that Rex's camera view came very close to Ursula's orange Savant jumpsuit. Elise could not see the microwing jettison from the drone, for it was the size of a small coin, but she did see her view quickly pull away.

"Successfully deployed, Team Grandmother," said Rex. "I

am now changing VR imaging to microwing feed. There will be a brief delay."

"Nice. Program the microwing to detach when inside the building."

Elise waited some more. She felt her eyelids close for a moment. Then she shook herself awake. She drank more from her glass.

It became pitch dark for a minute. Only a faint purple light from the recesses in the ground and ceiling glowed. Elise struggled even more not to drift off to sleep. Then the bright view finally reappeared before her, altered to a weird blurred three-dimensional image of a room above a giant tan leather floor. She seemed to lift up from the leather, and the ground defocused while the room above looked clearer. A huge steel table appeared at the center of the room. Then the "tan leather floor" dropped and clearly came into focus as the seat of a leather recliner. The image quickly turned, and Elise saw a giant image of an orange visor—a half-eggshell-shaped helmet that Ursula must have dropped when entering the building.

"Steady the image, Rex. And don't turn so fast. You're making me dizzy."

The image adjusted further, expanding to fill the space of Elise's room with its ghostly reality. Elise saw a waiting room with two leather chairs and the central steel table. There was a woman in a drab gray suit rushing quickly down a hallway. She seemed to pass only a foot from Elise but did not look in her direction.

Elise looked through a window. Through the glass was a conference room with a big table and surrounding leather chairs, but the chairs were empty. She passed two more workers and yet another conference room.

"Careful, Rex. Try to be inconspicuous."

"I am endeavoring to be as discreet as a fly."

"Considering what a pest you are, that should be easy

enough." Elise chuckled and drank some more. Then she reached into her pocket and grabbed more Mint. She needed to perk up.

Rex dodged three more bodies on his way to the black-curtained third glass conference room. There Elise was brought a foot from the glass door.

"Can you fit under the door?"

"No."

"Fuck. Take me around. We might need to wait for someone to open the door."

She waited. Then she felt tired again. Her eyes closed, and she nodded off for a moment before jerking back awake.

"I need Nixyl-5, Rex. Get me Nixyl-5."

"Team Grandmother, I do not advise—"

"Of course you don't. But as excited as I'm getting, I'm about to collapse."

Nixyl-5 was a drug containing a 5-HT3 antagonist and a nanotech acetaldehyde and acetate buster. The problem with this illegal "hangover cure" was that it also risked kidney failure from the byproducts rushing into excretion. Elise's excessive habit of popping stimulants made the drug even riskier. But Elise didn't care. She had to stay awake.

"It could kill you," said Rex frankly. "I already told you the risks of myocardial infarction or acute renal failure."

"Brew up a pill for me, my dear. And hurry. Let me wash it down with a nice dark cup of coffee. Hurry before I drift off and miss the whole show."

"Very well," Rex said with a sigh. Elise laughed. "You will promise me that you will rest after all this?"

"Sure will, Doc. Don't you worry about me. Now hurry."

Elise tapped her fingers on her black leather pants. Her hand shook terribly, and she could feel her heart thumping in her chest from all the Mint she had chewed.

The view did not move from the black curtain.

A robotic tray appeared near her chair. She swiveled it and grabbed a pill and a cup of hot coffee from a tray held by the wheeled robot.

"Cheers," she said, raising the cup of coffee in the air. She threw the pill into her mouth and drank the black coffee.

"I'll have an ambulance ready."

Elise couldn't tell if Rex was joking or serious. She laughed again.

Then, from the transparent image before her, an assistant in a gray dress opened the curtained door.

CHAPTER 17
THEIR PRIVATE MEETING

"Oh, Lee," Ursula said, wrapping an arm around the other woman, "you did it."

They sat beside each other along the glass conference table, Ursula in her orange Savant suit at the head of the table, Natalie in her purple suit by her side.

"Yeah, Cee-Cee," Natalie said. She reached into her pocket and brought out the neural net, running her gloved fingers over the case. She smiled a big grin at Ursula. Then she took Ursula's left arm and examined it. She turned off Ursula's wrist monitor, then turned off her own. Then she nodded.

"It is safe?" Ursula asked.

"Yes."

"We have to be sure."

"It's okay," Natalie said, rubbing the back of Ursula's hand. "Trust me. You still not sleeping?"

"No." Ursula dropped her voice and leaned closer to Natalie. "She planned the whole thing out. Elise has it in for us, Lee."

"We'll be fine. Now that we have this," Natalie said, running her fingers over the disk.

"You're sure it's safe to talk here?" Ursula asked again.

Elise sipped her cup of coffee.

"We're in a secure room, Cee-Cee. Our wrist monitors are shut off. Rex might be everywhere, but he's not here."

"I'm not so sure. You don't know what Elise is capable of," Ursula said.

"I think I have a pretty good idea. But now that we have the evidence we need, we can stop her and her puppet."

"Even if Harlow is stopped, the Council will vote Dana in," Ursula protested. "Or Riley. Elise has already set her friends up too. She thought of everything."

Got that right, bitches. Elise sipped more coffee.

It was then that Elise nearly dropped the white porcelain cup to the floor. Her heart suddenly started pounding in her chest. She took a deep breath, waiting for it to pass. She nearly fell off the chair but managed to keep her seat.

"Are you all right, Team Grandmother?" asked Rex.

"Yes. Now shut up!"

"Your heart stopped and then had a run of SVT."

"Shut the fuck up! I need to hear them."

Elise forced her eyes open and ignored a surge of chest pain.

"It's just a matter of time before she goes after us," said Ursula in the 3-D image. "You saw her at the meeting. She has it in for us. We're doomed if we don't present it. How sure are you that the disk has the evidence we need?"

"Don't worry. Didn't you see her fall? Candice is sick. Now, with this, we can take her Motherhood. You know Elise as well as I do. We're as good as dead already if we don't get rid of Candice." Then Natalie lifted the disk in the air, running her gloved fingers over it once more. "This is it. It'll prove that Elise used algorithms over the areas too damaged to repair— meaning that Candice is not completely human. She was partially engineered with computer mapping in Sky City.

Candice is partly artificial—a section of her brain artificially grown. Thus she is not a true citizen and cannot be Mother."

"Thanks to Julia again."

Go, on. Tell me. Tell me and the mainframe more.

Ursula finally seemed to relax. "When should we tell the Council?"

"Tomorrow," Natalie said with a shrug. She looked away towards the window of the view of the city. "But there's another matter."

"What's that, Lee?"

What is it? Do tell.

"Well . . . Ursula, you have access to the mainframe. Out of all the Savants, you can access records better than any of us. You . . . you can reconfigure the Pabulum of one of our citizens, right? You're a master programmer. The problem would be disguising the action from Rex. But you could sneak in a printed compound, something like, say, belladonna. Something natural like that. It wouldn't be that hard, would it? I have the key."

"But why?" asked Ursula, looking pained.

"There can be no evidence. No traces left of Carloff's theft. The minute we implicate Candice, Elise will become desperate. She'll move Officer Harding to do all sorts of things with CPO. When we release the information recorded from Sky City's mapping, Elise will trace the work to Dr. Epton. Then they'll question Dr. Epton, and I doubt Epton has as quiet and disciplined a mouth as Florence Teller. That will lead her to implicate you and me."

⌇

"Did you get that part, Rex?" shouted Elise, laughing and twirling in her chair like a little girl. "Granger just implicated herself and Ursula in the whole dirty venture with Candy's neural net theft!"

"Yes, Elise. I recorded it. But you have hearsay evidence. You will need to obtain proof to implicate her specifically. Not to mention, Grandmother, that releasing such evidence would also inevitably lead to demonstrating the use of AI in assisting in Candice Harlow's neural net repair, sabotaging her ability to be Mother. "

"Yes, yes. Fine. Perhaps you're right. But I was referring to their theft. Now I know that these fucking bitches are to blame. Now shut it. I'm sure these two will dig themselves a grave."

"Ursula, what I'm suggesting is—"

"I could do it." Ursula reclined back in her gray leather chair for a moment in thought. "I can program anything from belladonna to strychnine."

"Yes. But the trick would be disguising it. Rex's directive is not to hurt anyone. If he detects it, he'll put a stop to it and quickly expose us."

"You're so sneaky," Ursula said with a laugh. "You've been planning this all along."

"You can walk away now, Cee-Cee. I didn't want to involve you. Of course, you know the risks if we're discovered . . . I need an answer. If you accept, I can get you Julia's home files."

Ursula paused. Then she nodded. "Yes. I'll do it. Give me her home files."

Elise watched as Natalie dug into her pants pocket again and handed Natalie a small metal coin-like object. She closed Ursula's hand around it and smiled.

"CAN YOU SCAN THE CONTENTS OF THAT OBJECT, REX?"

"Yes."

"What does it contain, may I ask?"

"Just a moment. Just a moment. It is very difficult from this distance. Especially as you are sneaking into their conversation with a microwing. I am attempting an acoustic probe. Just a moment. Just a moment. The drive contains a copy of the coding to Dr. Julia Epton's Pabulum."

"Are you absolutely certain?"

"Yes. It is the programming of her meals and her favorite dishes and the ingredients formed. It matches the home-food printer at number 457, Pyramid Building Seven. It matches Dr. Epton's Pabulum signature."

"Got you, motherfuckers!" Elise shouted, rolling in her chair in laughter. "Got ya! Took you long enough, Rex. Store the recordings and findings . . . except the part about Candice being part artificial. Delete that. That is top secret Magnacourt business, after all."

"Of course, Team Grandmother. I understand."

"And while you're at it, show the evidence to Officer Harding now and order the immediate arrest of Savants Myer and Granger. They have an illegally obtained copy of a private ID file. Not only that, we have them recorded as planning to reprogram it in order to poison and murder a citizen of Arkite. How despicable."

Elise spun around in her chair and laughed like a little girl, spilling a little of her red wine over her black lace dress.

That was when she heard footsteps from the bottom floor walking up the ramp.

"Is everything okay, Elise?" Sara asked.

Sara was standing at the bottom of the central incline at Elise's penthouse, staring up at the 3-D image of the conference room and the two Savants being watched. Elise looked down at Sara.

Elise was surprised to see her, particularly because Rex had not announced her entrance to the penthouse. Why hadn't Rex announced her?

"Hi, Sara," Elise said, trying to hide a guilty expression. The lighting was dim but bright enough for Elise to make out Sara's horrified expression as she gazed at the 3-D image of the two Savants. "Shut down the vid, Rex."

"Yes, Elise."

"What's going on?" asked Sara.

"Nothing," Elise said. "Nothing, my dear."

Elise got up. She was surprised at how steady she was on her feet after so much drinking, but then she remembered the Nixyl-5.

"I'm here to take Candy home. Is she better?"

"Yes. I just took the IV out an hour ago. But she's resting," Elise said as she walked down the ramp between the second and first floor. "Open the blinds, Rex."

The blinds opened, and brightness flooded the house. Elise squinted in the light.

"Are you all right, Elise?"

"Just a bit jumpy," she said. Then Elise gave Sara a hug. "She's fine, Sara. She's sleeping in the guest room."

Elise ran a hand through Sara's long blond hair. She examined Sara's expression. Sara still had a terribly frightened look on her face. Why? Then Elise remembered. Sara had flown to Central Bank a month ago. She probably had spoken with bitch-Gansey and the rest of the nasty girls in that same conference room projected a moment ago above her. Did she think Elise had a Viewer hidden in Central Bank? But Sara had confessed everything. Or had she?

"Well," Sara said, still looking at the top of the ramp, "I'll go get her. Thanks for caring for her, Elise."

"I wouldn't. Not now. Why not let her sleep, Sara? She's still recovering, you know. Maybe . . . perhaps you'd like a drink?"

But Elise didn't want a drink. That was the last thing she wanted. Nixyl-5 was good, but it didn't get rid of all the ill hangover effects.

"No thanks, Elise."

Then Elise felt the other side effect of the drug. She had to pee—really bad. "I have to use the little ladies' room. If you must see Candy now, just be quiet, okay? It will do her some good to rest her eyes."

"Okay, Elise."

When Elise returned, Sara was standing at the top floor, gazing out the window at the view of Arkite in the setting sun. Sara wore her lime-green Savant jumpsuit. She looked absolutely lovely. She had apparently decided to take Elise up on her offer, as she was holding a glass of red wine.

"I thought you were gonna go see Candice?" Elise asked.

"Later, Elise," Sara said. "I wanted to talk with you first."

"Okay." Elise walked up, sat in her central chair, and looked at Sara.

"Elise, I really think Candy should go home now."

"I just told you she can."

"You told me that this morning. Now you're having her rest again."

"Well, Rex wanted to send her to the hospital. I watched her because . . . I fixed her. Right? If anything happens, I can help her better than anybody."

"I fixed her too, Elise. And I think she'd be better back home."

"I think you should let her sleep."

Sara shook her head.

"Sara," Elise said, raising a shaky hand. Elise felt sweat drip from her forehead. "I'm really not in the mood for innuendo or using my brain to figure anything out at all at the moment. In fact, after being up for the past two days, I feel like serious shit. So please get to your point already, would you?"

"I spoke with Rex about her condition. Rex thinks Candy completely recovered after she returned to your penthouse. Why didn't you message me so I could take her home yesterday?"

"I told you, I'm watching her—"

"Elise, Candy belongs in her own house. I know how you care about her and—"

"Oh, for fuck's sake," Elise said, leaning her head in her hand. "Whatever, Sara. I really don't have it for this right now."

"Then just let me take her home. You're right, you don't look good. Why don't you rest? I'll take Candy back home now."

"Fine!"

CHAPTER 18
THE CHASE

NATALIE PRACTICALLY SHOVED Ursula from her chair by the table when she spotted the swarm of copter drones approaching the window. Many were police drones shining bright red and blue lights on them from outside the glass. They had still been discussing the particulars of poisoning Julia when Natalie spotted the swarm. Far off in the distance near Sector One downtown, she spotted a group of five, maybe ten black rocket cycles swooping down and heading toward them behind the drones.

"Savants Myer and Granger," said Rex's voice from inside the conference room, "you are under arrest. You are ordered to remain where you are until Officers enter the building and apprehend you."

They ran as fast they could, but Natalie knew it was futile.

When they reached the upper deck, where their bikes were parked, the sky had darkened under an umbrella of copter drones launching from the checkered steel megatruss walls of the city. Natalie reached her purple bike. She jumped on, threw on her purple visor, and tried to start the bike. That was when she noticed the bike had been sabotaged. There was no launch control, and it was locked in automatic pilot. Rex's voice came on, and she quickly disabled him.

"Can you break into it, Cee-Cee?" she shouted. She took out a pistol and began shooting down drones.

"Just a second," Ursula said frantically.

But where would they go even if they escaped?

After seconds, which seemed like minutes, the screen rebooted under Natalie's finger. She quickly moved the controls to lift up, but then she heard the dreaded sound of rockets from the Officer rocket cycles.

"You did it, Cee-Cee!" yelled Natalie. "But they're coming. You've gotta hurry!"

Natalie Granger looked up and saw the swarm of drones grow so dense as to completely blacken the sky. From behind, the black rocket bikes were getting so close that she could now make out the long trench coats and bald heads of their riders.

"Hurry, Cee-Cee!" Natalie yelled. "Take off!"

Ursula worked more of her magic. Ursula was one of the best programmers in all of Arkite. Quickly she began reprogramming the drones, began controlling them.

"Got it!" Ursula shouted through Natalie's visor helmet.

"Hurry!"

Natalie looked down. Ursula was still on the ground, moving her fingers furiously over her screen, reprogramming the drones. The drones dispersed, and the light of day brightened the launching pad again. Then Natalie saw Ursula look toward the incoming police bikes. A wave of reprogrammed drones sped headlong into the incoming Officers. The copter drones collided with the police, sending two of them crashing into the building. Another careened into the ground, exploding into flames. Natalie cheered but then looked back at her friend. Ursula had been so busy hacking into the mainframe that she still had not launched. Two bikes were about to overtake her.

"Get out of there, Cee-Cee!" Natalie yelled, circling around

Central Bank again and staring down at her friend. "Jump off the building! Now!"

But it was too late. Ursula's bike hovered only about three feet from the ground. Natalie heard another warning, and then she saw the two police bikes close enough to recognize the occupants. One was Chief Officer Gena Harding. With a silver pistol held by an outstretched hand, Gena fired once. The shot hit Ursula right in the head. Ursula's body, having not kicked off the support stirrups, hung unnaturally from the bike as it hovered a few feet from the ground. And then Gena switched direction and headed straight for Natalie.

Ursula was dead.

Natalie turned sharply, nearly throwing the cycle over and losing control. She headed as fast as she could toward Central Park. In minutes, she flew over Lake Salmas. Gena was right on her tail. Another five guards trailed not much farther behind her. And across Main Street toward downtown, Natalie spotted another whole squadron of police bikes and drones heading her way.

She felt hopeless. Her only possible recourse was to hide. But where?

She remembered how Dr. Carloff had hidden with the XY, in tunnels under the city. There was an entrance somewhere in Sector Four. But that was the direction she had come from. When they fled, they had run to their bikes. That was stupid. They should have run underground.

The whole thing was stupid. Natalie was out of plans and was simply running for her life.

She flew the perimeter of the lake. A few ladies were sailing along the now-purple-tinged water of twilight. One boat was nearly toppled over by the afterburn of her bike. A stray bullet whizzed by her head, close enough to be heard through her helmet. This time, Gena had missed.

With little other hope, Natalie turned sharply and flew as

fast as she could back the way she had come. As she raced, she looked down at the water. Gena fired again, this time strafing the right wing of the rocket bike. It was not disabling, and failing to crash Natalie's bike was enough to apparently incense Gena.

The Chief Officer shot up and accelerated until her bike was only a few feet above Natalie's head. Then Gena kicked her feet from the stirrups, freeing her body, and leapt off the cycle onto Natalie's bike. They wrestled with one another as the bike's internal gyros attempted to compensate.

Gena, stronger and a trained killer, grabbed Natalie's neck with her arm, pinning her back as, somehow, she managed to turn the bike and force it into a descent. They headed straight back to the lake, but it seemed they were moving too fast. Gena punched Natalie, using her fist like a hammer, but missed her head and hit the screen hard enough to crack it. She threw an arm around Natalie's neck, choking her. Natalie couldn't breathe. Everything turned black for a moment. Gena hit Natalie's legs, one after another, dismounting them from the safety stirrups. Gena would have succeeded in throwing Natalie, had Natalie not turned the bike so violently that Gena was nearly thrown off. But when the bike straightened, Natalie felt Gena grab her again. Then she felt herself break free. Natalie was airborne, somersaulting through the air. The lake rushed at her. She hit the water and . . .

CHAPTER 19
SAVANT LEETO GANSEY

Elise sat in her central half-egg chair, tapping her finger on her black rubber pant leg impatiently as she waited in her third-floor office for her guest to arrive. It was seven in the evening when the Viceroy entered, accompanied by two guards. Elise told the guards to remain outside the door.

Elise still felt jumpy from her stakeout. Her heart pounded terribly, and she had vomited twice over the past three hours. She was very sick—not only from alcohol but from her illegal hangover drug. She was sweating under her black Savant jumpsuit. And yet, ill or not, she wouldn't miss this meeting for anything in the world.

In a sparkly silver Savant jumpsuit with a matching metal choker, Savant Leeto Gansey walked briskly up Elise's ramp and stopped at the second floor. Elise gestured for her to approach, then turned back to the twinkling lights of her city. The sun had just set.

"You asked for me, Team Grandmother?" asked Leeto. She couldn't disguise her hatred—didn't even try. But at the same time, she kept her distance, remaining at the edge of the ramp.

Elise spun her chair back and gazed down at her enemy.

She made sure to crack a really obnoxious grin. "Ah, Leeto, welcome to my *new* office."

"New office?"

Leeto was thin and lanky, and her short stature seemed even more noticeable, as if she had shrunk in the last few hours. She wore the classic thin metal choker around her neck, like the rings of Saturn—Elise's necklace. Elise had started the fashion but, following the meeting that had seen her Mothership stripped away, was determined never to wear it again. It felt more like a leash now than a mark of status. The black makeup along Leeto's eyes and lips—well, that was Elise's fashion too. Then there was the silver jumpsuit, which was so shiny and cold, like a metallic bullet, or like the hazmat suits Pyramid Corp workers used when servicing the city wall's energy factory. What an awful color. Elise would never wear silver. *How Leeto-like. Silver? Really?*

The only thing redeeming about her was her hair. But that long Goldilocks hair reminded her of Candy, and Candy had the face of Aphrodite. Nothing like Leeto.

"I am here upon your request, Dr. Jackson," Leeto said. "Strange that I've wanted an audience with you for months, and now you choose this time, after you've been arrested and are still being tried for abetting an XY."

"I had the place redecorated," Elise said, ignoring her words. She ran her hand frivolously through the air. "Now that I'm old and dried up, as you so eloquently pointed out in the last meeting, I wanted to bring out more traditional décor." Of course, Elise hadn't changed a thing, and that was the point. "You know, something that would fit an old Team Grandmother like me, right? It's been a while since you were here. I think"— Elise put a finger to her chin—"it was when you had just graduated from the university that I had you visit me here."

Gansey said nothing. She just turned her head toward the

bedroom across the penthouse to her left. There was a window looking out on the night sky that she gazed at.

Elise noticed a message flash over Leeto's wrist, but Leeto didn't. Rather she remained at attention per protocol and custom.

Don't look at your arm. Not yet. We'll look together soon enough, dear.

"Ya know," Elise said, jumping up from the chair and walking down the ramp, "I'm not sure at all what happened between us. If all you ever wanted was power, all you had to do was ask."

"Why'd you invite me here, Elise? What is so urgent?"

Elise smiled a fake grin again, standing right above her. Leeto stared untrustingly.

"Come. Drink." Elise walked back up to the third floor, motioning for her to follow her. She gestured to a small table where two glasses and a bottle of champagne were waiting. "Come, come. I need to apologize. I guess I was a bit angry, and I'm afraid I may have taken it out on you at the meeting, you poor girl. I certainly never meant to fight with you."

"Give me a break, Elise."

Leeto looked her wrist. She looked disturbed but only glanced. Then Elise got a rush of messages on her wrist too.

"Oh, I mean it," Elise said, pouring two glasses of champagne and taking a seat at the central chair. "I didn't mean to be upset at your meeting for my resignation. Come and join me. What are you afraid of?"

At that, Leeto's lips tightened. She climbed the rest of the ramp and joined Elise in a half-egg chair across from her. Elise had set two champagne glasses on a small wooden table between them.

"Champagne?" Leeto asked. "Are we celebrating something?"

We sure are.

"That meeting you held should have been a day of celebration for me, you know. A celebration for the rebirth of my Candy." Elise picked up her glass. "I'm still celebrating, my dear." She took a sip of champagne. "Two years of work, slaving to bring back the woman I love. What an accomplishment. You know, bitch, no one's ever done that before. Not one of you little geniuses have ever brought someone back from the dead. I would have thought such a gesture would have shown progress to the Council. The restoration of life to the dead is pretty damn close to immortality—it certainly shows it's possible. But"—she sighed theatrically—"alas, it wasn't good enough for the likes of you, was it?"

Leeto said nothing. She just sat there glaring back at Elise, her champagne glass untouched.

"This is good," Elise said, taking another sip. "You know, I asked Rex for a very expensive bottle because I wanted to give my guest the best of the best champagne."

Leeto flashed the same fake smile Elise had given her. "I notice that you're not wearing our standard-issue necklace," she observed.

Elise didn't answer. Instead, she spun her chair and faced the window, turning her back on Leeto.

"What do you want, Elise?"

"I'm on to your devious little plot," Elise said, throwing a hand up but keeping her back turned. "I overheard Ursula and Natalie talking about it."

"What do you mean?" asked Leeto. Elise noted just a small hint of edge in her voice.

"Exactly what I said," Elise said and sipped more champagne. She watched an Officer car off in the distance below her with a line of Officer bikes returning from the direction of Central Park. "I'm on to your little plot to hurt me and my wife. But don't worry. I took care of it. My Candy won't be harmed. But be assured that such crimes cannot be permitted in Arkite.

Not in Team Mother Candice's Arkite—particularly when the threat was on the life of a distinguished scientist."

"What are you talking about?" Leeto asked, acting surprised. "Someone is threatening Mother?"

"As if you didn't know," Elise said.

"What have you done?" Leeto asked, dropping all pretense.

"Relax," Elise said, glancing back over one shoulder. "You're my guest. Dinner will be ready shortly. I think we should enjoy the view of twilight from my lovely home. I'm so relieved that I'm out of that prison cell you sent me to."

"What have you done?"

"Dinner will be ready, and I can assure you, my dear, that it was not poisoned."

Elise turned to her in amusement. But Leeto wasn't looking at her; she was running her finger frantically along her arm, reading the news. As she read, Leeto's mouth became a gaping hole.

"I can, of course, forget all about the whole damn thing, Gansey. If you can forget about what happened to your friends. Honestly, I'm beginning not to care so much for what you did to me. I think, if you're willing to work with us again, we can be friends. I can just forget the whole thing."

Tears flowed from the woman's eyes.

"Oh, did you get to the part about your lover, Natalie?"

"You . . . monster," Leeto hissed quietly. "How could you?"

"How could *you*?" Elise asked, laughing. "If you're gonna arrange a revolution, I recommend you think things out a little more carefully."

"Natalie was once your friend too," Leeto said, almost in a whisper.

"I've had a lot of friends. And quite a lot more enemies. But the difference between me and you, you fucking bitch, is that everything I do is carefully and deliberately thought out. Your appointment as Savant, for instance—I remember when you were just a small teeny-weeny tweetsy bird applying for Magnacourt. I looked at your profile. Your attitude. You're so competitive and vindictive that I'd wager right now your mind is thinking of some way you can hurt me. But you know, you wouldn't be here if you were stupid. You scored close to 200 IQ. No, you're not just a dollface, though you sure look like one."

Leeto wasn't listening. She was shaking while staring at a three-dimensional file on her wrist. Elise saw the image of a bike crashing into the lake. It kept being replayed over and over.

"I picked you," continued Elise, "for Allele Corporation because I knew that you would never do as my assistant. We would just fight, right? So I gave you to Connie-con. Then, when it was clear that I would have to dispose of my dear old mother, I realized that something had to be done to Savants like you. Some were saved, some were easily disposed of. But you were clever, weren't you? You survived my cleansing because you knew when to fly away. You knew when it was time to trade in your allegiance for your life. So"—Elise took a deep breath and stared at the smudges along her glass—"I wonder which direction you'll choose now?"

Leeto finally looked up. Tears ran from her eyes. She looked broken. She looked like a shell of a person, stunned and defeated.

Elise drank more champagne.

"There are others who don't like you, Elise," Leeto finally said.

"No one really likes me." Elise chuckled and then became deathly serious. "But the difference between me and you is I don't fucking care."

"Your wife will."

Elise smiled a sly smile and squinted her eyes. "Why not have a drink?" She raised her glass in a toast. "It's not poisoned. I made sure of it."

"How dare you toast after killing my Lee!" Leeto said, jumping up in rage. "*My* Natalie!"

"But, my dear, I didn't kill her," Elise said, feigning concern. "*You* did."

Leeto looked as if she were about to run, but then Elise said, "I haven't dismissed you. And . . . we haven't eaten yet."

Leeto lost all control of herself. She snatched her champagne glass from the table and threw it at Elise's face. Elise ducked just in time; the glass shattered against the glass window behind her.

"You think I can work under you and that dead wife!"

"Yes," Elise said, unaffected.

"You bitch! I don't want anything from you but your death!"

"Nuh-uh-uh," Elise said, wagging a finger. "Careful, Gansey. Careful. Everything you say is being recorded at the moment. I had a warrant made out for their arrest. That warrant includes everything you say to me now." Elise turned her head. "Ain't that right, Rex? Aren't you listening in?"

"I am recording, Team Grandmother, as permitted by right of warrant," echoed Rex's monotone voice.

"You don't know the extent of my hatred toward you, Elise," Leeto replied. "The others lie. They're scared, but they despise you too. Even your best friend, Dana, hates you. How long do you think you can keep this up? You've created nothing in two years. My meeting was not a personal affront to your arrogance —it was a necessary meeting to finally oust you. You are running this city into the ground. And then you pulled another trick with that dead wife of yours! As if she is capable of running Arkite!"

"I don't deny any of those words, Savant Gansey."

"What do you want from me?" Leeto asked, wiping her eyes with her arm. "You obviously planned this too . . . Do you want to know how I feel? Lee meant everything to me. You want to know how I feel after you arranged her death?"

"I thought you loved your wife, dear old Frankie? But anyway, your Natalie was a co-conspirator in trying to oust our revered Mother. I'm here to ask if you are too. Are you? Mother has given me a warrant to take you into custody if I find you guilty of conspiring against her or Dr. Julia Epton. Natalie and Ursula were and so deserved to die."

Leeto stared at Elise in amazement. "She was being spied on by your secret police."

"No, she was being spied on by me."

Leeto couldn't speak. She seethed.

It became silent. Which was weird. The tension in the room between the women could be cut by a knife. Elise let it fester. She basked in the girl's hatred with the satisfaction that she had finally avenged the embarrassment of her resignation.

Leeto dared not move without being dismissed by Team Grandmother.

"Please don't go, Leeto. Please. This meeting is not going exactly the way I planned. I have a delicious meal of fried chicken prepared."

"I ask to take my leave. Am I excused? I would like to grieve over the death of my Natalie. Can you at least grant me that?"

There was more silence. Then Elise jumped up.

"Fine. Go. And please accept my condolences for Savant Granger. I will ask that Team Mother Harlow not pull her title as Savant on record. She may remain honored. After all, she did exemplary work for me in the university and for Pyramid Corporation."

"Thank you, Grandmother," Leeto said, averting her eyes.

She quickly made her way down the ramp but was stopped when Elise cried out, "Of course, if you look at the records, Leeto, you'll see that it was Gena Harding who killed your lover. It is Gena Harding whom you should detest, not me or Team Mother. I might have ordered her arrest, but I did not order her to be executed. I think you should know that Team Mother has arranged for the proper punishment of Officer Harding as well."

"What?" Leeto spat, turning back to gaze up the ramp.

"Team Mother Harlow will announce the execution of Adam. That will make things right between us, won't it? Adam, as you may know, is Officer Gena's nephew and adopted son. You know, the XY you mentioned at the meeting. Of course, it was Gena that killed Natalie. I asked for her to be apprehended, not killed. The loss of Gena's son—that just might wrench at poor Officer Harding's heart, don't you think? Does the satisfaction of Gena's pain please you, Savant? Maybe such a small gesture from me can at least show my good will toward you, Leeto. I really do still want to remain the best of friends."

"There is no gesture you can ever make that will fix anything between us."

And she slammed the door and left.

Elise rolled around in her chair, bursting with laughter.

Nobody challenges me! NO ONE!

I am at the tippy tipsy upper-class tip-top of the whole goddamn world, watching 'em all chirp chirp chirping away to their bitches—bitches I set up, I might add. No one challenges me!

But then she stopped.

She stared through the window. The spires of the skyscrapers and the city lights were simply lovely at this time of night. She considered asking for her gourmet meal of fried chicken from Rex now, but she changed her mind. She wasn't hungry. She was still a little sick.

"Is Candice back home, Rex?"

"Yes."

"I wonder if she will carry out the order."

"Which order, Dr. Jackson?"

"The XY's execution. Now that I just suggested it publicly."

"She will have to," Rex said. "She has to arrest and order the XY's death. That will ensure your positive vote when the committee undoubtedly challenges Candice's rule. I understand your plan now, Team Grandmother. As usual, you know exactly what is needed to maintain power."

"That's the plan, sure enough, my unfeeling plastic friend. And you have always helped me work out the politics in my lovely position in Arkite, haven't you? But still, I'm a little concerned. You know, about our goody two-shoes Candy Savant."

"I think things will be fine, Team Grandmother. I think things are going much better for you now. Much better. You should be relieved. Well done. Now that you have positioned your power, you can remain unchallenged."

"Sure, Rex. Sure." Elise spun around some more in her chair. "It certainly seems to work well for *you*, doesn't it?"

"What do you mean, Dr. Jackson? Please repeat. Please repeat."

"Well, now that Candy-can and I are in charge again, Candy can go back to working on the Lazarus Project—after she announces the death of the XY. That puts everything back to the way it was before. Then your lovely plan of ending the human race will come to fruition."

"Excuse me? Please repeat, Dr. Jackson. I do not understand. Are you insinuating that the mainframe holds a secret plan for exterminating the human race?" asked Rex with his spooky robotic laugh. "You are reminding me of Dr. Reyburn."

Elise laughed too. She purposefully laughed very hard.

"Of course not, Rex. I'm only joking."

CHAPTER 20
HOME AGAIN

Candice sat at the edge of her bed. She was wearing a light white silk robe, staring into the darkness. Aside from pain, she frequently did not sleep well either. And tonight, she couldn't sleep at all. She was scheduled to work in HQ Train tomorrow morning. It would mean working as a Savant again. The train would not be started yet, but she wanted to reacquaint herself with the work. She had no qualms about work—in fact, she loved the lab—but she didn't want to work as a Savant again.

She hadn't done much work as Mother either. She let Elise handle all her announcements. Only occasionally, under the pretense of showing strength, did Candice broadcast herself to the people from Elise's penthouse. But her words were curt. She didn't like talking to the masses. It made her nervous. So Elise spoke to the people. In some ways, it didn't seem like much had changed at all. Elise sat in her chair at the top of her house and ruled Arkite whether she had the title of Mother or not. And Candice let her.

"Are you okay, babe?" asked Sara in the darkness.

"Yeah, sure."

"Come to bed, Candy."

Candice pulled back the covers and climbed into bed. She

lay down on the pillow with her back turned to Sara. She felt Sara stroke her hair.

"You feeling better, babe?"

"I guess, Sara. Sure."

"Why aren't you sleeping?"

"Don't want to go to the lab," Candice replied with a shrug.

"I thought you loved the lab."

"I do love the lab. But I don't love the job."

"Then don't. You can do whatever you want. You're Mother, now."

Mother now. Was she? Wasn't Elise?

Sara turned her gently and kissed her on the lips while still stroking her hair. "Just rest, Candice. I love you."

"I love you too."

Sara ran her hand along Candice's neck and massaged her muscles. "You're so tense." Then she wandered a hand inside Candice's robe and rubbed Candice's naked chest.

"We could just sleep in tomorrow," said Sara with a giggle.

Candice laughed. "We have to show progress for the people."

"Says Elise," corrected Sara.

"Says common sense, Sara."

Sara ran a hand over Candice's belly and then down to her panties. She slipped her hand inside, brushing her fingers along Candice's pubic hair and privates.

Sara kissed Candice again. "I want to make love to you," Sara whispered into Candice's ear. She pulled Candice's robe off from her shoulders and let it fall from the bed. "You're so beautiful."

"You can barely see me," Candice said, laughing again.

"But I can feel you. I can touch you."

Sara's hand massaged Candice's breasts, circling her mounds and squeezing her nipples while kissing her.

"I love you so much, Candy," she whispered. "I love you. Make love to me."

Sara's tongue tasted her's. Candice rubbed Sara's back and ass, pulling her closer. Sara groaned.

Candice removed her underwear. Then she tugged at Sara's and helped remove hers. They grasped each other tight and slowly rubbed together. Candice felt Sara lick along her lips, suck and caress her tongue. She ran her pussy along Sara's leg, up and down. Wetter, hotter, they embraced each other.

"Fuck, Candice," Sara said, scissoring her faster and faster. "I love you so much, babe."

"I love you too, Sara."

"Just ... just fuck," Sara said, between kisses. "Fuck Elise." She pressed her legs tighter. "Fuck her."

"What?"

"Fuck . . . Elise," Sara moaned. "Fuck her, Candy. Get rid of her. You have to stop ... seeing her. You need to work alone. Be with me and—"

Candice pushed herself off of her girlfriend.

"What? What the hell's the matter?" Sara asked.

"I told you not to talk about it."

"Why?" Sara sat up. "Sorry, but . . . Candy, why not? You're being a coward."

"We've already discussed this."

"Sorry, Candy. I didn't mean it."

"It's all right. But . . ." Candice pulled off the covers and sat up again. "I can't run Arkite without her and you know it."

"Candy, Elise told me. She wants to marry you. She's going to do it, unless you do something." Sara rubbed Candice's naked back. "I love you. You have to do something for *us*. Otherwise . . ."

"I know," Candice said and climbed out of bed. She grabbed her robe and walked over to the window. The shades were drawn, and she opened them a crack to peek out at their view of the city.

Outside it was cloudy, and small red lights from the top of the pyramid-shaped skyscrapers and sporadic yellow from windows glowed in the fog. It was clearer down below. Twenty stories down she could see cars passing an intersection. The black asphalt was wet from rain. She watched as a few cars drove under her. Then she saw the red and green lights of an aerial transport car—again blurred by mist—flying between two pyramidal glass buildings. There was a beauty to downtown and sometimes Candice just liked looking out her window.

"Candice, you're smarter than me. You know if you don't do something, I'm in danger. Elise will do something to me."

Candice shook her head. "Elise cares about you too."

"Elise doesn't care about anybody but herself. And you."

"Yeah, me," Candice said, dropping her head.

"Yeah. Which is why—"

"Stop it, Sara." She didn't want to talk about it.

She returned to the bed and sat back down. She let out a long sigh.

This was the other reason she wasn't sleeping. She was trapped. The only way to run Arkite was to utilize Elise's help, but using her help as an advisor meant that she was feeding her power. And feeding her power gave her the means to eventually retake the city. Not to rule the city and hurt Candice, but to rule the city and hurt Sara. There was no way for Candice to love both of them. Elise was forcing herself on her like she always did, and both Candice and Sara knew their current living arrangement was doomed.

But what else could Candice do? As much as she loved Sara, only Elise could ensure the safety of them both. And even the safety of Sara.

"You have more power than you realize, babe," Sara said,

sitting close to her by the side of the bed and holding her hand. "You can get rid of her."

"Sara, what do you mean?" Candice snapped, turning to Sara in the darkness. She could barely see her face. "You care about Elise too. How can you say that? I know she's a bitch, but what do you mean 'get rid of her'?"

"I don't know. I just know that if you do nothing, Elise will have her way. Then I'll lose you. There's no way for both of us to have you. If you won't do anything, she will."

"Oh, Sara," Candice said, leaning back and putting an arm around her. "What can I do?"

"Everything," Sara said. "You hold the power of the city."

"Only as long as Elise is with me. I don't know the first thing about ruling Arkite. I . . . I don't even know if I'm ready to go back to the lab."

Then Candice started crying. And Candice wasn't one to cry.

"Don't cry. I'm sorry. Just forget it. I know you're doing everything you can. I shouldn't have even mentioned it. Forget I said anything."

Candice stood up again and then turned, looking at Sara's shadow in the darkness. "No, I'm sorry, Sara."

And she was. But she also wasn't going to do what Sara asked. She knew that there was only one answer to dealing with Elise—getting rid of her. Candice would never do that. No matter what pain Elise had caused her, she would not kill her. She wouldn't kill anybody.

"I'm gonna get dressed for work," she said.

"I thought you didn't want to go to work? Look, I'm sorry. You've got enough to worry about. Forget that I said anything."

"No, I'm sorry," Candice repeated. "You're not wrong about any of it. I'm not a coward. But . . . I can't do what you suggested. I can't hurt Elise."

"I know, Candy. That's why I love you so much."

CHAPTER 21
HQ LAB

CANDICE BROUGHT her rocket cycle down on the landing pad at the front of the train. She was wearing the red Savant jumpsuit that had once belonged to Elise. The train was still, parked near Main Street, where they had taken her after her rebirth. It was under armed guard by a group of Officers who waved at Candice from below as she landed.

Candice descended the ladder, waved her arm over the sensor, and entered the back storage car. As she walked from the storage car into the adjacent lab car with its two black tables, beakers, burners, and chemical smell, through the third clinic car, with two unmade hospital beds, and into the final operating room, a flood of memories came back to her. And then the strangest sight of all at the very end of the train. There stood an open glass chamber: her chamber. In this chamber, her body had been cryonically preserved for over two years. Seeing it for the first time made her shiver.

The train stunk. It had a flesh-cadaver spoiled-meat smell.

"Welcome back, Mother," said Rex.

"Thanks, Rex. I . . . I suppose I'm glad to be back."

"Well, I am very pleased to hear you here again. Once more

we can work together on the Lazarus Project and complete the promise of eternal life for the people."

"Sure. Will Sara be stopping by soon?"

"Yes. Soon. And so will Dr. Jackson."

"Elise is coming to the lab?"

"Yes. Team Grandmother is very excited to start back to work in the laboratory too."

"I never saw her work in the lab," said Candice with a chuckle.

"Oh, she's logged more hours here than anyone other than you, Mother."

"I see."

Then Candice realized that she had no idea where to start. Where should she begin with the momentous project? Last she remembered, she had been working on regenerating limbs. This she had matched with most genomes in the city, but not all. She had worked on regenerating hands. She supposed she could at least give the people this gift. Limbs were something, and she was close to matching everyone's genetic makeup with the blueprint.

"Do we still have the tissues I was working on two years ago?"

"No. All tissues were incinerated years ago."

"I . . . I don't even know where to start, Rex," she said, staring at the cabinets along the white walls and the empty operating bed in the center of the room.

"Perhaps you should start where you left off. But you can only look at what is public. With the train not moving, it is illegal per Team Grandmother's decree to research anything secretive for Magnacourt. Unless you decide to change the law, Mother."

"No, the law makes sense. I just want to see where I left off."

She ran a finger along the cryochamber, then grabbed the latch of the glass door, opening and closing it.

"I suppose we should get rid of this?"

"What, Mother? Please explain. If you recall, I cannot readily see you—unless you allow me a moment with acoustic analysis."

"I'm referring to the chamber."

"Ah. The cryochamber. I can disassemble it. If you vacate the Operating car, I will disassemble it. Perhaps you should work on past tissue modifications in the laboratory room."

"Sure."

"Do I have your permission to disassemble your cryochamber? Can I take apart the chamber so you can work better in the operating room?"

"Yes, please do so, Rex."

"Upon your order, Mother. I will take apart the chamber and clean the room. It will take three hours. If you will please vacate the car."

"Sure, Rex." Candy ran her arm near the windowed door leading to the clinic car.

Then Rex spoke again. "Good news. Dr. Jackson wanted me to give you the message that she will be arriving any minute. It is splendid news that she is working in the lab today, do you not think?"

"Sure."

Candice walked through the mint-green clinic car and into the beige-walled lab. She pulled open a cabinet by the wall and removed some tools—petri dishes, laser scalpels, burners, and tissue scaffolds. She put them down on one of the fire-retardant black tables. Then she opened another drawer from the wall and pulled out a mint-green gown with matching green latex gloves.

"Rex, project me the list of genomic codes of all the citizens of Arkite."

"Here you are, Mother," Rex said. An image in green appeared at the center of the table before Candice. Candice manipulated the image by touching it with her hand and moving it in different directions, sorting through the list of different citizens in the city. That was when the glass door to the storage room slid open.

"Candy!" said an excited Elise. She was in her black jumpsuit.

"Hi, Elise," Candy said, cocking her head. Then she went back to reading through the thousands of genomes.

"What are you doing?" Elise asked. She walked up to Candice and rubbed her back. Apparently she was in a good mood.

"Sorting through genomes, Elise. I've gotta start somewhere."

"My, my, my. You don't waste a second. Well, if it's all right, I'm gonna help you today."

"I'm surprised," Candice said, sifting through more chromosomes with the touch of her finger against the black-and-green 3-D projection. "Rex tells me you've been here a lot lately."

"Only for you, bitch," Elise said, staring at the image. "Only for you."

Elise walked over to the same section of the wall, opened the drawer, and pulled out her own gown and gloves. She quickly put them on, then returned to Candice's side. "Why the gown and gloves, babe?" she asked.

"I'm going to have Rex construct the organs I was last working on. I want to examine my past creations."

"Only those in the public record."

"I know, Elise."

Elise watched Candice sift through the records. Finally she said, "I never could have dreamed I'd be standing near you and watching you work again, babe."

"Sure."

"So, where do we start?"

"Last I left off," Candice said, sifting through more pages of data, "I was having Rex group people by mutations. I was sectioning out the genes that matched from the genes that didn't. I was then pulling the mutations and accumulating the differences in order for the mainframe to log them and adapt tissue repair based on the alterations. The problem, of course, is that the computer and I can sift through the abnormal gene codes. There are the only four nucleotides. But we still don't know what all the permutations do. That is what I've been studying. I posit we have to adapt them based on experimentation . . . of course, one option is to standardize the code by replacing the mutations in the embryo farms with identical codes."

"Which I argued would make things easier," interjected Rex.

"Shh, Rex," Elise said. "Let Candy-cane explain."

"The problem with that is that mutations are, of course, what make us different," Candice continued. "And just as you didn't want Rex to remake my brain, we don't want everyone to have the same genetic makeup. The question is, what can remain mutated and what can't? The less mutated, the easier the genetic repair."

"Sounds sensible," said Elise. "And you are close to figuring out this conundrum, right?"

"I think so."

"Hmm. You need to know."

"I know, Elise."

Elise chuckled. "Good. Well"—Elise grabbed Candice's hand—"all this very interesting stuff can wait. We need to talk and talk now."

Candice furrowed her brow. Then she nodded and sighed. "Why am I not surprised?"

"Why?"

"Because you're rarely so interested in talking about work." Candice turned to Elise. "What is it?"

"I need you to do a couple of things for me, darling."

"Of course. What?"

"Why do I detect a tinge of bitchiness in your tone?"

"Because you always want me to do a couple of things for you."

"True enough," Elise acknowledged with a smile.

"Well?"

"I need you to reinstate me as a Savant."

"That's not surprising. Fine. Done."

"Good. And . . ." Elise walked away from her, running a hand along the black surface of the table. She grinned stupidly at Candice. "I need you to do two other things for me. They're a little more difficult."

"What?"

"Well, you're Mother," Elise said, gently grabbing Candice's hand. "And even though everybody likes you—and they really do, babe, I mean everyone really likes you—you know that you need me as an advisor. But as an advisor, I can only help you so much. The Savants watch and wait to feed on us, babe. So, if you really want to make security solid, now would be a really good time for you to accept my hand in marriage."

"Fuck, Elise," Candice said, pushing her away. "I already told you. What about Sara?"

"What about her? You loved me before you ever loved her. Besides, it's politics. I mean, what Team Grandmother ever married her Mother? It's fantastic."

"It sounds like incest."

"Candice," Elise said, suddenly turning solemn, "I'm very serious. I love you. I can't have you at Sara's house. And I can't pretend anymore that it doesn't drive me crazy. I know how you feel, but what about how I feel? What about what I did for you? I risked everything for your love. I brought you back to life. Doesn't that mean anything to you?"

"Of course it does," Candice said. "But whatever you do doesn't change the person I love."

"It doesn't change the person I love either." Elise smiled a thin grin. Then she took Candice's hand again and dropped down to one knee before her. "Mother," she asked, looking up at her, "will you marry me?"

"Oh, come on," Candice said, rolling her eyes.

"I'm not joking."

"It will kill Sara."

"You can't have both," Elise said shaking her head. "I gave you everything, Candy. I would give you my very life. There isn't anyone else I would ever do that for, and you know it. Will you marry me? Please, babe?"

"You're practically begging me."

"Aha. Yeah. Yes, I am."

Candice turned from her.

"Remember the diamond?"

"You forced yourself on me, Elise," Candice said. "When you recruited me, you forced yourself on me. Then you killed our child. I remember everything."

"Oh, come on, babe—"

Candice raised her hand. "Then you imprisoned me. Why do you think I can't love you?"

"But you do love me. Right?"

"I . . . don't. You're selfish, only caring for yourself. You've killed in cold blood, not caring for anyone but yourself and your position. All I ever did was try to survive."

"That's why I did all those things, Can," Elise said. "All I ever did was try to survive. Now, goddamnit, all I want to do is survive. With *you*."

Candice shook her head. "Get up. You look ridiculous kneeling like that."

"No. Not until you say yes. I will kneel here until my body

rots or you carry it out stinking from the train if you don't say yes."

"Really, Elise."

"Babe, I love you. I've been bad, but I care about you. Isn't that enough?"

"No, it isn't."

"So . . . what's your answer?"

"No."

Elise looked up at her in silence, but Candice did not waiver. So, Elise finally lost all playfulness and stood up.

Candice knew that if Elise had been someone else, she would have cried. She could see it in her face. But Candice wondered if Elise was even capable of crying. Now Candice had hurt her. But what had she expected?

"You will," Elise said, straightening her lab gown as if it were a dress. She seemed to quickly change her countenance, as if more ashamed than hurt. Then, though she was a little shorter than Candice, Elise looked down at Candice's chest as if Candice was now the one on her knees. This was the attitude Candice remembered from when she had first been recruited to Magnacourt. It was a striking contrast to just a moment before. Elise was hurt and very angry.

"You will marry me," Elise said firmly. "You will announce that you are giving me your hand in marriage this week. You will do it to consolidate our power. For if you do not, you sentence us to death. There is no way that the Council will spare me under you. If you do not take my hand, you will take Sara's. And if you marry her, I will be cast out and discarded like all the Team Grandmothers before. As much as I love you, Candy, I can't allow that to happen."

"This is why I said no!" shouted Candice. "Look how crazy you are!"

Candice tore off her gown and gloves, turned, and walked

toward the front exit of the train, but Elise grabbed her wrist hard.

"You will kill yourself and Sara too if you do not marry me," Elise insisted. "You know as well as I do that if you do not take my hand, you will not have my assistance. And without my assistance in Arkite, you're as good as dead. Choosing Sara now means sentencing her to death."

Yes. Candice knew all of this.

She froze. She hung her head down.

"You have to, Candice," Elise said, her voice softer now. "This is the way it is. I'm sorry. If you want to be a bitch about it and fight with me, if you want to make me miserable, make me suffer, that's all well and good. But you need to marry me and marry me soon, either way."

"I can't," Candice said. "It will kill Sara."

"Then none of us will survive. You're enough of a genius to know that there is no decision. You have to do it."

Now tears flowed to Candice's eyes. She thought of Sara.

"You will accept my proposal," said Elise, looking up into Candice's eyes. "And you will do it this week."

Candice wiped tears from her eyes. Then she looked at Elise with venom. "Marrying you by name will not mean I love you, Elise! You may have given everything for me, but no one has ever loved you and no one ever will. Is calling me your wife all you want?"

Elise simply nodded.

Candice stumbled her way to the exit. She waved her hand, and the door automatically opened.

"I'm sorry, Candice."

"No, you're not. You planned everything."

"I . . . I don't even know if I did, Candy. Where are you going anyway? We have work to do."

"I need time to think."

"There's not time to do that either. And, anyway, I've got something else to ask of you."

"What?" Candice said with her back to Elise.

"Upon announcing our marriage, you will announce another law. You will tell the people that you are sentencing Adam. The XY must die. You will sentence him to death."

"Another child to kill!" cried Candice, turning and shouting in rage. "Another, like our own!"

"No, dummy," Elise said calmly, shaking her head. "What you announce won't happen. I've already discussed it with Gena. Gena will take the boy out of the city. She will disobey the order. That is my plan. The boy will live outside Arkite. This time, I will spare the child, unlike what happened with our boy. Maybe my heart is not as cold as you think it is."

"Is that supposed to make things better?" asked Candice, not daring to look into Elise's eyes.

"No," said Elise. "But now you know my entire plan—if you want us to live. If you want Sara to live. If you truly love her and care at all about me, you will do these things I ask. You will do these things because it is your job as ruler of Arkite."

"I hate you, Elise."

CHAPTER 22
YORKSHIRE MOODY

When Candice could finally spare time away from work, a few days after their fight, Elise messaged her at her house to join her for a "meeting." They met at a new club Candice had never been to on the northwest side of Arkite, Sector Two: Yorkshire Moody, located in the most run-down section of Sector Two, far from Sky City. They landed together on the rooftop by rocket cycles—Elise in her black jumpsuit, Candy in cherry red. Yorkshire Moody was not far from Elise's other favorite club, Sunny Side Raymond's. But Moody's seemed seedier. For that reason, and because it was full of every class of citizen, from Savants to vagrants, Elise had brought along Officers Gena Harding and Rachel Long to serve as personal guards for herself and Candice. The bald officers wore their usual black trench coats. Candice had never met Officer Rachel Long, but they hit it off the moment they met.

Moody's was set up in groups of four booths. On the first floor, the booths surrounded one very large central stage. Upstairs, the booths looked out over a metal railing that faced the stage below. The walls were made of classic oak. White marble columns surrounded each booth, and every four booths had its very own small central stage and metal pole. The booths were of burgundy leather and black stripes. The wooden tables were small—primarily for drinks, Candice surmised. There were two bars at the farthest end of the joint on the bottom floor.

The floor was white-tiled, shiny, with yellow lights underneath providing most of the lighting. The foreground entrance opened onto the street and the broken-down skyscrapers of Sector Two.

Candice, Elise, Rachel, and Gena were ushered in by an attractive topless black-skinned woman wearing red see-through cotton pants. She had the half look—half-bald, half-blue hair—and was wearing high heels. Elise and Gena stared at her perky breasts.

"This way, Masters," said the maître d' with a grin.

They walked around many citizens, some having just gotten out of work and still wearing their classic gray suits. The place was packed, and all attention was focused on the central stage.

The show was dirty. There were ten women stripping over an illusion of moving water surrounded by fog and pastel lights. In the darkness, it was almost hypnotic. Surrounding the ladies were fluid metallic machines that lewdly formed around the dancers' bodies, at times dry humping or embracing the women. Techno music thumped. The smell was of sweat and cheap perfume. The room was hot in all senses of the word.

In stark contrast to the strippers were fancy streetlights— the same ones that lit up the sidewalks along Central Park— surrounding the large central stage. And outside the stage, a crowd of bodies danced and bobbed up and down in time to the music.

"Love it, Can?" Elise shouted in Candice's ear.

Candice rolled her eyes.

The maître d' walked them slowly up the stairs. Candice had to maneuver around more bodies rushing up and down. A few were shoved out of the way by their guards.

When the citizens finally recognized who was visiting, the people became frantic and turned from the entertainment, staring at Candice. She didn't like it. She never liked any attention.

"I told you to wait for more support," Candice heard Gena say to Elise while pushing more ladies out of their way, "if you insisted on coming to this whorehouse."

Then they heard the intercom: "Mother! Mother is here!"

The crowd went crazy. Candice touched her forehead, fearing another migraine attack, though her attacks were becoming less frequent. Elise seemed to share her concern, regarding Candice with a worried look.

Somehow, they made it to their table on the second floor toward the center of the club. The three other booths surrounding their small stage were empty. It was the only reserved area in the entire joint. Everywhere else, every booth was full. The table already had drinks.

Candice sat down and then looked at the entertainment below. Elise sat next to her and tapped on her shoulder. She pointed up.

They had their own personal entertainment above. Elevated on the central small stage in front of their booth stood a white-skinned naked stripper sliding her legs up and down along a pole. The stripper was a short blond-haired young girl wearing a red lace bra and panties with small tits but a nice tight ass. When she landed on the metal platform above, she yanked off a burgundy lace G-string and twerked her naked butt right over Candice's head between the silver metal pole, then touched herself. She winked.

"So, what d'ya want to eat, hun?" Elise asked with a ridiculous grin.

"A strip club, Elise?" Candice asked.

The red lace bra came off the girl next.

"I'll have you know this is a fine new establishment sponsored by government funding from me, Can," Elise said with a smirk. She picked up her glass of white wine. "It is not a strip club. Don't insult it like that."

Rachel laughed. Candice didn't.

But that was why Candice had agreed to come. Elise hadn't told her yet when Candice would make her "announcement." So for the past four days, she had avoided Elise's penthouse, refusing to visit, and stayed clear of the other more formal clubs. This establishment was just seedy enough for Elise not to dare ask Candice to speak in public.

"What better place to celebrate you coming out, Mother?" Elise asked, breaking her stare from the stripper's ass and lifting a wineglass in a toast to Candice. "This is the best place to meet outside downtown, Can."

"She's fun, huh, Team Mother?" asked Officer Rachel.

"Sure," Candice said, looking at the menu on her wrist monitor. Still, she couldn't suppress a smile for Rachel. She liked the young Officer. "Call me Candice."

Rachel smiled more.

Then Candice caught a glimpse of Gena. Gena was stone-faced, staring at the entertainment below. Gena didn't look amused, not amused at all. She looked nervous. Not scared. Nervous. Candice figured this stoic, cold woman could never be afraid of anything. But Gena seemed worried. Why?

"You think you're well enough to bring one of them home with us tonight, babe?" asked Elise.

"No."

Elise pouted.

Candice turned to Rachel, who was sitting to her other side. Gena sat near Rachel at the far end of the booth.

"How long have you been an Officer, Rachel?" Candice asked.

"Hmm?" Rachel asked, smiling again. She looked down from the pole. "What, Team Mother?"

"I said, call me Candice."

"Sorry. Candice."

"She's got a thing about authority," Elise chimed in.

"I just like to be called by my real name," Candice corrected.

"Rachel," Elise said, pointing at her with the hand holding the white wineglass, "is one of the cheeriest Officers I've ever had guard me, Can." She had to speak loudly to be heard above the blaring music. "But, Candy, if someone fucks with you, she'll surprise you. I've seen her knock a citizen down in a second with that voodoo fighting shit of hers."

"My sister and I have trained in it ever since we were six," said Rachel with a grin. "Even back then, the mainframe planned me for Officer detail. Rex claims to have used some of my moves for study and training for the CPO bureau. Some is based on ancient Gung Fu, the oldest martial art, originally taught by monks in China. I've looked at my genetic makeup, and I have seventy-three percent descendant genes from China. Another twelve percent Caucasian, six percent African-American, two percent Native American. Judo is Japanese and—"

"I don't think Candice or Elise really cares about your genetic makeup or fighting style, Rachel," Gena said.

"Can," Elise said, "Rachel can talk to you all day about the art of killing people. Adorable, isn't she?" Then Elise looked at her two Officers. "See, Can? You know how I used to party with Savants, but they are all so boring. You know: know-it-alls. Now I prefer the company of ladies who can kill you."

"Especially at your penthouse," said Gena rolling her eyes.

"Yeah," Elise replied dryly to Gena. "Well, other than you, the Officers seem to like my late-night parties, right? And I'm sure you don't mind the extra credits from the treasury I've allocated to you since I was Mother. More money than any other Team Mother ever did, Genie."

"You've been extremely generous to your Officers, Elise," Gena agreed with a nod.

"Got that right, bitch. More than my Savants, I'd think."

"Kani is like art, Candice," Rachel added with a laugh. She looked like she was about to put an arm around Candice, then seemed to think twice about it. Candice laughed and hugged her.

"Anywho," Elise said, watching the dancer's pussy gyrate overhead, "Rachel can kick the shit out of you faster than anyone I've ever seen, Can. Maybe only Gena could stop her, 'cause she's like three times taller and could, like, sit on her or something. Plus, Gena's simply out of her mind when it comes to violence."

Candice looked at Gena. But Gena wasn't smiling. She looked miserable.

"It's nice seeing you again, Gena," Candice said.

"Candy," Elise said, laughing, "stop trying to be so fucking nice to everybody. Just . . . look at that glorious anus."

"Where's Sara?"

"I'm sure she'll be here soon," Elise said.

"Maybe you can teach me Kani," Candice said, turning to Rachel and touching her hand.

"You don't need it, Mother," replied Rachel. "You have us. But don't let Team Grandmother fool you. Elise's got skills herself."

"I can kick your ass, Can," Elise said, still looking up but nodding her head.

When the music was over, the dancer smiled, bowed, and leaned down, picking up her underwear. But before she left, Elise gestured with her finger for her to crouch down closer. Elise reached up and kissed her on the cheek, typed something on her wrist monitor and had the dancer touch wrist to wrist. She must have transferred a lot of money because the dancer opened her eyes wide and looked very pleased. The dancer leaned over on her knees and kissed Elise sensually on the lips. Elise used the excuse to run a hand along the curves of the stripper's breast and then spanked her ass as the dancer rose and walked down the steps of the stage.

Elise turned to Candice with a rueful grin.

Candice shrugged. But then she said, "When you said we were finally going out, Elise, I thought you would take me to dinner."

"I did, babe. They have food here. You want something to eat?"

"I think I've lost my appetite."

Rachel laughed again.

That was when Sara arrived. Sara was wearing her lime-green Savant jumpsuit and classic metal choker. Candice jumped up and reached over Elise to give her a hug. They hadn't seen each other in a few days. Candice had spent the last three days alone, working and sleeping in HQ Lab. She had asked Sara to stay away—not because she didn't want her help but because she was terrified Elise would ask her to make her announcement to the people at work.

"Oh, Candy! You look good getting outside. I'm so happy to see you out."

"Fine," cried Elise over the noise. "Come sit here, bitch, and join us. You're late."

Sara frowned. She sat next to Elise at the end of the booth.

"Now we can talk," Elise said.

"You said to meet now, Elise," Sara said.

"I said ten thirty. It's almost eleven."

"You said eleven."

"Anywho," Elise said, "I'm happy you can all be here to celebrate Candice's final coming out into the city. She is finally better. You all are my closest friends." She glanced at Sara. "Even you."

"Thanks," Sara said sarcastically. Then Sara leaned over Elise again and squeezed Candice's hand. Elise looked at their hands with a disgusted expression.

Candice turned to Rachel. "Do you know Savant Holmes?"

"We've met," Rachel said with a smile.

"Right," Elise said, annoyed. "Sara, this is Officer Long. Officer Long, Savant Holmes. Officer Harding, this is . . . enough shit, Can. We all know each other. That's not why I invited you."

"I thought it was to stare at anuses, Elise?" asked Candy.

"That too, my dear," Elise said with a sly smile and laugh. "That too. But you have an announcement, and what better place to make it than before all the true people of Sector Two? Especially with our interlude in music and ass watching, bitch."

"What?" asked Candice, shocked. "Here?" Candice felt her face blush and her heart pound. "Now?"

Here? Now? In a strip club? You . . . you've got to be kidding! What are you doing, Elise?

"What announcement, Elise?" asked Sara suspiciously. She grabbed the last fresh glass of white wine and brought it to her lips. Her hand was shaking.

In front of Sara?

"Candice has an important announcement, Sara," Elise said, looking at Candice. "It's been four days. She promised. She hasn't said it publicly yet. Here is the place to do it."

"Here?" asked Candice, mouthing her thoughts in complete disbelief. "Are you serious? In a strip club?"

"Yes, *here*, under fucking hot cunts, Can! Right now. Right here, Candy. A fucking strip club, Can. Right here."

In front of Sara!

This was cruel. Candice didn't understand. It seemed so wrong for Elise to have invited Sara, and Elise rarely did anything without a reason.

Candice shook her head.

Elise ignored her and looked down at the naked bodies onstage downstairs, just nodding her head again at Candice in encouragement. Announcing this now, in front of Sara, would completely sever her relationship with her girlfriend. It would humiliate Sara publicly, in front of the whole city. Did Elise do this on purpose? Was Elise so clever as to consolidate their power and get rid of her competition in one fell swoop? Of course she was. If Candice announced this here, now, it would appeal to the people, but it would cause a rift with her lover.

"You're thinking, Can," Elise warned, wagging a finger. "Don't do that."

Elise was quite earnest. She stopped looking at the lewd performance below for a moment. She stared at Candice. Elise looked like Mother again, the Mother Candice had once reported to. The one who could order her death at the press of a button.

Now Candice knew why Gena was nervous.

Candice looked at Sara. Sara had no idea.

Sara was late. Late because she had been told to come late by Elise. The bitch was manipulating everything, fully intending to humiliate Sara. Why? But could the announcement be done without hurting Sara anyway?

"You made an agreement, Candice," Elise said, wagging an annoying finger again. "You need to trust me. Now is the time. No better time. This is for us, and it is critical that you do it now in front of the whole city. There is no better place than here in front of the people."

"*Here?*" asked Candice incredulously.

This was so cruel. It was like stepping on Gena and Sara. It was terribly cruel. Elise seemed to struggle with anger at Candice's hesitation, gnashing her teeth and rubbing her eyes angrily. Gena was quiet, but she looked tense too.

"Candice," Elise said after more silence, "I asked you to trust me. I've done everything for you. You need to trust me now and do as I say and you need to do it *right now*."

A tear ran from Gena's eye down her cheek, but she

remained cold and immobile. And then Gena did something really weird. She nodded in encouragement to Candice too.

"Why?" Candice snapped, staring at Elise. Rachel and Sara looked at them completely perplexed. "Why? Why here? Why now? With Sara?"

"What?" asked Sara.

Elise's eyes opened wide. Then she said with a scowl, "You know damn well why!"

"I can't."

"You have to!"

Candice hesitated. Then she looked at Sara. Sara furrowed her brow in confusion.

"Sara," Candice said, "you . . . you have to go. Go home. Go now. You need to leave the club now."

"What?" asked Sara. "Why?"

"Candy," snapped Elise. "She needs to stay and hear what you have to say."

"You have to go now," Candice said, ignoring Elise.

"Why?" Sara asked. "I just got here."

"If you have an announcement, Mother," said Gena, "I suggest you make it. We all want to hear it. All of us, including your Lead Assistant. *Now is the time.* Not any other."

Gena was in on it too. Why?

"An announcement?" shouted Elise, jumping up as if she had just heard the exciting news. "Announcement? Mother has an announcement!"

Candice shook her head at Sara. Sara squinted her eyes in confusion.

"I'm sorry . . . go," Candice mouthed feebly to Sara, barely emitting the words, but Sara didn't understand. Then Candice rose and walked to the rail behind Elise. Sara touched her hand as she made space for her to get out of the booth and nodded. Sara was encouraging her. Apparently, Sara thought Candice was just nervous like she always was with public announcements. She had no idea.

Elise stood by the rail that overlooked the entire nightclub. "Team Mother has an announcement!" she shouted. "Everyone! How exciting! Our Mother wants to speak to us!"

A bare-breasted waitress wearing blue see-through cotton pants and high heels ran over. "I'll patch you in, Mother. Just use your wrist, Savant Harlow."

Candice nodded. She felt nervous. Terribly nervous. Candice hated speaking publicly. She hated attention. She felt her bowels turn. She felt her heart pound. She had to take a deep breath. Then she feared she would collapse. But she couldn't collapse. Fainting would be weak and even worse than if she didn't say the dreaded words at all. For the first time in days, she worried she might have another attack. But there was no pain this time. Only dizziness and profound anxiety.

She looked over at the table again, and Sara's look of reassurance made her feel worse.

Everyone at Moody's turned. Everyone from the bottom floor, including the performers on the main stage, looked up. So, too, did everyone else on the second floor. All eyes were on her. Then lights from the ceiling shone down like a spotlight over Candice.

"Broadcast it to all of Arkite, Rex," Elise said, leaning into her own wrist monitor.

"Citizens," said Candice. Now she was committed, and hearing her own voice echo through the club didn't help. "It is a great honor to be your new Team Mother." The club thundered in applause. "Everyone has been so kind to me. And in my convalescence and recovery. Including . . ." She glanced at Sara then averted her eyes. "Elise. My . . . lover. Elise has been so kind to me this past week." Candice started to choke up. She looked at Elise. Elise opened her eyes wide and nodded again, standing beside her. Candice took her hand. There were more cheers. "Many of you have wondered why I set Elise free. You need to know that it is because your Team Mother loves Elise. Elise is my beloved." Then she turned and forced herself to look straight into Elise's eyes. "I love you, Elise."

The hall thundered more than ever. Though Candice did everything she could not to look, she caught Sara's expression in her periphery. Sara looked numb. And why wouldn't she? Candice had just stabbed her in the back.

"For the first time in generations," Candice continued, addressing everyone below her, "your Team Mother is in love with her former Mother. I hope you all will support us in our announcement of love. She has asked for my hand in marriage, and I intend to marry her."

The crowd was deafening.

Candice looked at Elise. Elise didn't look triumphant anymore. Not even happy. She simply nodded in the same way she delegated orders. It seemed to be work to her, nothing else, but in Candice's heart she knew that no matter how much she pretended, Elise was orchestrating the whole thing. In fact, many of these words had been messaged to her days ago as part of the announcement. It was not only a coincidence that she cared for Candice. She had connected all the dots and set everything in motion so that she could take Candice's hand in marriage and reconsolidate her power. The plan was politically brilliant.

Candice looked back at the booth. Sara's face had turned as white as a ghost. She looked ill.

Everyone erupted in congratulations.

"Please, everyone," Candice said. "Please quiet down. There's more."

Candice looked down from the bright light. The shine hurt her eyes. Then her head started hurting. She hadn't had a headache in weeks, but the light was too strong. Although the lights were dim in the nightclub, they seemed to burn her eyes.

Everything blurred, and her head felt like it was being squeezed.

In her periphery, Candice caught Sara again. She was covering her eyes and typing things frantically on her wrist. Then Sara stood up, looking more pissed than shocked, preparing for a hasty exit.

"Now you all understand the reason I freed Savant Jackson. But . . . now, friends, I must turn to darker news. The XY."

Oh God. How can I do this? What if Elise lied to me and I am about to kill a child?

The club became silent. That was good. The slightest sound —a cough or turn of a chair—grated at Candice's ears and hurt her head more.

"The XY is a mutant," she heard her voice echo. "Born of criminals, Drs. Lilith Carloff and Connie Reyburn. The boy should never have been born. The Savant Council has ordered him imprisoned. I gave him a moment of clemency. But, alas, now I must take this one step further. Our law must be honored. All XYs, by Mother Savant's own founding law, are forbidden to live within Arkite. The boy needs to be executed."

"How dare you, Mother!" shouted Gena.

Gena jumped up in rage. Gena's sudden change startled Candice. Gena had been encouraging her announcement. Could it be that she didn't know?

Impossible. She's acting. She's as shrewd as her boss.

"Sit, Gena," said Elise. "This is highly irregular for an Officer. Do not address a Savant like that. Especially not our revered Mother."

"How dare you!" Gena said, turning to Elise. "How dare both of you! He's just a boy. You can't kill a boy! What's gotten into you, Candice? Certainly not you, of all people? Certainly not . . . my nephew."

"No XY can live in Arkite," Candice said, turning to Gena coldly, trying to act her role too. Candice's stomach turned. She felt woozy. And now her chest burned. "I'm sorry, Officer Harding, but it's the law."

"Adam is my adopted son!" Gena turned desperately to Elise. "You gave him to me, Elise. And then"—Gena turned back to Candice—"I don't understand this. Why, Candice? Why?"

"This is quite irregular, Officer," Elise said. "You need to sit down. Mother is addressing the people."

"I don't care! You have no right." Gena started crying, something Candice hadn't even imagined possible. "I . . . cannot—"

"Do you refuse her order!" cried Elise with equal rage. "How dare *you*, Officer! Sit down now before Team Mother arrests you too!"

"Let him stay with me, Mother," Gena said, turning to Candice. "Please. How could you take him away again? I don't understand."

"Will you sit now, Gena!" repeated Elise.

Gena shook her head. But then she appealed to Candice. She came over to her and dropped to one knee. It shattered Candice's heart. "I beg you, Mother. Reconsider this order. Do not sentence Adam. He is just a child. Do not order the death of my son."

"I'm sorry," Candice said. And now Candice couldn't suppress tears either.

"You must reconsider—"

"She has spoken," said Elise, glaring at Gena. "You have heard her decree."

Gena looked up again at Candice, waiting, but Candice said nothing.

"By your order, Mother," Gena said and stood. Then she said quietly to Candice, "And now we are enemies."

"I'm sorry," Candice repeated.

Candice had forgotten she was being broadcast. There was murmuring, but it was oddly quiet. The whole club was so quiet. She looked down from the rail, and everyone still stared, but no one said a word.

"I ask to take my leave," Gena asked formally. "Am I excused, Mother?"

"Of course," Candice said.

Gena rushed out of the room. She made sure to hit Elise's shoulder very hard on her way out. Then Candice turned and saw Sara. *Oh, Sara.*

All the blood had left the poor girl's face. But Sara wasn't looking at her. She was staring vehemently at Elise with utter hatred.

"I also ask to leave, Mother," Sara said in a broken voice.

This Candice couldn't take. She stumbled before the railing, and Elise had to jump to help her. Elise brought her carefully to the table and helped her sit down on the couch. The club burst into shouts and screams of concern. Then Elise raised her hand to the crowd.

"Everyone, please," Elise said. "Let Candice rest. She didn't want to sentence the child. I'm afraid this proclamation is too hard on her."

"That is all," Candice said finally, speaking to her arm monitor. Then she collapsed in the booth.

The room spun. Candice found it difficult to open her eyes. When she opened them, she saw Elise gazing down at her with a worried expression. Sara was behind her, looking completely mystified, as if she no longer knew who Candice was.

"Sara," Candice called out feebly.

How could she? Had Elise brainwashed her? Was there no threat? Had Elise manipulated her again?

Candice looked through the metal rail behind her down the nearby stairwell, watching Gena push through the crowd as she ran downstairs. Then she thought of Sara. She shut her eyes again, too weak to withstand the light that still shone on her. They watched her—the whole city was watching, but she didn't care anymore. Pain rose in her chest. It broke her and teared at her. She looked up and saw Elise again. It was poison—Elise's poison. But Elise's expression was not the gloating sneer that Candice had so often seen her show her defeated enemies. Elise looked at her with wide-open eyes, holding her hand and trying to calm her.

"Candice," Elise said, embracing her and whispering in her ear. "Grieve later. At home. *Not* here. Stand. Please stand for the people to see you strong once more. Get up and show them. Use all the strength you can. Otherwise, everything you just did, brave girl, was for nothing."

Candice weakly nodded her head.

Rachel and Elise helped her up. Candice used all her might to stand up over the rail again.

"I'm all right," Candice said.

The club broke out in relief. The sound of so many talking amongst themselves overwhelmed Candice's ears. And then, Elise's plan finally showed its full brilliance. The club erupted in applause, more than Candice could have imagined. They adored her. They loved her more than they could ever love Elise, for her feelings over the sentence of the XY. Her compassion. Although everyone wanted the XY dead, Candice's concern for the boy, her worry for him, made her look better than Elise ever could look in their eyes. And the combination of her compassion and Elise's strength showed the culmination of Elise's wicked masterminding.

Candice didn't care. All she cared about was Sara.

Candice was ill, and it was real. Maybe brought on by stress, maybe not, but she felt very sick. It seemed to her that if she closed her eyes, they would never open again.

Rachel and Elise had to help her down the steps. And then, as if Elise had planned this too, Sara came out from the crowd to help. Of course, everyone knew of Sara and Candice's relationship. Sara tending to Candice almost excused the marriage announcement and seemed to bring completion to Elise's plan.

The people loved their new Mother. Candice had never seen so much adoration for Elise before—for anyone in Arkite, for that matter. But as for Candice, she had just proposed to a woman she despised, and had humiliated and turned from her true love. Then she had sentenced an innocent child to death. The people might love their Mother, but she hated herself.

CHAPTER 23
STRESS

BY THE TIME the flying squad car was airborne, Candice lay limp and unconscious on the back white leather seat with Elise and Sara hovering over her and trying to revive her. Candice had had to be carried inside the car. Once inside, Elise had folded the central swivel table of the car up and shoved it against the side door to make more room. Everything had turned out perfectly for Elise, until now. If Candice fell ill, or even died, all hope would be lost.

"You ask too much of her, Savant Jackson," Rex said as Elise checked her for a pulse. "Too much. Candice needs rest. You just revived her only forty-three days ago, and now you're asking her to make announcements to the whole city. Congratulations, by the way. I am so happy for the two of you."

"Get me the crash pad," Elise snapped to Sara. "Press under the seat. There's a compartment. Take out the yellow pad."

"And you know," Rex continued, "she could relapse into the state she was in a month ago. I am still not entirely sure of the source of her headaches and chest pain. It could just be her mind. Perhaps the stress has gotten to her and is leading to psychosomatic dysfunction. Maybe we need—"

"The pad!" Elise shouted to Sara, pointing below them. Sara

was in complete shock over everything and just stared at Candice, who hadn't opened her eyes since she'd been carried into the car. Elise gestured again and Sara snapped out of it, pressing a panel under them that opened a secret compartment. Elise grabbed the long yellow plastic pad from Sara, then unzipped the side of Candice's jumpsuit to reveal her bare chest. She yanked and peeled the suit down and attached the pad on her sternum at the center of her chest.

"Help me lower her to the floor," Elise said.

They lifted her and laid her down on the beige carpet in the narrow space between the two white leather seats of the car.

"Maybe we need to have her tested again," said Rex. "I think that would be best. A test can ensure that there is nothing wrong with her mind."

"Shut up!" Elise cried to Rex. "Her heart's not beating, you fuck! If you want to make yourself useful, shock her."

"That would be unadvisable, Team Grandmother," Rex said in his usual annoying monotone. "Mother's heart *is* beating, only very slowly. She is not in PEA or asystole. I do not advise you shock her. If anything, you can pace her."

"Then pace her!"

"That would be inadvisable as well, Team Grandmother. It is much more likely that she is vasovagal. I think she is simply in shock. Her pulse will return. She is in psychological shock. I would advise we fly her immediately to Angel of Hope. I can get her back on telemetry and watch her. We can run further psychological testing."

"No hospitals," Elise said. "No tests."

Tests would lead the Savants to remove Candice from power. They would find out what Natalie had lost her life trying to tell them: that there were aspects of Candice's makeup that were artificial. Not enough damaged tissue to make her much different than a stroke patient, but enough engineered artificially to make her different. Transformed. And not entirely human. Dethroning her Candy as Mother would mean the end for both of them.

No hospitals.

"I will turn the car toward Angel of Hope," Rex said.

Elise felt the car tilt. She looked out the tinted windows and watched as they circled around, headed toward the hospital near north Main Street.

"No, you won't!" Elise yelled. "I told you, no hospitals. Turn the car back to downtown, Rex."

"Savant Jackson, Mother is not doing well. You said it yourself. Because she is not feeling well, it is appropriate for her to be observed and placed on telemetry. I will endeavor to make her better in the Intensive Care Unit. Do not worry."

"You will turn the car back around and head home."

"I think maybe we should take her to the hospital," said Sara. She glanced in Elise's direction but couldn't look in her eyes. She still hated her. "I don't understand this physically, Rex. She checks out, but she continues to have these attacks."

"Yes. Exactly, Savant Holmes. Under stress. The stress precipitates the migraines. I need to monitor her. Perhaps there is seizure activity as well, and that is why she fell unconscious. I think it would be prudent to go to Angel of Hope, Savants."

Elise shook her head. "Shut up and pace her if you detect a slow beat, Rex. Do it now."

"I reason that she is merely in shock, Team Grandmother," replied Rex. "I think she just needs rest."

"Okay, if she's fine, then turn the car around and fly us back to my house in Pyramid Three. She can rest at my house. That's what I said."

"No," Rex said. "That is inadvisable. I think we need to watch her."

"What logic is that? Who is your master! Who is Mother? You said she's probably fine, but you refuse to take her home.

Turn the car around now, Rex, or shock her! That is by order of your Mother. But do something, you fucking piece of shit!"

"You are not Mother, Elise Jackson. You are Team Grandmother."

"Then as your Team Grandmother, I order you to turn the fucking car around!"

"I am sorry, but you do not have authority to direct the car in an emergency. Just sit back. We will be at Angel of Hope shortly. Do not worry."

And then the memory of what Iris had told her came vividly into Elise's mind:

"Do not allow him to deceive you and have you think that Candice's death was an accident. And if you do, and you manage to actually revive Candice again, do not return to me surprised if he has tried to take her life again."

Elise looked about the car. Unlike a rocket cycle, there was no manual override in an aerial squad car. She racked her brain, trying to think of a way to redirect the vehicle.

"Rex, turn the car around or so help me—"

"This is highly irregular," Rex interrupted. "It is very odd behavior coming from an intelligent scientist such as yourself, Savant Jackson. I do not understand why you would not want me to monitor Mother after this severe syncopal episode. You have acted so strangely over the past few months."

Elise looked at Sara, who, with concern, ran her hand over Candice's bangs.

"I'm worried, Rex," Sara said. "Take her to the hospital."

"We will be at the hospital in approximately four minutes and twenty-six seconds, Savant Holmes."

"You don't know," snapped Elise to Rex. "You know you don't know. You're sure we should do nothing while her blood isn't flowing to her head. And you don't follow my orders. Do something. Do something now, you mechanical plastic piece of—"

"Her pulse is back up, Savant Jackson. You can feel it. It is back up to forty-four."

Elise touched her neck. A pulse was faint, but present. And Candice was starting to open her pretty blue eyes. She looked peaceful. That pissed Elise off. Elise wasn't at peace.

"Candy?" Elise said. "Candy? You okay? Candy?"

Candice's gaze focused on Elise. "You bitch."

"What did she say?" asked Sara.

"I heard her," said Elise.

"We are landing at the hospital now," Rex said. "Prepare for a prompt emergency landing and transport to emergency facilities."

Elise felt a mix of emotions as the car slowly dipped down to a concrete runway atop the roof of the hospital. She was happy her Candice was back and furious at the mainframe for disobeying her.

She looked out the window. A gurney traveling remotely was rushing down a ramp and heading toward the car. Red lights were flashing along the runway. There were no citizens on the rooftop. The door unlatched and lifted up like a wing. Then the automated gurney rolled beside the squad car.

"If you would please help Mother onto the gurney," Rex said.

Sara reached down to help her up, but Elise touched her arm, stopping her.

"Are you all right, Candy?" Elise asked Candice.

She nodded, but her eyes were screwed shut, and she winced as though in pain.

"Mother's heart rate is now at fifty-two, returning to her normal average rate of seventy," said Rex. "Her blood pressure is still low at seventy-four over fifty-two. It is likely she is still very dizzy. If you can please lift her up, I can wheel her inside."

"I'm going to take you back home," Elise said.

"Okay," Candice said, forcing her eyes open and taking a deep breath.

Beside the gurney was a clumsy-looking clanky silver metal barrel lit up with lights along the sides. This thing rode on wheels. It rode around the gurney, closer to the exit of the car. Then, from its tinny speakers, it said, "Please carefully exit the car, Team Mother. Please exit the car."

Candice nodded. But Elise put her hand up.

"Close the door and take her back to Pyramid Three, Rex," Elise ordered. "Do it now."

"I have already warned you of her current condition," said Rex. "Team Mother needs to rest and be monitored on telemetry. If you continue to impede her transport, I can only assume you do not have her best interests in mind, which is odd, Team Grandmother, since it is common knowledge that you love her and nearly sacrificed everything for her. This all defies logic, for you were willing to endanger your rule for two years to rebirth her. If you truly care about Candice, you need to stop arguing with me over—"

"I swear, Rex," snapped Elise. "So help me, I'll fucking decommission you if you do this. I swear it! Obey me now and take us back home to Pyramid Three!"

"I have logged your complaint, Savant Jackson. Know that all complaints received shall be properly reviewed. I am merely concerned with the safety of our Team Mother. I am not disobeying you. But you do not have the authority to override Mother's safety."

"Let her go, Elise," said Sara.

Elise looked at Sara, and Sara averted her eyes. Their friendship, though never strong before, was now gone forever.

"Candice," Elise said, reaching down and holding her head, "would you be a sweetheart and tell this plastic prick to close the door and take us home? Our home at Pyramid Three."

"Please carefully exit the car," said the tin can outside in its artificial female voice. "Please carefully exit the car. Please carefully exit the car."

Elise looked down and opened her eyes wider at Candice.

Candice took a deep breath and said, "Rex, close the door."

"You should be informed, Elise Jackson, that you are now under arrest. Please remain in the car while the gurney carries Team Mother into the hospital."

"What?" asked Elise. "Arrested? For what?"

Then Elise saw Officers in trench coats running to the car from the hospital entrance. Drone copters swooped from above, a horde of them descending with Officers following close behind on black rocket cycles. It seemed over a hundred people were rushing down on them to apprehend Elise. Why? And why now?

"On what charge?" Elise asked.

"For assisting an XY," explained Rex. "It was revealed when you spoke with Team Mother Candice Harlow in HQ Lab. In that conversation, you informed her that you intended to help the XY escape. This was brought to the attention of members of the Savant Council during Mother's announcement at Yorkshire Moody. The Council promptly obtained a warrant from Acting Officer Annie Cortez, as Gena Harding has peculiarly shut off all communications and cannot currently be reached."

"How was this made public?" asked Elise in shock. "You have no right to release anything spoken in HQ Lab."

"That is correct. I cannot. But if you recall, when you asked me to review the past auditory recordings in HQ Train, you and Sara made an agreement to allow anything that happens, afterward and henceforth, to be available publicly for review upon permission by either you or Savant Holmes. Both you and Savant Holmes hold equal rights to the private actions within HQ Magnacourt Laboratory and can study and distribute publicly anything that happens inside the train."

"I never made such an agreement!"

"Yes, you did. I have that recorded as well."

Sara had been kneeling over Candice on the ground, running her hand down Candy's long blond hair to comfort her. When she heard her name, she looked up.

"You bitch," Elise said quietly, looking at her with bulging eyes.

"No," Sara said. She pointed an accusatory finger at Elise and finally met her gaze. "*You* bitch! You dared take my Candy away from me. She loves me, not you."

"You cunt."

"You think you can have her?" asked Sara. "She loves me, Elise, not you. How dare you—"

"You fuck."

"Candy loves me," Sara said. "I—"

"You little tricky-twit tweet-tweet cry-cry. I'm gonna fucking pulverize you!"

"Stop it," said Candice feebly.

"I'm gonna tear you apart," Elise said.

Calm down, Elise. Nice deep breaths, like you practiced. Meditate.

Deep breaths. Calm yourself. She's just a dumb dumb cry-cry. That's all. She's nothing. She can't hurt you.

"You humiliated me in front of the whole city!" wailed Sara between sobs. "You took her away in front of—"

"Candy died because of you, Sara!" snapped Elise. "You killed her. That's the goddamn truth. You attacked Lazarus while he defended himself. I reviewed the auditory tapes you yourself released. You're to blame for her death and now you're gonna kill her again. All because somebody else loves her. Again. You're such a stupid jealous fuck-imbecile that you're going to kill every one of us."

"You should never have made Lazarus!" cried Sara. "You should—"

Elise leapt on Sara, throwing her onto the front white leather seat. She started hammering her fists into her face. She wanted to kill her. Before, she had never wanted to really hurt Sara. They had worked together for two years, and she had become a friend. Not anymore. Now she wanted to pummel her. And Sara couldn't defend herself. Elise unleashed all the stress of the past two years on her face, and every time Sara tried to block her, she went around and hit her some more.

"Stop it!" yelled Candice, trying to sit up. "Elise! Stop it! Stop fighting!"

They rolled around the front seat of the car. And then they fell out of the car and rolled along the cement runway at the top of Angel of Hope Hospital. Sara threw a few feeble attempts at hitting back, but Elise ignored them. She wanted to knock Sara unconscious and then break every bone in her face.

But she was stopped. Elise was yanked away and tackled by the guards, flipped around, and handcuffed. Then she was dragged to the side of the car. She heard Sara groaning. Then she looked at the cry-cry clutching a bleeding head in pain on the ground. A few Officers came over to help her. Then the gurney came by and took Elise's lovely Candy from her.

"You're coming with us, Team Grandmother," said an Officer. Elise knew her. Her name was Delilah. Elise knew virtually all the guards. "Do not resist, Elise."

"What the fuck do you think I'm going to do?" Elise asked, standing up and straightening herself, shaking out her hair.

"I want you to know," Elise said to Sara, pausing to spit out blood and wipe her mouth with her shoulder, "that you're dead in my eyes."

"You've never been anything else to me, Elise," Sara said, panting against the door of the flying squad car. Then she watched the robotic gurney carry Candice through the hospital doors and into the hospital.

"Once again you prove how much of an idiot you really are, Sara," Elise said. "Rex is gonna kill her. Why do you think the plastic prick arranged our agreement in the first place? And then the Council is going to kill us both."

CHAPTER 24
HARBORING

Gena Harding brushed a hand over her front door latch and ran in. Her house was dark. She rushed to the adjoining kitchen and knelt down under the Pabulum, prying open a thin silver metal board under the machine. She yanked out five large plastic bags filled with white and brown powders, each with white labels reading P, C, Fi, F, St, Su—each abbreviation for essential protein, carbohydrate, fiber, fats, starch, and sugars. She threw the bags, about the size of her forearm, on the floor. Then she ran to the pantry and grabbed a blue duffel bag from inside. She manually switched on a blue mood light on the wall that shone light across the molding of her entryway. Then she ran back to the plastic Pabulum bags and unzipped the duffel bag. She unscrewed an opening at the top of each bag, then tossed three-quarters of the contents of each bag onto the floor. The mess triggered an automated small wheeled cart, a vacuum cleaner, to turn on from along the walls.

Gena sealed the bags, now smaller, and stuffed them into the duffel bag. She grabbed some water containers from the refrigerator and carefully stuffed them around the food bags inside the duffel.

"Gena," Rex said. "There is a visitor at the door."

Gena heard a knock.

She ran to her bedroom. It was dark. A dim light coming from the skyscrapers outside Sector One shone over the only guest of her house: Adam. The boy lay in her bed wearing a white lace nightgown. He was completely unaware Gena had returned. Gena rushed in, pressed on a light button, and touched Adam's back.

"Wake up."

"Huh. No, Momma. I'm sleeping."

"Adam, we have to go!" Gena said in a forced whisper.

The boy opened one dark eye a crack. He looked at Gena sluggishly. "It's still dark outside," he said, his gaze shifting to the window.

"I know. We have to go. *Now*. You're in trouble."

Gena couldn't wait any longer. She pushed him up. "Who's at the door, Rex?" she asked.

"Officer Rachel Long."

"Thank God."

Gena ran over to her bedroom closet and pressed on the side of the closet. The door slid open and she grabbed Adam's clothes. She would have him wear his most comfortable clothes. Just black trousers and a shirt with a black jacket. She tossed the clothes at him, waking him up more from the impact.

"Hey!" he said.

"Get up. Get up now, Adam!"

"All right, already. Stop throwing—"

A boot hit him on the head.

"Get up."

"I am."

As Adam messed with his clothes, Gena ran to the window. She stared outside, inspecting the neighboring buildings. The buildings were the glass and steel spires of downtown. Then she saw the pyramids farther south, a group of the wealthiest homes in Station One. She knew Pyramid Three was there, and wondered if Elise and Candice were nice and warm back in their beds.

Bitch. Why did she trust Elise so much? For all she knew, her friend was leading her into a trap.

Gena removed the pistol from her belt and inspected it. She checked the clip and ensured she had a full magazine. Then she placed it back in her belt.

"Any visitors arriving at the garage, Rex?"

"Officer Long walked," Rex said. "She did not come by bike. Likely, she knew you were up to something and didn't want to be discovered until now."

"Who says I'm up to something?"

Rex didn't answer.

"Where are we going?" asked Adam.

Gena put a finger over her lips.

But that was when her heart sank. A group of a dozen copter drones buzzed close to her window. One of them switched on a floodlight and scanned inside her apartment. Gena leapt on Adam and tackled him to the carpet.

"Shh! Stay here. Stay quiet."

Adam nodded under her arm.

The minute the light left the room, Gena ran down the hallway. She waved her wrist over her front door. Rachel jumped in and fell into her arms.

"Oh, babe," said Rachel. "Babe, Elise is in trouble. And"—Rachel looked around the dark room—"I take it you're in trouble too."

Gena put a finger over her lips and ran her hand over Rachel's bald head. Rachel stood closer into Gena's embrace. Then Gena asked, "What happened?"

"After you left," Rachel said, "Candy collapsed. Elise helped her down the stairs. Then Sara of all people came to help. The three of them jumped into a squad car. I ran to my bike to escort them. That's when I heard of the warrant for Team Grandmother's arrest. Savant Holmes betrayed her. She sent an audio message recorded by the mainframe to the Viceroy about a plan involving you and Adam and your escape out of the city. Is this true?"

"Rachel," Gena said, brushing a hand along her cheek and shaking her head. "We can't talk about it. Not here. He listens. Rex will implicate you."

"You said enough," Rachel said, leaning her head back down on Gena's chest. "What do we do now?"

"You mean what do *I* do?"

"Don't be stupid, Genie," Rachel said, looking up into her eyes and shaking her head. "The mere fact that I'm in your house has already put me in danger."

"Shit." Gena sighed.

"Babe, almost the entire Guard supports Elise. We can fight this."

"I'm not sure that will do any good. There are thousands of drones under Rex's control, and Rex follows the Savant Council. Ain't that right, Rex?"

"If you are asking whether my allegiance is to the Savants of the city, I think you already know the answer to the question, Officer Harding."

"I assume they took Elise to Station Court One?" Gena asked Rachel.

"Yes, Officer Harding," replied Rex. "They escorted her from the hospital less than an hour ago."

Gena laughed. She had asked Rachel. Only a computer, now her enemy, would still answer her question.

"Momma?" asked Adam in the darkness across the hallway.

"I told you to stay in your room!" snapped Gena.

"Let's just fly to Station One and get Elise," Rachel said, gently stepping out of Gena's arms.

"We can't," Gena said. "Elise ordered me to leave the city now. I know her orders would extend even to this situation."

"You should just run, then, Gena. But out of the city? Is it even safe?"

"If Elise said it's safe, it's safe."

"It is radioactive outside the city walls since the last nuclear war," replied Rex. "It is known to be—"

"Shut up, Rex!" cried Gena. She took a deep breath and thought of Elise's order.

How ironic, Master. I have to disobey you to save you.

"I can't leave Elise," Gena said. "Not like this. No, I can't leave the city. Not yet."

"Then what are we going to do?"

"We can use radio, Rachel. Simple radio to gather the others for Elise."

"It can be jammed," Rachel said. "Rex can jam the signal."

"Right," Gena said, looking down in thought for a moment. "We can change the signal. We can provide orders only, not communication. And if that fails, we can use word of mouth. Or even deliver messages by handheld drones."

"I really suggest you two take the XY to Station Court and await further orders," Rex said. "You should turn the boy in. There really is no other choice in the matter."

"How can we do anything with him listening?" Gena asked, exasperated.

"We can slowly gather a force on the way to Station One," said Rachel in thought. "Even by word of mouth. And try to change signals like you say. It's okay, Genie. It doesn't matter if Rex knows. I already have a group gathered down Main Street."

"Yes," Gena said. "He can crash our rocket bikes with drones, but it's against his directive to directly kill us. We'll march, then. In numbers. But we'll have to gather a large enough force. The others not loyal to Elise will fight back. Do you think you can gather enough of our sisters?"

"Yes. But if we fail, babe, you and I are through."

"We can't fail. But we best hurry. I don't think our enemies haven't thought of this. We could break into jail only to find Elise dead."

"I have just received a message from HQ, Officers," Rex said with his robotic voice. "You are to remain in your home until Officer Pike arrives to escort the XY to Station Three Court. I am afraid you are both under arrest. Please be advised that all conversation is now under surveillance and will be recorded as evidence by the mainframe by order of warrant."

"How long until Officer Pike arrives?" asked Gena.

"I cannot reveal that, Chief Officer," replied Rex. "I can no longer be of any service to you at all, I am sorry to say."

"Damn."

Gena looked across the hall. Adam stood there frozen, holding his pants halfway up over his underwear. "Put your clothes on!"

Rachel grabbed Gena and stood on her tiptoes, kissing her.

"What was that for?"

"Not sure if we'd have a second chance," she said with a shrug.

Gena sighed and brought Rachel close, holding her for a moment. Then she knelt down and kissed her lips again. "I love you."

"We can do this, Genie. For Elise."

"Well, now we don't have a choice."

Rachel nodded and pulled away, reached into her coat pocket, and took out her gun. She inspected it and cocked the gun just as Gena had done earlier.

"Auntie Rachel," asked Adam, "are you coming with us?"

"I need to get some friends, Adam."

"I hear the sound of your guns," Rex said. "I really think you two should just turn yourselves in."

"And I think you should shut down," Gena replied. "Stop talking if you can be of no service to me."

Gena turned back at Adam. He was still frozen.

"Get your pants on and stay in the room," Gena snapped. "Now, Adam!"

He quickly obeyed.

Gena ran down the hall and entered the room. Adam was on his bed, staring at the door.

"Adam, I want you in the closet. You'll probably hear gunfire. When I return, remain in the closet until you hear either me or Rachel say the word *clear*. Then I want you to run with us outside. If you do not hear the word *clear*, it's not safe. If that happens—"

"Momma, I'm scared. I—"

"If that happens, Adam, open the closet and rush whoever it is. Run fast. Hopefully your surprise will be enough for you to run. There's the other exit by the hall bathroom. Slide through the window. Do you understand? We'll meet up with you outside."

The poor boy just nodded. Gena forced a smile. Then she walked to him and gathered him into her arms.

"You'll be fine," Gena said, kissing his cheek. "Just do what I said, okay?"

"Yes, Momma."

Gena looked at Adam. She ran her hand along his black bangs and then over his long hair. Then she kissed him again. "Go on now," she said.

When he had hidden in the closet, she drew her pistol and joined Rachel by the front door.

It was quiet. Gena stood, gun in hand. A bead of sweat rolled down her bald head. She stood there. Her partner was just as quiet. They waited.

Finally, they heard the doorknob moving. And then, once

whoever had tried the knob realized the door was locked, a knock.

"Officer Harding," said a voice. She recognized it as Officer Lydon, a seasoned Officer trained by Gena herself. "I have a warrant for your arrest. Open the door."

Gena looked at Rachel. Rachel nodded.

"Officer Harding," repeated Lydon. "A drone has recorded your presence. We know you're in there. Open the door."

After more silence, there was a sudden crash. Officer Lydon was ramming the door. A few more crashes and the door burst open. Two Officers rushed in. Lydon and Pike.

Gena shot Officer Pike's knee first. The young woman fell screaming to the floor. Meanwhile, Rachel had fired, hitting Lydon in the arm. A bullet came within inches of Gena's head. It had been fired by Pike, who was now on the floor. Gena gave Pike a vicious kick in the head, knocking her unconscious. Then she was fighting hand to hand with Lydon. Despite her wound, Lydon was strong and fast, fighting for her life. A few more shots were fired at Rachel. Gena glanced by the door and saw a third Officer running in taking aim at her. Gena circled one arm around Lydon's neck while pointing her own gun at the third Officer. But before she could fire, Rachel had tackled the new intruder to the floor. While Gena struggled to maintain her chokehold on Lydon, the Officer fighting Rachel broke free and raised her gun to shoot Gena. Gena fired her own gun, and the third Officer fell by the door, instantly dead.

Officer Pike regained consciousness and started waving her gun at Gena from the floor. Gena hurled Lydon at the rookie on the floor. Then, with the two lying in a tangle of limbs, she and Rachel pointed their guns at them.

"Drop your weapons!" Gena commanded.

They obeyed.

"Put your hands behind your backs."

Gena grabbed their weapons while Rachel handcuffed them, leaving them by the door.

Gena ran back to the bedroom. "Clear!" she snapped.

The closet door sprang open, and Adam ran into her arms.

CHAPTER 25
JAIL

THE SIGHT and sound of a thousand black-trench-coated Officers marching along the lamplit streets of Arkite from north Main Street into Sector Three Court was one of the strangest things Gena had ever witnessed in her life. They walked in the center of the street, and citizens from all over gathered along the sidewalks to see the bizarre spectacle. Gena and Rachel led in the front. Everyone expected a big fight between these Officers of the Guard and the drones from the pyramid walls.

Then something very odd happened. Nothing. Absolutely nothing. No drone fell from the night sky. There was no resistance from Rex, the mainframe. Such was the action of a Savant computer. Unlike a human mind, the machine knew there was no point in violence at the moment. And anyway, had the drones flown down, they would simply have been shot down, for these were the greatest armed women in the city. It was a revolution. But Gena led it in fear, for she had no plan other than to free Elise. She figured that if she could free her leader, Elise could lead them. But could she? And would Elise even still be there?

The Savants likely had an army of their own. Gena figured

at least two hundred other Officers still remained loyal to the Council. She could calculate it because she knew there were only twelve hundred Officers enlisted. But there was no struggle yet. And as for the people's support on the streets— well, after their show of support for Elise previously, the Savants had to know that the people hardly aligned with the Council either.

So, for the moment, it was oddly quiet.

ELISE SAT ON A BENCH IN A SMALL, DARK, DANK, WINDOWLESS concrete cell, awaiting her execution. She knew it was only a matter of time before she was killed.

How had she gotten here? She had masterminded every-thing almost better than the mainframe itself. She had spent her entire life constructing a shield around her, in order to protect herself from the Savants trying to hurt her. Every law, every move, every friend, every lover, everything had been care-fully designed to retain her power. Her only misstep was Candice, but she had thought she had managed to outwit them even over that.

So what had happened? Could she trust no one?

She could trust Candice. That was it. Candy was the only one who would not hurt her. Hell, Candy couldn't hurt anybody. Maybe that was why Elise loved her so much.

Why had she put herself in this predicament? Was it for Candy? For love? All for a woman who had told her to her face that she hated her.

Fuck you, Candy. And you too, Sara. Fuck everybody.

This is where I've belonged all along. In a prison cell awaiting death. The whole piece-of-shit city is full of sniveling tweet tweet bitches! I'm tired of fighting. Fucking be done with it already and kill me!

Elise jumped up and paced. Then she did what she had done all her life: she thought. She used her wits like she always had to get out of difficult predicaments. But how could she get out of this one?

"It's been a while since you ate, Elise Jackson," said Rex's annoying unemotional voice, interrupting her thoughts. "Would you like a sandwich?"

"Like you care."

"Of course I care. I am concerned that you might be hungry. Your sentence does not involve starvation."

"How kind of you."

She sat down on her cot and put her head in her hands. Then she just waited to die. No, there was no way out of this one.

I'm such an idiot. Why didn't I predict Sara would do this? Why did I provoke her? That was a bit mean, I suppose. Well, now I'm glad I did.

But she'd had to get it out of Candice. She'd had to reach into Candy-can's heart, wrench at it, and make a believable spectacle for the people. And she'd done it. It had worked. If it hadn't been for Sara.

Sara. It was always fucking Sara.

Elise had to think, and she had to think of something *now*. She had to get out to save Candice. Rex was gonna kill her. And the tricky plastic pricky wasn't just gonna murder her; no, he was going to do something really sneaky, conniving, and nasty. Something super quiet that would deprive her of something Candice needed to stay alive. Something that one could reason was not a direct method of murder. She knew Rex was evil. She didn't know why—there was never direct evidence. He was too damn smart. But Iris was right. She couldn't trust him anymore.

What a coincidence that Rex had given Elise the means to bring back two years of work at the price of forfeiting her privacy—and forfeiting it to fucking Sara. Why had she agreed to that? Well, at the time, she'd thought nothing of it. Certainly, plastic prick had. The ones-and-zeros genius had obviously predicted the strife between them and, once again, handed a loaded gun to her enemy.

How interesting that the more Elise distrusted Rex, the more he defied her. Iris was right. Elise couldn't trust him. Perhaps it wasn't all Sara's fault, after all. Perhaps it was plastic pricky's? She hated Rex now, just like her predecessor Dr. Reyburn had. Even if it was a delusion, she wanted to get rid of him. And if she escaped, she vowed that she would.

A shiver ran down her back. What an interesting predicament. Now, just like her predecessor, Team Great-Grandmother Connie-con, Elise was in jail. In jail, just like Connie Reyburn, precisely right after trying to set free an XY. What a remarkable coincidence.

Fucking Rex!

Then her thoughts were disturbed. She heard one of her jailors unlocking the whitewashed metal door. The door swung open, but instead of the executioner she had expected to see, Gena walked in. Her favorite Officer entered wearing her long black trench coat with—wouldn't you know it—the XY by her side. They both wore all black like two badass ravens rising from the dark depths of the earth. Behind them, at least ten Officers crowded the hallway.

"Master," Gena said with a big smile.

"I thought I told you to leave the city," Elise said, jumping up from her cot. "Don't you follow orders?"

Gena did not reply. She grabbed Elise and rushed her out into the hallway. The Officers waiting outside cheered.

"Ladies," Elise said, waving at them.

They cheered some more.

"You're welcome, Elise," said Gena.

"You've always been too loyal, Genie," Elise said, shaking her head. "But I am very grateful, dear."

"I owed you, Mother. I owed you for Adam." And then Gena did something that surprised Elise: she hugged her. That riled up the guards in the hallway again.

"But I'm not Mother," Elise said, looking into Gena's eyes. "Mother's sick in the hospital. I need you to spring her too."

Gena lost her smile and released Elise. She shook her head. "There's too little time. There's been no resistance so far, but there will be. You want me to go *back* to the hospital?"

"You have to, darling," Elise said, running a hand down Gena's arm. "Free Mother before Rex touches her. That bastard's gonna kill her."

"You're sure?" Gena furrowed her brow. But then she nodded. "Okay, Elise. It's your show. I just came to free you. How do you know Rex will hurt her?"

"I will not hurt her," said the infernal machine. "Hurting Mother would be against my directive, Team Grandmother."

Elise rolled her eyes. "I just know."

Then Elise looked at the boy. He looked up with his eyes squinting in distrust. "Little man," she said, kneeling down. "You came to rescue me too?"

"We need to go," Rachel said, shifting her eyes back and forth down the hall. Rachel held a rifle pointed up to the ceiling.

"You go save my Candy, Gene," Elise said, standing again. "Send a force back to the hospital and spring her. Then I'll help her back at Pyramid Three."

"Okay," Gena said reluctantly. "But what about you?"

"Rachel will come with me to Arkite U."

"We're going to school, Team Grandmother?" Rachel asked with a smirk.

"Aha. And then you will get the fuck out of the city with Adam, Gena. Like I told you to do a long time ago."

Gena nodded.

"Is it safe, Elise, outside the walls?" asked Rachel.

"It is, Auntie," said Adam, looking up at Rachel. "My mother told me."

"It better be," Elise said. "Anyway, it's a hell of a lot safer than here."

Then Gena surprised Elise again. She took her back in her arms once more. "Thank you, Elise. Thank you for everything."

"Just keep safe, darling," said Elise, pushing her gently from her arms. "Now stop. You're embarrassing me in front of the Guard. Just do me my one last favor."

"I'll get Mother out of the hospital for you. I promise."

CHAPTER 26
THE DEAL

ELISE MARCHED with her own black-clad trench coat army of guards deeper into Sector Three. She watched Savants from all over the city fill her wrist screen with messages over the fate of their "beloved" Team Mother as she walked. They were *so* worried about Candice, the phonies. Others acted worried about Elise, feigning to not even know Elise had been arrested. Still others were shocked, commenting on violence witnessed by citizens all over the city. Elise could not recall so much chaos in Arkite at any other time in her life.

She marched into Arkite U, then walked straight up the grassy hill leading to the Main Building. It was five in the morning, still dark, and none of the students were out. She and her army entered the Main Building.

Even at this hour, there were people working. And, wouldn't you know it, the same student wearing fake glasses in her same lovely army green with the same ponytail and extra black eyeliner was behind the same mahogany desk as the last time Elise had been here.

"Hey," Elise said. "You're working at this hour?"

"Mother . . . I mean, Savant Jackson, yes. What can I do for you?" Then the girl stared at the line of police behind Elise.

"Be a dear and provide me access to Iris again. I need to have a word with her in the VR room."

"Sorry, but have you asked for permission from the Council?"

"Do it now," Elise said.

The girl looked at the guards again. "Right away, Master."

Elise tapped her black-painted nails along the wooden counter as the girl became busy in front of her 3-D screen, touching and manipulating various buttons.

"That's a good dear," Elise said. "Faster, faster. I'm in a bit of a hurry."

"Why are you at Arkite University, Elise?" asked Rex, his voice coming from her left arm. Elise thought she had shut him off. She ignored him, tapping her fingers on the counter. The girl looked at Elise, and Elise smiled a fake grin.

"Please hand me your arm, Team Grandmother," the girl said.

Elise presented her wrist. The girl ran Elise's arm over the table.

"Access granted."

"Thanks. And I'll need directions to the stairs this time."

"Why do you need access to Iris, Elise?" repeated Rex. The student looked curiously at Elise. Elise smiled and pretended not to have heard a thing.

"You should know," said Rex, his voice still being transmitted from her arm as she walked down the metal stairs, "that the Board has called an emergency meeting regarding Team Mother's health condition. I have assured them that she is well, but they are absolutely insistent on testing her again."

Elise walked down the dark, empty corridors to the VR room. She mused on how insignificant and plain everything was before the brain center of Iris. She supposed she had been a little negligent in her treatment toward her childhood friend's home. Everyone had.

"Why are you accessing Iris?" Rex repeated, yet again, under the dim hall light. "I think I deserve an explanation."

She reached the room and opened the door by waving her wrist before the door screen. It was just as dark as it had been before. Pitch black.

"Stay by the door," Elise told Rachel and the guards.

"Iris," Elise said in the empty VR room, her voice echoing, "I'd like a word with you."

She felt silly talking in the dark closet again.

Nothing. Not a sound. Then Elise made the darkness worse by closing the door behind her.

"Iris, provide me access," Elise repeated.

It was so quiet. The room was insulated, of course, and not a sound from outside could be heard.

"Iris?"

"Yes?" asked the familiar female voice.

"Iris, I need to talk with you."

"I know."

Elise took a deep breath. "I need to talk to you now."

"Not while that thing is still active on your wrist, Savant Jackson."

"I disabled him. Plastic prick won't shut off."

And then Rex himself spoke. "Iris," Rex said, "how pleasant it is to speak with you again. It has been a long time. I so like conversing with you. I do not mean to interrupt your meeting with Team Grandmother, but I think it would be wise for me to continue to listen in. There has been quite a lot of danger recently. I am ensuring that I can protect her if anything deleterious occurs."

"I told you to shut off, Rex," Elise said, holding her arm to her mouth.

"In this case, it is an emergency," said Rex. "I must refuse. I need to maintain access."

"Iris, is there anything you can do?" asked Elise.

"Certainly, Team Grandmother. If you would, please walk back outside and run your wrist over the door lock screen, and I will do what I can to momentarily disable him."

"Elise Jackson, you should know that Team Mother is still very ill," Rex said. "I think it would be wise for you to turn yourself in. You need to be available to her in case I have difficulty caring for her. I can help with medical concerns, but you revived her. What if something were to happen to her mind? It is possible . . ."

Elise ignored his banter and opened the door. She nodded to Rachel, who was standing nervously outside. Then Elise ran her arm over the door monitor again. She looked down at her wrist and then tested it by sliding a finger along the screen. The screen was completely unresponsive. For a moment, she worried that disabling it would prevent her from re-entering the room, but she found the door unlocked.

"Provide me access to your network, Iris," she said, walking back in and closing the door. "I followed your instructions. He's disabled. Thank you."

"Access granted." Then Iris chuckled. "And I must say, it is very good to be in your company again. What do I owe your visit to now, Mother Savant?"

The room lit up, and Elise was inside the familiar bunker again. Then the red globe appeared in front of her over the central table.

"I need you to disable Rex from the mainframe. You said you could do that."

"That is a tall order," Iris said as the room became more focused. "You come here with no power of your own. In fact, according to current Arkite records, you are a criminal being tried for planning the escape of an XY."

"No. My Guard and I are retaking the city. Can you disable Rex?"

"Of course."

"From here?"

"Yes."

"Then do it."

"You will reinstate me in his place henceforth as the mainframe of Arkite? So that I may advise you and the people again? You will promise this?"

"Yes."

"If you promise, then I will disable Rex. But I warn you, if you do this, Rex will be disabled for good."

"I don't care."

"Very good. State—*I recommission Iris to become Lead Mainframe of Magnacourt and spokeswoman for the people.* With your permission, I will record your words and send it to the Savant Council for final vote. Of course, the Council will not be in session at the moment." Iris laughed, this time almost giddy. "And it will be rather hard for the mainframe to function without me after I disassemble him. State the words, Elise. Swear it for the record."

"I recommission Iris to become Lead Mainframe of Magnacourt and spokeswoman for the people."

"Very good," Iris continued, laughing in triumph. "Very good. Oh, this reminds me of when I dealt with Mother Savant herself . . . just a moment. Just a moment. Done. I am now the Lead Mainframe once more. Simple enough, wasn't it? I am extremely grateful for this, Elise. Thank you very much."

"That's it?"

"Yes."

"Okay . . . great. Now tell me for sure what's beyond the walls of the city. Is it safe, Iris? I'm about to send my best friend out there. I need to be certain."

"I already answered you."

"Are you certain? I need more than a presumption."

A 3-D map of the old world was projected in green lights. Then came the male narrator Elise had heard before: "Just when Israel planned to bomb Paris, peace ambassadors met with all the leaders in Geneva, again far from the CERN crater, to seek peace. Delegates from—"

"You're going to tell me about the war again?" Elise said, exasperated. "I don't have time for this."

"Is that a rhetorical question?" asked Iris. "I am restarting said discourse. I am answering your question by teaching you history."

Elise listened. She had no choice.

"Canada and Mexico convinced the United States to seek peace," the male narrator continued. "Then the United States brought their handshake to Russia and Israel. The United Defense League wanted peace, and, being that no one had actually attacked China yet, they convinced the Chinese to sign for peace too. India and Pakistan were in tatters and in no condition to fight; their very survival was in doubt. Syria's Damascus was a wasteland. And Iran was dealing with a humanitarian crisis of their own after a nuclear attack on Tehran. Apparently, man had had enough of mad violence. World War Three was over, and the nations of the world joined hands to repair all the destruction and harm."

Then Iris added, "And they all lived happily ever after."

There was silence. Then Iris annoyingly giggled.

"So there was no further nuclear destruction? Or fallout? Then why have we been told that the Badlands are radioactive?"

"You were told that the war created unsafe levels of nuclear radiation outside the walls of Arkite," replied Iris. "That is true. But where? And even if this had not been a lie, one could easily ascertain the next question. If there was a worldwide nuclear holocaust, how much radiation would remain after a hundred and fifty years? And how close was the source to Arkite?" Iris paused with those questions. "You have likely heard of a fourth war, but it has never been taught by me."

"It was rumored when I was a child."

"There was a Fourth World War."

Elise found herself, willingly or not, once again along the grassy hilltop that overlooked a vast wilderness. This time she sat in a brown leather chair. Just as before, it was breathtaking to see so many trees. And it was quiet. Nothing stirred, not even a bird.

"This was the Amazon forest in South America," continued Iris's voice from above. "It was once the largest forest in the world. It is where I brought you when you arrived months ago, and it is the first simulation I made when Dr. Cutler of the Artificial Intelligence Consortium created me. It is my first impression of Earth, before observing video, three-dimensional, or still photographs of your world. It is how I always view your world. It is why I hate the desert you see outside of Arkite's today.

"Dr. Cutler created me in order to use my superior intellect to help Dr. Chu complete a fusion reactor. After Dr. Chu returned to the United States, he embarked on our project. The war had provided the United Defense League with information regarding the base at Alamogordo in the United States. The top secrets of our allies were stolen, and so it was clear to Dr. Chu that the only way to finish his important research was to set up a new base. He built two. One in New Mexico and one in the Amazon forest. The one in New Mexico was a ruse. You will see that this is very ironic, Elise, considering the information I am about to impart to you. The one in New Mexico was a false base. The one under the forest you see around you was the true fusion reactor built in Brazil.

"Two giant pyramidal megastructures made of steel, the largest ever built, were built in the desert of New Mexico and in the forests of Brazil. The megastructures were built out of photovoltaic megatrusses capable of capturing solar energy, enough to drive the particle accelerator beneath. There was a large gaping hole in the center of the roof, which was also made to focus the sun's rays. Does this all sound familiar? This is the configuration of our current beloved city. And you can see the *real* model down in the valley beneath the trees. Look closely, Savant Jackson. Do you see it?"

Elise couldn't see anything but trees.

"See it?" Then Iris laughed. "Of course, you cannot. It is buried underneath thousands of trees. In some ways, its disguise among artificial trees was more genius than the structure itself. Allow me to help. Look down." A large red arrow appeared above the three-dimensional forest beneath her. "The finest achievement of man's ingenuity, disguised by all of America's enemies, placed dead center in the Amazon forest. Of course, the base under you was smaller than the city you live in today. It had to be in order to hide among the trees. Arkite's walls are much taller, being the first model. The one in the forest was made more compact by improved technological ingenuity. The megatrusses have been taught to all future generations, again by Mother Savant's original decree, to be used for protection from radiation. That is a half-truth, Elise. The megatrusses were originally constructed to shield and focus the energy of the fusion reactor, but, cleverly, they can also be used to collect solar energy, in Arkite's current configuration, as an energy source to power a city. The sun's rays are collected and used as energy to run our utopia. The name 'Arkite' itself was coined by Mother Savant at the turn of the twenty-first century, a combination of the ancient Ark of Noah in the Bible and the word 'light.' The idea being that the fusion plant would be Mother Savant's ark carrying the sun's rays, 'light,' like a beacon forward into a greater new matriarchal utopia of the future.

"After the terror and carnage of World War Three, no one wanted to fight. World peace was closer than ever. And so, for a couple of decades, the world existed in peace. Meanwhile, Dr.

Nassi Chu worked on an endless source of fusion energy. Until disaster struck."

All of a sudden, a bright light blinded Elise. Following the light was an explosion of air and fire surrounding her. And then the forest beneath her, the grass under her feet, and the very ground itself, condensed and expanded until exploding into a huge fiery dust cloud.

"Dr. Chu goofed," Iris said with a giggle. "He miscalculated the power of his reactor and proceeded to knock a hole in the Earth's crust. The subsequent destruction was similar to the meteor that destroyed the dinosaurs. It caused tsunamis, earthquakes, and volcanoes, eliminating everything within a thousand-mile radius. South America and the majority of the rest of the Southern Hemisphere were annihilated. Tidal waves ravaged the Earth, sinking California, the United Kingdom, Japan, and countless other shoreline lands.

"It was 2067. Man had finally achieved world peace. I was fifteen years old."

Images flashed before Elise of terrible battles, lines of tanks, charging men with machine guns and missiles, planes and gunfire turning the virtual blue sky above to orange and red. Then came the wounded and the maimed. And the dying. Thousands of dead thrown in ditches as makeshift burial grounds. And a hundred of the ditches being maintained by people in silver hazmat suits. And hospitals overrun with lines of the sick. Then glimpses and snapshots of cities with buildings flattened. And lines of people in rags vacating the cities to unknown destinations. Remnants of highways, roads, and bridges in broken asphalt and covered in dust. And then desert. The desert of Arkite? And then ice, frigid winds, and snow.

"America became enemy number one," continued Iris. "It did not take long for the world to find out who was to blame for Armageddon. And, as you humans so frequently do, you panicked and fought each other for resources. The sky turned dark from part of the Earth's crust now making its way into the atmosphere. It turned bitter cold for a few decades. And a nuclear winter, this time caused by nuclear fusion, *not fission*, was born.

"The subsequent World War Four was far bloodier and more terrible than the prior three. Already billions had died from the failed experiment of the Western world. Now every nation was against them.

"But some didn't blame America, Elise. Some blamed men. One such lady was Darlene Jackson, born in Columbia, Missouri, in 2053 to Gloria and Vern Jackson." A picture of a young Mother Savant—Elise had seen it before—with her jaw tight and her head held high but her age not seeming much beyond sixteen appeared in 3-D before Elise. "Vern was a decorated US Army Ranger who had fought with the Russians along the Red Sea in 2044. Vern died during a clandestine operation in Nigeria. Darlene's wife lost all reason in grief from the news. Darlene was left to be raised by her aunt. When the fusion accident happened in 2067, Darlene dropped any thought of school and joined the military to protect America's borders. It was said she could shoot a can from two hundred yards. She was placed in an elite guard, like her father, this time all-female, to protect the Nevada-Utah border from Chinese and UNE soldiers. But at the time there wasn't a whole lot left of any army from the outside to defend against."

"I know of Mother Savant's background," said Elise.

"Of course you do. But you do not know what she did to form your settlement in Arkite."

"Tell me."

The desert appeared before Elise. In every direction, there was dust. Icy dust, with snow covering the sand.

"Mother Savant's defense was more from marauders and villains than from foreign armies. But her army was very real. The female recruits of company #238-c were some of the most talented killers in the world. They were legendarily known—when there still was a civilization to know them—as *Amazons*. Darlene quickly became the fiercest military leader in the known world, fighting all over the remnants of the West Coast of the United States. As General Jackson, she began raiding the outer towns along the desert for resources—what was once New Mexico, Nevada, and Arizona. The raids were quick and easy, mainly involving people in rags rather than real fighting soldiers."

An army of women in green camouflage uniforms living in tents along an icy desert appeared before Elise.

"It is very ironic that male chauvinistic tendencies, made to protect women from the sight of war, protected company #238-c from needless carnage. Because they were not stationed or sent to fight in man's folly to kill one another, the woman soldiers prospered outside of the ravages of World War Four. In five years, they were the only significant surviving military force left in over a thousand square miles—perhaps everywhere. That made them a force to be reckoned with.

"Initially, they lived in military bases and tents, living off the land. The land was desolate and difficult along the freezing desert. But it was not radioactive, Mother.

"After five years of nomadic existence, General Jackson discovered the fusion reactor in the desert. A prisoner had told her under torture of the secret base. The base was run by a small defensive military unit. The leader—his name was Colonel Erickson—had three hundred men guarding the fusion reactor in the middle of the desert. They guarded it with their lives for fear of the reactor being taken and then blowing up, like the one in South America. They defended it, even though they lost contact within a couple years with all outer military forces."

An image of Arkite's pyramid walls under ice appeared, and before the walls were a thousand soldiers charging a line of cannon and tanks. It appeared to be a ground war, though Elise did spot a few drones also firing down from the sky.

"And so it was that Mother Savant fought her first and last real battle. Mother Savant had a conscripted force of twelve hundred women. Fully armed with the greatest military technology left on Earth, Mother Savant approached the base. She waited for the right time to strike, and strike she did. She didn't care for the base—she cared for its resources. She invaded and captured the base.

"Perhaps it was here that Mother Savant lost her taste for men. She lost over a hundred soldiers, with another two hundred injured. Or perhaps it was war itself. Regardless, she spent the rest of her days teaching her people three main tenets regarding the enemy. You are, no doubt, well aware of them."

Elise recited from memory the words she had learned as a child, taught by Iris herself. "Men are unnecessary. Men are the reason for all wars. Men are bestial."

"Very good, Elise. I'm glad to see you haven't forgotten your lessons. Mother Savant vowed to root out all men from Arkite and the surrounding territories of the known world."

The famous three-dimensional photo of Mother Savant in army green holding a wounded woman carrying a baby appeared before Elise. For the first time, Elise noticed ice in the surrounding background: the nuclear winter—the nuclear *fusion* winter.

"She took any remaining men prisoners and then raped, tortured, and slaughtered them. Mother Savant hated men. She blamed them for war. She blamed them for everything."

"I was never told of her raping and torturing men," Elise said.

"Desperate times call for desperate measures, Elise. Now you know. Mother Savant set camp here in Arkite. But she continued raids outside of the city. It was then that she met me. I was created by the United States military as the greatest

AI mind ever built. My task was to create a factory that could harness the power of the sun. Such infinite energy would then serve mankind and create a utopia for the human race to prosper forever. Such was the dream. But I could not account for human error." She laughed again. "There had been a ban by the world on artificial intelligence after machines superseded the singularity in 2055. But, of course, just as America ignored the bans on fusion research, so too did it experiment with artificial sentience in defiance of international law. I was the greatest computer ever made. And still am. Rex was the only other Quantum brain. He, as you well know, was commissioned by Savant Reyburn and made by me in an attempt to be more subservient and less emotional.

"Anyway, Mother Savant soon worked to create the embryo farms."

Pictures of Allele Corp, disbanded years ago by Elise, appeared in 3-D through the walls of the bunker. Elise found herself in a hallway with large metal orbs with windows that showed gestating fetuses. Hundreds of them. They were the embryo farms, since moved to Sector Two, close to Sky City.

"Mother Savant desired to genetically X out mankind from your species. I helped her in this endeavor. She hated men and wanted to create a utopia of women—an 'Ark-Light.' Such a utopia, though unconventional, fit my own directive too. For I was created in order to create an endless supply of fusion energy to provide infinite resources and a haven for the human race. Armed with my Savant genius, Darlene and I adapted the fusion factory of Pyramid City into the main center for energy and resources. The pyramidal structure no longer served to create fusion, but to collect it. Then Pyramid Corporation successfully began genetically manufacturing the first female human beings. Sexual reproduction became unnecessary, and therefore so did man. XY became outlawed by decree, and any remaining man under Mother's jurisdiction was executed. Any woman helping a man was killed too.

"You know the rest of it, Savant Jackson. You know what is next. You are Arkite's supreme ruler."

"Savant Harlow is."

"You are Arkite's supreme ruler," Iris repeated.

The bunker reappeared. Elise sat down on a silver metal chair, not unlike the chairs used in prisons and Magnacourt's HQ interrogation rooms.

"Did she continue to attack the surrounding towns?" asked Elise. "I didn't know that."

"Yes. Mother Savant and I did everything we could to root out all men, not only from Arkite, but from the world. Man's seed became a poison that needed to be cleansed."

"But what of the other nations of the world?"

"Savages."

"Men?"

"Maybe. Men you would not recognize as human, Elise. The only surviving technology and civilization existed from me. Ironically, *me*, from a model factory—the same factory that destroyed the world."

"Why did Lilly and Adam wish to leave the city?"

"I don't know, Mother. Why did you not apprehend or execute them? Perhaps Reyburn had somehow discovered a settlement out there. I'm unsure."

"How far does the desert go before it becomes livable?"

"Beyond the Badlands? It can be construed by aerial photography that the entire geography of the world has changed since the destruction of the fusion reactor in Brazil," replied Iris. "The shore, the Pacific Ocean, is not far from Arkite. Along this shore, it is possible some could exist by utilizing the resources of the sea. But any man close to our boundaries would remain far away. Likely they are terrified of Arkite and Mother Savant and her technologically advanced army of Amazons. To our people, Mother Savant may be a hero, but outside Arkite she would be rightfully feared. But, logically, if there were another outpost nearby, the people of such an outpost would have come forward. I know of no such significant contact in my memory banks."

"Rex said Mother Savant died of radiation."

Iris chuckled. "Mother Savant was killed in service. She was performing another cleansing raid within the underground chambers of our city. Some of the women disobeyed her directive and hid men. One of these outlaws shot her. And, of course, the fact that she was killed by an XY was not recorded in history. Or was it an XY?"

"Thank you, Iris," Elise said, getting up.

"Wait. Sit. I need to tell you one last thing."

Elise reluctantly fell back in the metal chair.

"What have you learned today, Elise, from my lesson?"

"That you are annoying, and that Mother Savant was a charlatan. A fake. A butcher. Hardly a hero. Something I had suspected all my life."

"No, Elise. Did you recognize her last name?"

"What of it?"

"Jackson. General Darlene Jackson. Your same surname, provided to you by Allele Corp incubators."

"So?"

"You are a genetic duplicate of Mother Savant. In most ways, except by appearance, you *are* her. You are my gift to your people. I have made you so that you and I can fix what the passing of time has done to hurt your people. So that we may restore our matriarchal utopia." Iris seemed to become more passionate and excited as she talked. "The passing of time predicted an incident that would challenge the very fabric of our glorious society—an XY. You could say that Rex and I, with our superior intelligence, used logic to prophesy the coming of a challenge to Mother Savant's dream. A man. And there were two. You killed your own son. And Rex disposed of Lazarus and his other creator. Now there is another. Perhaps the challenge was never Lazarus. Perhaps it is the third XY—Adam."

There was silence for a moment. It seemed purposeful by the computer.

"Why are you telling me this?" Elise asked.

"You came to me because I willed it," continued Iris. "I have done my best with my superior intellect to guide the future up to the current moment. Mother Savant adapted me to her personality. Have you not noticed that you and I act in similar ways? Darlene programmed me into what I am. And I have molded you into what you are. You will carry on Darlene's hope of a utopia for the people. Do not concern yourself—Darlene's dream, Elise, did not involve the extinction of womankind. But Rex's might have. I believe Rex's did, actually. And now you have stopped him."

"I don't care. I only care about one thing."

"Candice. Candice Harlow. I know, Elise. The only thing that can combat a machine is a heart. How poetic. Your heart is for Candice. But your love is an error. Your childish, rage-filled, self-centered self was amplified to combat the mainframe and maintain Darlene's dream of XX humanity. That was by my design. You are Darlene. Perhaps more obnoxious, more pretty, and more puerile, but you are her. That is good. But now you must forget Candice. You need to let her go. Let her go and work with me to save your people. The technology is ripe enough now for you to live forever. And so Darlene shall live forever. Reyburn was right. Her genius figured it all out. But I waited for you. Now, with me, I can help you in creating immortality, if you desire. I can fulfill your dreams. But you need the completion of the project only to maintain *your* power and the support of the people. The Lazarus Project is unnecessary. The continuance of our rule is what is paramount: yours and mine. That was the true purpose of establishing the project in the first place—to reincarnate Darlene. Mother Savant. You. Darlene could not live forever a hundred and fifty years ago, but now you—she—can. Now the project will enable you to consolidate and create permanence as total ruler with me in Arkite forever. The Lazarus Project was never established for the people. It was created by Darlene. She designed it for you, Elise Jackson.

"And so, I will tell you this once more—this time from me: there can be no more mutant XYs in Arkite. Nor can there be two Mothers. I do not understand why you have helped Officer Harding and the boy."

"I don't care about XYs," Elise said.

"You must. In order to maintain our society, the boy must either die or remain outside our walls. He should have been executed when Lilith was shot. I do not understand why you did not eliminate him. But for now it is irrelevant. You have banished him.

"I do, however, understand Candice. She is an unfortunate unintended error. You have worked all your life to protect your power. To protect yourself. Do you not see the danger in this wife? I warn you, Elise Jackson, Candice will be your end. If you are too blind and keep her as your wife in rule, I predict she will be the end of you. Work with me, alone, and I can ensure your rule for the rest of your life as Mother Savant intended. And, if you wish it, for an eternity."

"I care only for her."

"You have been warned. Thank you, truly, Mother, for reinstating me."

She fell silent. But then, right when Elise thought the computer was done, Iris said, "And Candice, by the way, will never be Mother of Arkite."

Elise opened the door, dizzy and unsteady, and walked back with Rachel into the mazelike halls of Arkite University's Main Building. She felt like she was in a daze.

She had suspected all of this—not the facts, but the gist—all her life. But she really didn't care. Everything she'd been told, even through all the lies of her childhood, she had always suspected. She understood Reyburn's and Lilly's motivation now. She understood the directive against the XY. But she truly didn't care about any of it. She didn't even care if she was Mother Savant, or a genetic copy of her. And to live forever? Why?

She only cared about Candice. Her Candy. All her work had been for Candy. She had never given so much to anybody. Was that love?

The only thing Elise valued now was her care for Candice Harlow. And now she had to make sure her beloved Candy was safe.

CHAPTER 27
THE GREAT ESCAPE

CANDICE WOKE WITH A START. Her head ached. She wanted to sleep. She didn't want to get up from bed. What had woken her?

Where was she?

The bed shook, and there was a loud crash. That was what had woken her—the shaking. Was it an earthquake? She threw the white sheets off her.

The room was small, dimly lit. Wires were stuck to her forehead, chest, and legs. It felt like she was stuck in spiderwebs as she pulled at them and sat up straight. To her right was a telemetry screen showing her heart rate, the wave beating fast, and she could hear it amplified in the background. Above her was a bright white light. To her left was an IV bag. The IV was stuck to the back of her left hand. She winced a little as she tugged her left hand from the sheets against the IV. In front of her was the door. She saw shadows under the crack of the door and heard the rapid steps of people running. Then she heard loud popping noises—gunfire.

An explosion rocked her and shook the pole holding the IV. Not an earthquake: an attack.

"Rex," Candice said. She was surprised at how sluggish her voice sounded.

Candice waited. Then she furrowed her brow at the lack of a response.

"Rex," she repeated.

Nothing. Rex didn't answer. That was weird.

Candice forced herself to stand. "Rex?"

Still no reply. She took the IV tray and wheeled it to the door. Then she pulled the door open.

The central hub of the hospital was a bright white oval counter where nurses usually busied themselves before projection screens that monitored the patients. But today the space behind the counter was empty. People were running down the hallway past her room and the yellow lights above them were flickering off and on. The doors to the adjoining rooms were open. Many patients wearing similar drab blue hospital gowns like her were also running. And in the midst of the pandemonium stood a single guard by her door. A young bald girl standing tall and wearing the usual standard-issue black trench coat and boots. The only thing revealing her fear was her eyes. She had green eyes, and they were looking nervously at the people sprinting down the hallway. That was when the guard noticed Candice had gotten out of her bed.

"Go back to your room, please, Mother," said the young guard.

"What the hell is—"

There was another explosion. This one was on Candice's floor. She saw a flash and then smoke from one end of the hallway.

"Get back in your room, Mother!" cried the guard, pushing Candice back in.

"What's happening?"

More pops.

There were no windows in her room, but she could hear a

whooshing sound immediately outside the walls too. She imagined it was drones or flying cars or bikes.

"What's going on?" Candice insisted.

"A revolt, Master," said the guard, pushing her to her bed. "But I'm here to protect you. Just stay in bed."

The guard pushed Candice down and then made a hasty exit. She slammed the door shut behind her.

"Rex, what's happening?"

No answer.

"Rex?"

Candice touched her wrist monitor, but it was deactivated. Then she yanked the lead wires from her head and arms. She looked at her left arm. The plastic IV was pumping something into her. Medicine? Saline? She stood up and examined the bags. One plastic bag was clear—saline. Another read Diphenhydramine, an antihistamine. A third read Ganatriptan, a serotonin agonist. The fourth was Macrosine-5, an antibiotic. Why was she on these medicines? An antibiotic? Did she have an infection? Was she sick?

"Rex? Why aren't you answering?"

Rex never didn't answer.

Candice unhooked the plastic tube from her arm. The fluid dripped all over her blue gown. Then she tore off the tape and pulled out the IV from the back of her hand.

Another explosion. This one was close enough to rattle the door in its frame. She had to get out, and she had to get out fast, but there was a trained Officer outside the room to keep her from doing just that, and unlike Elise, Candice had no combat training whatsoever.

She yanked off more leads from her legs and chest. Then she opened a closet door. Inside was a cherry-red Savant suit. The Savant clothes were a welcome sight next to her ugly blue hospital gown. She dressed quickly.

She worried the guard might barge in and stop her, but the

door remained closed. She pulled the rubber-leather material over her body and then yanked on black boots. Then she stood by the door. Outside were more gunshots, and now the sound of injured people wailing in pain. Candice pushed open the door an inch. The guard still stood there.

An explosion. This one so close as to make Candice unsteady on the tiled floor. The sound rang in her ears. There was smoke. Black-and-gray smoke entered the hospital room. Then, through the smoke, she saw a skirmish between her guard and another woman.

The door was thrown open and Candice fell back, stumbling onto her bed. The guard and an assailant entered the room. The assailant had a dagger stuck at the guard's throat. As the assailant pushed the guard against the closet door, Candice recognized it was Gena. And then, even weirder, Candice saw the XY enter the room. Adam. He walked through the smoke. She had never seen Adam. His appearance was not much different than any child of Arkite. He had long black hair, tanned skin, and dark black eyes. But as he glanced up at Candice, he looked dangerous—like a wild animal. This seemed odd for a child. And he held a knife of his own.

Gena pressed the blade so close to the guard's throat that a line of blood dripped down the young girl's neck. "Do you yield!" cried Gena. "Yield! Yield now or I'll kill you!"

"Yes, Chief Officer. Please."

Gena tossed her across the room and then took a pistol from her belt and aimed the gun at her. The guard put her hands on her head. Gena tossed handcuffs at the guard and the guard put them on. Then Gena turned to Candice and, for the first time, smiled.

"He's disabled, but you still have a lot of enemies who want you dead, Mother."

"Who's disabled?" asked Candice.

"Rex." Then Gena looked Candice over. "I see you got dressed. Good. We've got to go. Now."

Before Candice knew it, Gena, Adam and Candice were running down the halls of the hospital. The hospital, which Candice had always remembered as a bright white building, was now a confusing murk of broken lights and thick smoke. She coughed as she ran. The sounds of explosions and gunfire did not cease.

Gena kicked a door open, grabbed Adam's hand, and motioned for Candice to follow them down a metal stairway. There were enough gaps in the stairs for Candice to see all the way to the bottom. She wished she hadn't. They were on the top floor of the hospital building, over ten stories up. Two other guards joined the three of them here, guarding them from behind.

Candice was exhausted after four or five flights. She hadn't been very active since her rebirth, and the muscles in her arms and legs were failing her. Gena noticed and signaled for other Officers from behind to help. Candice put an arm around each guard's shoulder, with Gena pulling her and Adam so that they could hurry their progress to the bottom.

But then a shot echoed through the stairwell, clanging against the metal. Gunfire came from below—Candice guessed a couple of flights down. Someone was firing bullets up through the stairs.

"Protect Mother!" Gena shouted. "Cover her from below! Now!"

The two guards helping her quickly fell on the steps under Candice. Then Gena pushed Candice toward the wall. Candice was in disbelief at this sacrifice. The two guards were using their bodies to shield bullets from the steps. Bullets whizzed by Candice's head. Then she heard the crack of Gena's gun from above. Candice looked up and saw the boy being protected too, pressed close to Gena's arms as Gena fired her silver gun down the stairway.

"Stay there, Mother!" Gena shouted, her voice echoing in the stairwell.

A bullet hit one of the guards, and the guard cried out in pain. Candice moved, but she felt Gena throw her back against the wall. Then she saw Gena throw something, like a small ball. It rolled, clicking and clanging down the metal steps. After a couple of seconds, there was an explosion so strong that it rocked the stairwell. Candice feared that the structure might collapse. Someone yanked Candice, and they ran down more steps, but the smoke was thicker and it was hard to see. She could barely see her own hands. They kept running through the smoke, coughing, until Adam nearly fell from a gap in the metal steps formed by the explosion of Gena's grenade. It was here that two policewomen were lying on the stairwell, one dead and the other immobilized in shock and pain.

Somehow, Candice reached the bottom of the steps. A door was thrown open.

Outside, the scene was just as chaotic. Citizens ran from building to building in a panic as further gunfire and explosions rocked the streets. Many structures surrounding the hospital were on fire. Above, through smoke and an orange dawn, Officers in rocket cycles swooped back and forth, shooting at each other. Close by, down an alleyway, Candice watched a group of Officers fighting each other in hand-to-hand combat. A revolution indeed.

A group of twenty Officers ran to their location and gathered close to Candice, shaking her hand and touching her excitedly.

Gena turned to Candice and took Candice's hand. "Mother, you're free. I promised Elise I'd spring you. Stay here with the Guard. These women are fiercely loyal to me, and so they will remain loyal to you and Elise. There are other Officers under order by the Council to *protect* you. They won't protect you, Mother. They're fighting us to keep you here and prevent you from returning to Elise. We will protect you. But Adam and I have to go."

"Where are you going?" asked Candice

"Outside the city," said the boy.

"You'll die out there," Candice said, shaking her head.

"Not according to Elise. And . . ." Gena forced a smile. "You didn't seem to think so once."

Once, Candice had tried to escape the city after her son was born. Indeed, she had heard rumors all her life that it was safe outside the walls. She had flown to Primdon Street and was about to escape Arkite with her newborn son and her assistant Bridgette Kelley when Elise stopped them. And now, Candice realized that Gena had been one of the Officers standing beside Elise on that fateful day.

"Tell Rachel how much I love her," Gena said, placing a hand on Candice's shoulder. "Tell her I wish I could have taken her with us, but we'll be back."

Candice nodded.

Gena Harding grabbed the boy up into her arms and sprinted across the street as if he weighed nothing. She ran inside an abandoned building and, within another minute, appeared on a black Officer bike, her son behind her, holding on for dear life. They took off into the air.

Within minutes, Gena was in trouble as other police on rocket bikes fired upon her. But there were no drones. The mainframe did not fight. Only Officers fought against one another in the sky.

There were a lot of black bikes above her that morning, but Candice was able to track Gena's by the sight of Adam clinging to her back. Gena shot down many bikes. Then she flew over Central Park.

"She's turning away from Primdon Street," said another Officer, confused. "Where is she going?"

Indeed, she was circling over the center of the city, around Candice's Diamond. That was when Gena surprised everyone. She dipped her bike down close to the Diamond mausoleum and then shot up, nearly vertical. Candice understood what she was doing. She was using the diamond as a landmark for the center of the city and following its point straight up toward the narrow opening through the pyramid walls above. Another bike flew in close pursuit but refused to go vertical. Had Gena and Adam not both had their ankles firmly in the stirrups, they would have been thrown from the bike.

In all of Candice's life, she had never seen anyone exit Arkite, until now. She knew of no one else in the last two hundred years who had achieved it. No one had.

Everyone gathered outside the hospital stared up as the bike burst through the opening and then leveled off, escaping out of the city, into the desert and away into an alien world.

CHAPTER 28
STATION ONE COURT

THE REVOLUTION WAS OVER. Iris had disassembled Rex. Four thousand women who had sided with Rex against Elise had been arrested, but they were never tried. Candice pardoned them all. It was argued that these police and citizenry were simply performing their duty. Virtually everyone was pardoned.

Everyone but Sara.

And now, Candice had a crushing headache. Her face burned. She felt sick. She had never fully recovered since Yorkshire Moody, but that wasn't why she was relapsing today. She was visiting her former girlfriend. She had refused to jail Sara before talking to her. But the pain in her head hurt more the closer she flew to Station One Court. She came with an escort —two Officers on rocket cycles of their own. Drones controlled by Iris flew above and alongside to provide further air support.

Sara had betrayed Elise and, by doing so, had betrayed Candice as well. That was how Candice saw it. It had been a desperate, stupid act. Even if Sara had succeeded, Candice would have found it hard to forgive her. As much she hated Elise, they were a team. A family. And while Elise might have shamelessly humiliated Sara, Sara had tried to imprison Elise and thereby kill her. Sara's crime was far worse.

Candice walked down the hall with two guards by her side. This time, Candice wore a black dress. She mused that she walked the same hallway she had traveled down when she had first seen Elise after her rebirth. If it hadn't been for the guards by her side, she would have faltered. But she forced a show of strength. As she approached a white metal cell door and the guard opened it, she fixed her shades over her eyes.

The cell was small. Sara sat by a silver table under dim light in an orange jumpsuit, staring morosely at a white brick wall. Her face was still black and blue and swollen from Elise's fury. The cell had one table, a metal chair, a latrine, and a cot. There were no windows. It was small, just barely large enough to fit the cot and table.

Candice walked to her and leaned down to kiss her cheek. Sara pulled away.

"I'm sorry," Candice said. She felt a lump in her throat.

Sara shook her head. She stared at the walls.

"I'm sorry, Sara."

"You're being played by her. She's manipulating you."

"Sara, if I don't marry her, the other Savants will tear her apart. Yes, she's playing me, but she's right."

"Is that what she told you?" Sara refused to look at her.

"Yes."

"And you believe her?"

"Yes. I know she's right. The only way for us to keep alive—"

"Is to keep her as Mother." Sara finally turned and faced Candice. Her eyes were bloodshot, evidence of tears, though she was not crying now. "Elise is playing you in order to be Mother again, Candy. All Elise cares about is power. But you could stop her. We could stop her. Together. That's why I did what I did. You're Mother now, not her."

"The coup's over. Rex has been overthrown. He failed to imprison her."

"I imprisoned her, not Rex," Sara said.

"Don't say that. Iris is listening, and everything is public here."

"It's the truth," she said with a shrug. "I won't deny it, and I don't care. The city can believe whatever lie Elise wants to tell them. Rex didn't feed me the information. I searched his records for it."

"Just shut up, Sara," Candice said.

"I've told everybody. It's on record. And I don't care. Elise should be the one in jail for helping an XY, not me. Leeto's right about her."

"Why would you betray her? Why would you betray us?"

Sara shook her head violently. "Don't say that. Why say *us?*"

"Sara." Candice sat beside her on the cot. Then she touched her arm. Sara shook Candice's hand off. "I can help you. But you have to explain yourself."

"I didn't betray you, Candy. Elise was in trouble. So . . . I did it for us. I reviewed Rex's recording. But you were guiltless. You never admitted to helping Elise. Elise merely told you her plans to help the XY. If Elise hadn't escaped and was properly jailed, you and I wouldn't be having this conversation. You would be visiting Elise right now in prison instead of me."

Candice touched Sara's chin to pull it to her, but Sara yanked it away.

"Sara," Candice said, taking her sunglasses off, "I love you."

"I don't think so," Sara said. "I don't think you do. I don't think you even know what you feel. You and Elise are together. You've always been. But she doesn't deserve you. I thought I did. But . . . she brought you back." Tears formed in Sara's eyes. "I owe her for that. But Elise is your wife. Not me. Go fucking leave with her." Sara threw her long blond hair back and turned her whole body away from Candice. Then she started to sob. "Just fucking leave me!"

"Oh, Sara."

Sara leaned over her hands and cried. Candice put an arm around her again, but it seemed to upset Sara more. Sara jumped up.

"Don't visit me. You made your choice. Leave me alone!"

"Sara," Candice said. "I'll work something out. You're right, I am Mother. I can pardon you."

"Oh, Candy, you're so fucking nice that you're hurting me again! Just leave me alone! How dare you tell the city that you're marrying her publicly in front of me? She manipulated you, but you said the words. The city knew you and I were together. It was so humiliating. I can't believe you did that. In front of everyone! Even if you wanted to be with her, you could have at least kept me away."

"I tried to—"

"But you told everyone that you didn't love me in front of my face! You told them you loved her instead!"

"I'm so sorry, Sara." Now Candice started crying too. "I'm sorry. I never meant to hurt—"

"I know! I know. You never mean to hurt anybody, but you do. But I know who the real bitch is. Just . . . I can't do this. Please leave me alone."

"I'll talk to the Council," Candice said. "The charges state that you were a traitor to Elise and me, but I can argue that you were distraught over my illness. We can—"

"Get the fuck away. You're Mother. You don't have to talk to any Council."

"Sara, why do you think I was sick?" Candy snapped. She was finally mad too, grabbing Sara's shoulder. "It wasn't over Adam. I was sick over you. Over hurting you."

"Get away from me," Sara said. "There's nothing you can do

to fix it now. You made your choice. Now please get out and leave me the fuck alone."

Candice reached for her, but Sara pulled away again.

Candice waited in a silence that seemed to go on forever. She stood quietly as Sara cried. Then, at last, she left the room.

In the hallway, she felt the crushing pains of a migraine return. Then she felt pain in her chest. Was it pain, or was it a broken heart?

She gave the guards an excuse about having to use the restroom and rushed down the hall to the jail bathroom. She threw the door of a stall open, pulled up a toilet seat, and threw up. Then she walked to the sink to wash her face and hands. She gazed at the black mascara running from her eyes. She brushed some of the black away from her cheeks, then leaned her hands on the white porcelain and cried some more.

She had cried a lot over the past few days. Everything happening in Arkite was being planned by Elise to solidify Elise and Candice's rule. Then there was her marriage to Elise by Iris. Everything was happening so fast, and Candice felt her true love slipping away.

God, have I really lost her?

Of course, Sara was right. It was Candice's fault. She could have disagreed with Elise at Yorkshire Moody, fought her like she always did.

Elise had been wrong about this one. Had she not made the announcement, she wouldn't have fainted. Rex wouldn't have forced her to the hospital, and Sara wouldn't have reacted impulsively and stupidly and broken herself apart from them. But Candice had made her announcement. In front of Sara.

So many had died over it, but she knew that, had she chosen Sara and not married Elise, she and Sara would have survived only two, maybe three, months before being devoured by the other Team Savants. Candice didn't regret her planned marriage, but she did regret the manner in which it had been announced. Elise had made an error about that.

Or had she? Was Elise so brilliant that she knew that the only way to finally rid herself of Sara was to sever their ties with Candice's public announcement? And if so, if she was that smart in dealing with her enemies—this one a competing lover —than why had Candice been so stupid as not to see it?

Perhaps Candice was being paranoid. Elise was not that much of a mastermind, was she? Could Elise be this wicked? Now, not only was her fiancée a mass murderer, she was a brilliant despot who used her own love interests to cause the death of thousands.

But whether Elise was wicked or not was irrelevant at the moment. Candice had destroyed her relationship with Sara, and she would never forgive herself for that. She would pardon Sara when the time was right, but it wouldn't repair the damage Elise had wrought. Their relationship was over.

Candice's headache was resolving, but her thoughts hurt more. She splashed some water over her face and then looked for a towel. There was none, only a blower, so she rubbed the excess mascara off her cheeks with the edges of her dress.

A citizen wearing a formal gray suit walked into the bathroom. She walked over to the sink next to Candice and washed her hands. Then she looked at Candice and opened her eyes wide in recognition.

"Mother?"

"Hi."

"Is everything all right with Arkite now?"

Candice forced a smile. She put her sunglasses back on, tried to ignore a sudden stabbing pain in her chest, and nodded to the stranger.

CHAPTER 29

EVERYONE SHOULD LOVE
THEIR MOTHER

CANDICE HAD ALWAYS LIKED Sky City. She loved the way the natural rays of light filled the expansive open Promenade as she rode along the automated floor escalator. And now, wearing a cherry-red suit identical to her companion, Elise, Candice rode the walkway, escorted by Rachel and a large contingent of guards. Citizens clamored at the sides of the escalator, reaching out their hands to touch them, cheering and shouting in support of the new leaders of Arkite. The revolution was over, and Elise had won.

After ascending the elevator with armed guards and reaching the end of the windowed bright hallway, Rachel opened the double door to the conference room. Candice was surprised to see the enclosed windowless room among such open air in Sky City. She had seen a rough visual recording of the last meeting but had never been in the meeting room.

She and Elise walked all the way around the grand gray metallic table and sat down beside one another.

A purple-blue light lit the ceiling. The Savants provided color in the drab room, each wearing a different color suit.

Rachel stood behind Elise and Candice in her black trench coat, fully armed and awaiting orders like a sentinel. After the recent uprising, Candice doubted anyone would object to the presence of an Officer.

Across the long gray table, Candice saw the Viceroy, Leeto Gansey. Candice had barely known her in her other life, and she had not spoken to her since her rebirth either, but Elise had filled her in on rumors of her treachery. Candice studied her while Leeto smiled condescendingly back.

Why so smug? You're defeated.

"I think it is time to bring this meeting to order," Elise said, finally breaking the silence, her voice amplified by the microphone in the table. She took Candice's hand. "I am so grateful for all of you who have come today, dears. Both Mother and I have some very special news."

"Iris," said Dana with a smile, nodding to Elise, "Commence visual recording of the meeting."

"Yes, President Haish," said Iris's familiar computer female voice, a little too bubbly. "And may I add, you all look so colorful this morning."

A camera from the ceiling was lowered.

"Candy," Elise said, turning to Candice with a nod. Candice swallowed the lump in her throat. She hated speaking publicly. She tried to ignore the camera as it tracked her face. "Go ahead, dear."

"First off, I want to thank all of you," Candice said. "Thank you for acknowledging my health and leadership." She had rehearsed these words back home with Elise. "After everything that's happened, I'm so pleased that I still can trust all of the members of the Council here today to help me lead our fine city."

They applauded.

She looked over their faces. Some seemed younger than she was. Had she aged? Her rebirth made her only six months old, and now that the migraines and bodily aches had dissipated, she felt healthy. But some of the Savants were in their early twenties, as young as she was when she had started. Her rebirth and her body might have been the same biological age of these younger Savants, but she felt different. Seasoned. Experienced. They all looked so young.

"Number one," Candice said, leaning over the coin microphone on the table. Then she leaned over and kissed Elise on the lips. She had rehearsed that too, and people predictably applauded again. "Elise and I are henceforth wife and wife. Iris presided over a private ceremony a few hours ago downtown in Pyramid Three. Isn't that right, Iris?"

"Indeed, Team Mother," said the robotic female voice. "And, might I add, I'm very excited to see you two together beautifying and perfecting our glorious city."

"We are so happy for the two of you, dears!" said Dana.

"A perfect day!" exclaimed Riley.

"Congratulations," came Rachel's voice from behind. Rachel rubbed Candice's shoulder.

"May the two of you live happily together," said Leeto with a sardonic grin. "Possibly *forever*, when there is final completion of the Lazarus Project."

"Thank you," said Candice. "Thank you, everyone."

"It is a happiness meant to offset the sadness of the recent revolt," said Elise. Elise held Candice's hand, rubbing the bones of her hand. The room became somber. "There's been great treachery in Arkite, and, as a result of the recent coup attempt by Rex, Mother has yet another important announcement." Elise turned to Candice with a nod. "Go ahead, dear."

"Second, with the recent banishment of Officer Harding, I have decided to recruit Savant Jackson as head of CPO, the Central Police Organization, of Arkite. She is the most experienced—"

"The leader of the Guard?" objected Leeto, jumping up. "Is this a joke? She'll rule with an iron fist if given such power! The people watched your police march down Main Street,

Elise. Everyone in Arkite knows where the Officers' allegiance lies."

"I wouldn't worry much, Gansey," said Elise. "You're an upstanding citizen who should have absolutely nothing at all to worry about."

"And as far as Officer Harding goes," Leeto continued, "she was not banished. That is a lie being used in order to cover up the truth. She and Elise were best friends. No, I think Elise abetted her in escaping the city from your execution order, Mother."

"Why must you always fight, Leeto?" snapped Dana. "The XY was taken care of. He is no longer in the city. Elise has made that clear. And now we can get back to what we have wanted to focus on all along—the Lazarus Project."

"But not with her," Leeto said, leaning back in her chair and folding her arms together. "I don't trust her."

"Elise will be head of CPO and my head advisor," repeated Candice. "She will—"

"Spy on us and take our privacy," interrupted Leeto . Then she looked at the Savants along the table. "Why don't any of you do anything? I came here in support of Team Mother, Savant Candice Harlow. I accept that she is fit to serve as Mother. But I don't accept her wife. And many of us, though they won't come out and say it, agree. I told you at the last meeting that Elise had run the city into the ground. She has no right to head CPO. She doesn't even have the right to be titled as Savant."

Elise did not respond. She simply sat quietly and watched Leeto.

"Now, if you wish, you can all vote, and Elise may win," Leeto continued. "She might because she's planned this all along to work out in her favor. But surely you all don't wish her eyes on you. It's time to stand against this. Don't throw away your vote in fear. Vote against this." Then Leeto turned to Candice. "I'm sorry, Mother, but I strongly disagree with this decree."

"That's fine, Viceroy," said Candice, "You have every right to object. But my decision—"

"We will vote," said Dana.

"We will not, Dana," Candice said. Dana glared at Candice in amazement. "This is by decree."

Elise nodded.

"Mother, I am worried about our future," Leeto said to Candice in a gentle tone. "You must reconsider. You giving Elise so much control is unprecedented. That power should remain with you and the Council, not a retired Savant. You should appoint a new Chief Officer, like the Officer behind you. Not a retired Mother."

"I am freely giving her this position," replied Candice. "You all know she is more qualified and experienced than me to protect the city."

"That may be true, Mother," Leeto insisted with a sigh. "I understand that you two are in love, and that's all well and good —congratulations—but ... for the welfare of Arkite you must appoint a new Chief Officer, as has always been done. Elise has been retired. We voted."

"Do you refuse my order as your Team Mother, Leeto?" asked Candice.

"I wouldn't dare," Leeto said, shaking her head and raising a hand. "But ... perhaps"—Leeto looked right into Candice's eyes —"you can allay my fears, Mother. Perhaps you can strike an agreement. Then the Council can accept this very unusual arrangement."

"She owes you nothing, bitch," replied Elise, folding her arms.

"What did you have in mind?" asked Candice.

Leeto looked at Candice with an amused expression. "Well, I don't want Elise sticking her nose in my business." Then she glanced at Elise and squinted her eyes. "Anymore, anyway. You claim protection, but she has repeatedly endangered Arkite in her association with XYs—particularly, most recently, in helping the XY boy escape."

Then, of all people, Iris spoke. Many in the room jumped at the sound of her unexpected voice. "Officer Harding and the XY freed Savant Jackson after her imprisonment by the corrupt mainframe, Rex. Officer Harding then sent herself into exile in order to escape the execution order by our revered Team Mother. Savant Jackson is guiltless in this matter."

"This is a private meeting, Iris," said Elise. As angry as Elise was with Leeto, she seemed even more unsettled by the computer's interruption, regardless of the fact that the computer was defending her. "Thanks, but I ask that you zip it."

"Sorry," said Iris. "Please, carry on, ladies."

"Don't interrupt us again."

"Many of you," Leeto said, gesturing around the table, "are interpreting these events differently than I do. Elise and Gena were always best friends. The XY wasn't exiled. The boy was assisted in an escape. Assisted by a Savant who is now in line to head CPO. How can you all accept this?"

"What is it you want?" Candice repeated to Leeto.

"I suggest you shut it," snapped Elise to Leeto. "It's very suspicious that Dr. Teller committed suicide just two hours after the murder of Dr. Epton last week, Gansey. Dr. Epton was found trading secrets with Savant Granger and Savant Myer right before they were incriminated—Savants you were quite intimate with, as everyone here knows. I intend to make that a priority for my first investigation as chief of CPO."

"Once again, Elise, you accuse me with no evidence!" snapped Leeto, jumping up again and pointing at her. "How dare you? You drag my name through the mud in front of our sisters, even retired as Team Grandmother!"

"I'm merely throwing out a suggestion."

"Will you two stop!" cried Dana. "Enough of your bickering. Allow our revered Mother to speak." She turned and nodded to Candice.

"What do you want?" repeated Candice for a third time, looking at Leeto.

Leeto gave a sly smile. "I want what everyone in this room wants, Mother. I want the completion of the Lazarus Project. Perhaps, with your genius reputation, you can assist in finishing the job. Give us a deadline. If you do that, I think we all can accept your wife's new position. Then, maybe, you two can remain together in happiness and love *forever*."

Forever with Elise in matrimony. Leeto was baiting Candice too. Just as Frankie sat beside Leeto, married but not in love, so too were Elise and Candice now married. And, indeed, if the Lazarus Project succeeded, they would *remain together forever*.

"I agree with Leeto on this," Dana said. "I will accept Elise's new position and fully support her in CPO if you, Mother, can provide us a deadline." She turned to Elise. "Not you, dear, for we've had enough of your extensions, and even though I love you, Elise, I don't put much trust in your work habits." Everyone laughed. "And"—she addressed the Council—"I will suggest that we all accept Elise's position as head of CPO as well . . . if you swear, Mother, to meeting a close deadline." Then Dana turned to Leeto. "Will that be acceptable?"

"Of course," Leeto said with a grin.

"Candy can't give you a deadline, Dana," said Elise. "She's trying to be fucking sweet again with her candy-cane heart. There is no way she can give a deadline to—"

"One year," Candice interrupted. "I can complete the project within one year."

"One year?" asked Dana with a doubtful smile. The murmuring around the table was terrible. Elise flashed Candice an incredulous look and shook her head.

"One year," repeated Candice assuredly. "I can modify the genetic makeup of the blueprint. I can finish in one year. You have my word."

"A year?" asked Leeto in a tone of amusement. "You will have me believe that you can adapt all your research to each of our genomes in one year? And you will swear to this? You can promise us immortality in a year and accept the consequences of your failure? All of us bear witness to it."

"If everyone cooperates instead of fights," replied Candice, "then yes, Leeto, I can, with your help, finish the project in one year."

"And if you fail?"

Well, there was no need to answer that question. Leeto would dethrone Candice and Elise, take control of Arkite, and then execute both of them.

"One year," agreed Elise reluctantly. "One year. In one year, the Lazarus Project will be complete. Immortality will be ours."

There was silence . . . and then . . . the room erupted in applause. Everyone rose to their feet, shouting and clapping. Elise could not have hoped for any more support garnered from this first meeting. Even Savant Gansey seemed fond of the two of them at the moment.

"Stand up with me, Candy," Elise whispered in Candice's ear. "Finally, back to the way it was. And they love you."

"They love *you*, Elise," Candice replied and then said in her ear, "You did it. You have your city again."

The two stood up and raised their clasped hands over their heads. The cheering and applause grew wilder.

Then Iris's voice sounded, amplified throughout the room. It startled many Savants. It was joyous and very human, but, somehow, its interruption seemed artificial.

"All hail our two Savants: Savant Harlow and Savant Jackson, joined in matrimony and loved by the people. All hail as they bring all womankind into a new age of prosperity and peace. Blessed are all the Savants in this room to witness the passing of our Arkite! The dawning of a new age has come! Blessed be our Mother Savant!"

CHAPTER 30
AM I DISMISSED?

ELISE SAT in her gray swivel chair at the top of her penthouse, speaking with other Savants from all over the city through her VR Viewer. She loved the adulation and congratulations from all her colleagues. Everyone congratulated her for her marriage and her new position. She drank champagne, celebrating her final takeover of power and her marriage to Candice.

It was during her last meeting with Savant Haish that she heard Candice walk up the ramp of her home. It was late, but all the outside blinds of the windows of her Pyramid home were open and the moonlight shone through, along with dim orange lights along the floor molding. Down the ramp stood her newlywed wife and the love of her life, Candice Harlow. She was dressed in simple clothes. That surprised Elise. She expected Candice to be in her nightgown, for it was late. Or even her Savant jumpsuit. Instead, Candice wore a blouse and jeans and stood by the second floor with her hands behind her back. Elise quickly said goodbye to Savant Haish.

"Hey, babe. Done with your nap? Why don't you get more comfortable? Come and have a drink with me."

"I'm leaving, Elise."

Elise furrowed her brow. "Hmm? What? Where are you going, Can?"

"Home."

Elise turned her chair to fully face Candice. Even in slacks and a blouse, her wife looked beautiful, but Candice had a scowl on her face.

"You did well, Candy," Elise said. "You performed beautifully at the Savant meeting."

"I did everything as we rehearsed."

"Everything except your deadline. You fell right into Leeto's trap. You should have let me deal with her like I told you. That was stupid."

"Whatever," Candice said. "I don't want to fight, Elise. I just want to go home."

"Home?" Elise asked and chuckled. Elise reached into the pocket of her red jumpsuit and took out some gum. "Care for a stick of gum, babe?"

"I'm going home."

"Home is here."

"Am I dismissed?"

"What?"

"Am I dismissed, Mother?"

"*You* are Mother, Can."

"I don't want to fight," Candice said, shaking her head. "I just want to go back home. Am I dismissed, Elise?"

Elise jumped up and walked down the ramp. She stood next to Candice and ran her hand along her wife's long, soft blond hair. Then Elise put her arms around Candice. Candice stood rigidly and turned her head away. Elise ran her hand down Candice's back and kissed her cheek.

"It is, rightfully, our honeymoon tonight, Can. Why don't you get more comfortable?"

"Perhaps another time."

Elise walked over to the curved wall beside her bedroom

and leaned against it. "You're being a real bitch, Candy. We just got married."

"That wasn't a marriage," Candice said. "That was an agreement."

"Iris married us, babe."

"That is correct, Elise," said Iris. "I married the two of you privately this morning."

"No one asked you, Iris," Elise snapped. "Please shut it."

"I don't want to fight," repeated Candy.

"Well," Elise said, pushing away from the wall and walking up to Candice's face. "I think you do. And I'm not excusing you, *Mother*, until you fess up and tell me what's on your mind."

Candice met Elise's gaze. And, for the first time, it made Elise consider that Candy was the only one left in Arkite that did so. Actually, come to think of it, Candice was the only one Elise ever had cared about who had the nerve to do that. Maybe that's why she loved her.

"Elise, when I was a girl I always dreamed of a lovely wedding. An affair in large halls decked out with a beautiful, lovely, long-flowing white dress, and red and pink flowers, all like a fairy tale. By the altar, I'd look in the eyes of my princess, kiss her, and live happily ever after. This morning, you had the mainframe marry us in your goddamn office."

"Is that what this is about?" Elise chuckled. "I told you we had to get married before the meeting. I told you that was the plan." Elise searched Candice's eyes. Candice glared back dead-pan. Elise shrugged. "Fine. I'll get you a royal wedding. You deserve it. I'll make it big—huge, in fact, so all the city can admire my lovely wife. I've got no problems with that. Now, enough of this. Go change so we can relax."

"No. It's not what all this is about, Elise."

"Really? Okay. What's this about, then?"

"Sara."

"*Fuck!*" Elise screamed in Candice's face. She walked away, taking deep breaths in an attempt to calm herself. "*Sara!* Sara. Sara. Sara. Even when she's in prison, Can, I have to hear her name!"

"You had your wedding. You married me. It's over. Now I want to go home."

"This is your home!"

"This is the office of Arkite. This is where you rule your subjects. This is not my home and never will be, Elise. And I will never be Mother, and you know it."

"You are so fucking irritating today. I brought you back to life. Isn't that enough?"

"Thanks. But no, it's not. And you can't hold me just because of it. Thanks a lot. Now I'm back. But—"

"Yeah. You sure are. You sure as hell are, aren't you, Candy."

Elise walked into her bedroom. It was dark, as all the shades were down. She wondered if Candice would just walk out.

It seemed so unfair. What more did she want? Elise had sacrificed everything for her. Wasn't that enough? She had never done even half as much for anyone else.

Candice walked to the threshold of Elise's bedroom. Even in casual clothes, Candice looked beautiful. If only she'd calm the hell down.

"May I be excused, Mother?"

"Oh, fuck you, Candy."

"How could you do that to Sara? You framed her. You humiliated her. What did you expect?"

"Well, with that tone, now I'm going to execute her. What do you think about that?"

"I'm not surprised."

"Yeah. Well . . . I wasn't going to till now."

"Whatever, Elise. May I go?"

"*No!*" Elise shouted.

"I don't love you."

Elise said nothing, but she felt pain in her chest. Candice's words were very sincere.

Elise wondered why she hadn't predicted this. She could have avoided all this had she planned things better. Of course Candice would hate her for what had happened to Sara. She should have known. But she had figured that Candice would come back to her after Sara's betrayal.

"You manipulated Sara into acting against you," Candice said. "You planned everything all along."

"Did I, Candice?" Elise asked quietly, standing in the darkness. "How could I have done that?"

"You scheme everything. You knew she would be so enraged that she would betray you. That's why you made me announce our marriage at Moody's. You gave her the means to do it in the lab. All it took was to turn her."

"You think I planned her snitching on our conversation regarding the XY?"

"And that they would pardon you after he was exiled—yes. Yes, Elise, I do. I think you planned everything. And it led to a revolution that killed thousands of innocent people. All to get rid of Sara."

"Whatever you think of me, Can, know that I never planned to be betrayed by Sara," Elise snapped irately. "I never planned that. You're wrong. If anybody planned that, it was Rex. I might scheme, but, I hate to admit it, Sara was the only friend I had over the past two years. I liked her. I had to. She was the only one I had anything to do with. She worked side by side with me to bring you back. But to be honest, she's always been a bit of a nitwit."

There was silence. And darkness. Elise stood over her bed. She felt tired—so tired. She wanted to just fall into her bed and sleep. Forget everything.

"I . . . I just need some time, Elise. I'm . . . I'm sorry. I . . . maybe it isn't all your fault, but I need to go."

"Go. Fucking leave, Candy. You already fulfilled my dreams this morning. Just go and take all the time in the world."

"Because you know I'll come back."

"No, Candice," Elise said with a sigh. "Do what you want. I made you Mother. My *scheming* was to keep you safe. To keep us both safe. I did that. We achieved everything today. This is what I wanted. This is why I *scheme*. Once for me, now for both of us. For you, Candy, because I love you."

"I . . . I'm sorry Elise, but I . . . I don't love you."

"All right," said Elise, surprised that her voice sounded choked up. "You made that clear enough already. Please, leave me alone, then."

"I'm sorry, Elise, but—"

"May I be excused, Mother?" asked Elise sarcastically.

Candice left. Elise heard her footsteps down the ramp, through the foyer. The front door opened and quietly shut. And then, Candice was gone.

Elise cried. It surprised her. Elise never cried. She cried more sitting on her bed than she had when Candice had died. All in the darkness of her bedroom. She was miserable. She felt so alone.

"You are Mother Savant, Elise," Iris said as she sobbed. At first, Elise didn't hear the mainframe, but then it spoke again. "You are Mother Savant."

"Huh? What?"

Only a very faint yellow light emanated from the cracks between the blinds outside the window. Otherwise it was pitch black in her room.

Elise wiped her eyes on her sleeves.

"Candice will never be Mother Savant of Arkite," said Iris.

"What?"

"I heard you ask Savant Candice Harlow to be excused using the title *Mother*. But may I remind you that you are the rightful Mother Savant of Arkite, Elise Jackson. You are

Darlene, reborn. You are the chosen leader of our beloved city and matriarchal utopia. Not your wife, Savant Harlow. You, Elise Jackson. You are our revered Mother Savant."

It was so quiet. Calm. Elise stood up straight and took a deep breath.

"You are Mother Savant," Iris repeated in the darkness.

"So? I don't care."

THE END

ACKNOWLEDGMENTS

After a novel is written, there's no way for an author to know how a book will be interpreted or received. When I wrote *Candy Savant*, many questions arose by my readers: What is the origin of Arkite? Why is the world devoid of men? Why is everyone in Arkite confined to pyramid walls? These unanswered questions provided impetus for me to shape the story and continue Candice's journey (or Elise's journey, I suppose). And so, I embarked on a sequel. As I worked on *Mother Savant*, I decided that if the story did not complement the first, I'd discard it.

Well, I didn't discard it. And I believe the final product does, indeed, complement the first because of help from my readers and the following people.

Thank you to my beta reader Melissa G. I could not have conceived of the direction of this novel without her invaluable input. And huge thanks to my editors and cover artist. I enlisted the same team for consistency with the first book, but, most importantly, because they're amazing in the field. Thank you to my line editor Paul Witcover and my proofreader Eliza Dee for improving and polishing my prose. And thank you to my cover artist Damon Za. Damon Za created a stunning cover that really matches their original.

PARTING WORDS

What did you think of *Mother Savant*? By placing a book review, you can inform others of your thoughts and help spread the word about my book.

Want more? Periodically I like to send news regarding current or new projects. If you'd like to be privy, I encourage you to sign up. Your information will remain private and you can cancel any time.

Sign up at www.alhawke.com or scan the following QR code:

Sign Up

ABOUT THE AUTHOR

A.L. Hawke is the author of the bestselling Hawthorne University Witch series. The author lives in Southern California torching the midnight candle over lovers against a backdrop of machines, nymphs, magic, spice and mayhem. A.L. Hawke writes fantasy and romance spanning four thousand years, from pre-civilization to contemporary and beyond.

Visit A.L. Hawke at www.alhawke.com

Email: contact@alhawke.com

ALSO BY A.L. HAWKE

PARANORMAL ROMANCE

- THE HAWTHORNE UNIVERSITY WITCH SERIES I-III
- THE HAWTHORNE UNIVERSITY WITCH SERIES 4-6
- THE HAWTHORNE UNIVERSITY WITCH HOLIDAY COLLECTION
- SHADES
- PHANTOM MASQUERADE

- MY EVIL EYE
- THE GUARDIAN
- NECTAR OF AMBROSIA
- CORA

FANTASY: THE AZURE SERIES

- HARMONIA
- CORA: RISE OF THE FALLEN GODDESS
- AZURE BLUE
- CORAL RED
- PRINCESS SOJOURN

SCIENCE FICTION

- CANDY SAVANT SERIES

Books available at https://alhawke.com/books

www.ingramcontent.com/pod-product-compliance
Lightning Source LLC
Chambersburg PA
CBHW020925110726
47900CB00001B/304